12/3

W9-BSA-122

A Place to Come Home to

MELODY CARLSON

HARVEST HOUSE PUBLISHERS
Eugene, Oregon 97402

OUACHITA TECHNICAL COLLEGE

Cover by David Uttley Design, Sisters, Oregon

Map illustration by Jan Cieloha, Springfield, Oregon

A PLACE TO COME HOME TO
Copyright © 1999 by Melody Carlson
Published by Harvest House Publishers
Eugene, OR 97402

Library of Congress Cataloging-in-Publication Data

Carlson, Melody.
    A place to come home to / Melody Carlson.
        p.   cm.
    ISBN 0-7369-0053-5
    I. Title.
PS3553.A73257P57   1999   99-14245
813'.54—dc21   CIP

All rights reserved. No portion of this book may be reproduced in any form without the written permission of the Publisher.

Printed in the United States of America

99 00 01 02 03 / BC / 10 9 8 7 6 5 4 3 2 1

PS
3553
A73257
P57
1999

In loving memory of my grandfather,

ORVIL H. HAGA,

*A man who could "do anything" and
took time to make me feel important.*

One

aggie scanned the words on her computer screen again—it sounded too good to be true. And usually that meant it wasn't. Her journalist's sense of skepticism kicked in as she called out to Skip in the cubicle next to her. "Listen to this one, Skippy. *Dream job in a dream location. Wanted: experienced and motivated newspaper writer/editor to manage small-town paper in Central Oregon. Benefits include but not limited to: tall pine trees, snowcapped mountains, peace and quiet...*"

"Where do I sign up?" asked Skip.

She laughed. "And while you're at it, I have a bridge I'd like to sell you."

Skip leaned over the divider and pointed his pencil at her accusingly. "Haven't you ever been a dreamer, Maggie? I'll bet there's an old-fashioned idealist hiding beneath that cynical reporter's crusty exterior."

She just shook her head and sighed. "Idealists don't survive in L.A., Skippy. At least not for long."

He grew thoughtful for a moment. "Maybe you're right. I'm still a newcomer here." Maggie watched as disappointment washed over his face and suddenly felt guilty for spoiling his youthful illusions. Maybe she was a little jaded.

"Sorry, Skip. I probably felt like that once too, but I suppose my brass ring has gotten a little tarnished-looking over the years."

He smiled and nodded towards her computer. "Any luck in your Net-search for a fledgling reporter who's willing to become a slave for peanuts, or are you just surfing for the fun of it?"

"Nothing much yet." She glanced at her watch. "Actually, I better call it quits. I promised Spencer that I'd start coming home before dinnertime this week."

"What a concept. Which reminds me, I'm running late too. See ya tomorrow."

Maggie returned her attention to her computer screen, but before exiting the ad section she stole one last look to see exactly where this "dream job" was located. Pine Mountain, Oregon. How interesting. She read the address again just to be sure. Pine Mountain...now that induced some wonderful childhood memories. Her family had spent several summer vacations on Silver Lake, just outside of the small town of Pine Mountain. Her dad's partner had lent them his cabin up there, a rustic affair made from hand-hewn pine logs and complete with a stone fireplace that smelled like real wood smoke. She'd almost forgotten that short but happy era. Even now it seemed like a time and place out of some juvenile book she'd read long ago. Places like *that* couldn't really exist. But even if it was only imaginary, wouldn't it be great to go there, if simply for a moment. How she would savor the clean fragrance of sun-warmed pine needles and the peaceful sound of water lapping gently against the dock on a hot summer's day—things she had taken for granted during their summer vacations. Suddenly she recalled how she and her brother would traipse through the little tourist town of Pine Mountain in search of an ice cream cone—two enormous scoops of the wildest flavors dripping down the side of the cone in the summer's sun. But the friendly shopkeepers hardly seemed to notice the sticky faces or grimy camp clothes and dusty tennis shoes. How unlike the immaculate designer shops in L.A.

where everyone and everything looked squeaky clean and perfect—at least on the exterior. Did places like Pine Mountain really still exist?

She blinked at the clock, remembering her promise to her son, and shut off her computer. Determined to start this week out right, she had to hurry if she wanted to fix a real dinner tonight. She'd even gone to the store during her lunch hour for fresh pasta and a few other ingredients she hadn't seen in her cupboards for months. Perhaps a feeble effort on her part, but when she'd learned from a teacher friend that Spencer was hanging with some kids who were not his old sports pals, she'd grown concerned. And according to the same teacher these were the kind of kids rumored to have gang connections. Naturally, Spencer denied all this, insisting that just because some of his friends dressed differently the paranoid teachers assumed they were "gang-bangers." Not wishing to engage in another useless argument, Maggie had held her tongue, hoping that he knew what he was talking about. And after all, he had always been sensible and dependable, always more mature than his peers. But at the same time she was haunted by the memory of how Phil had always said that kids who imitated gangs—"wannabes"—could be just as dangerous as the real thing. Maybe even more so. Oh, if only Phil were still alive. He'd surely know how to deal with this.

Maggie fought down a wave of sadness as she rode the elevator down to the parking garage. This wasn't how it was supposed to have gone. She had never intended to marry a cop. Everything sensible and rational inside of her had warned her against it. But those clear blue eyes, that disarming smile and hearty laugh, had all joined forces to defeat her on their very first date! Now Phil was gone, and it was her job, a thirty-eight-year-old newspaper reporter, to raise Spencer alone. And fourteen was a bad age. Other parents had warned her, but she had boasted that her son was different—reliable, responsible, trustworthy. Now she wasn't so sure.

She hardly remembered the commute home. Not because she'd driven it thousands of times, but because her mind was seeking refuge in the Oregon mountains. Once again she was a carefree child, splashing in the cold lake, teasing her little brother with a frog, looking at stars so close she thought she could reach up and touch them with her fingertips. She sighed as she exited the freeway. Skip was wrong, she hadn't always been a skeptical, no-nonsense reporter. Once upon a time, she'd been young, she'd entertained all kinds of dreams and ideals—

And then she saw them—flashing lights, police cars, ambulances, at least a dozen of them—all in front of her house! She parked her car without shutting off the engine, then leaped out and pressed through the crowd of gathering spectators and curious neighbors. Quickly she forced her way to where a number of uniformed officers were standing.

"Stay back, ma'am," warned a young cop she didn't recognize.

"Hey, Maggie," called Gordon Bender, an old friend of Phil's from the force. "Let her through, Kent."

She ran to Gordon, unable to form an intelligible sentence, searching his eyes for some sort of sign that everything was okay. "Is he…is it…Spencer?"

Gordon threw an arm around her shoulders. "Now don't worry, Maggie. Spencer is just fine—pretty shook up though. He's over talking to Lieutenant Harrell right now."

"Then what in the world is going on?" She felt tears of relief build in her eyes, but she was determined to remain calm. Putting on her reporter's reserved detachment, she would just get the facts.

"A drive-by shooting." Gordon exhaled slowly before he continued. "It's a kid…Brian Jackson."

"Oh, no…" Her hand flew to her mouth. "How is he?"

Gordon shook his head sadly. "He's dead, Maggie."

"No!" She could no longer hold back the tears. "Oh, no! I can't believe it! Not here, not in this neighborhood! This is a quiet subdivision…Phil always said it was safe…"

Gordon frowned. "No neighborhood is safe."

"Oh, poor Sandy and Tom...are they home yet?" Maggie looked over to her next-door neighbors' neatly landscaped yard. Tom kept the greenest lawn on the block. Now it was cordoned off with garish yellow plastic tape.

"The parents are on their way. They know about the shooting, but they don't know he's dead."

Suddenly Maggie's knees began to weaken. She didn't know how much more of this she could process. She felt sick for the Jacksons, but it also felt as if her own world was spinning more and more out of control. "I've got to talk to Spence..."

Gordon grabbed her arm. "Wait until they're done questioning him, Maggie. Let's get you inside. You need to sit down and pull yourself together."

As if in a dazed dream, she allowed him to lead her into her own house. This couldn't be happening. Not here in Oak Valley, where neighbors actually knew each other by first names and weren't afraid to walk their dogs after dark. She sank into the couch and closed her eyes, pressing her knuckles against them as if to press out what was going on all around her. She heard Gordon moving about in the kitchen, opening a cabinet, running water in the sink...

Why God? she prayed in silent desperation. *Why do you allow these things to happen?* Her pleading wasn't an accusation. She'd moved beyond the accusation stage long ago. God had been her lifeline since Phil's death, and she couldn't afford to shove him away now. And so she prayed wordlessly for Sandy and Tom and for Brian's older sister, Lisa, who was away at her first year of college. Maggie's spirit cried out for her neighbors and the sorrow that would soon overwhelm them. She knew that kind of sorrow. It could kill you if you let it.

Her chest tightened as she remembered Brian's impish smile as he shot baskets against Spencer in their shared driveway just a few days ago. The two kids were always comparing heights, but on that day Brian had been a hair taller

taller and all long and lanky just like Spencer—and then she began to sob uncontrollably.

"Mom, are you okay?" asked Spencer in a voice that didn't sound anything like her son.

She looked up. His freckles stood out on his unusually pale face and his eyes seemed blank, like the shades pulled down over a window. He stood over her, his large, bony hands hanging loosely at his sides. Suddenly he seemed so tall and gangly. When had he grown so tall? She stood up and reached out for him, and for the first time since Phil's death, they hugged and cried together.

"I'm so sorry about Brian, honey," she said when they finally pulled apart. "I just can't believe it."

He wiped his wet cheeks with his hands. "Me neither."

"Do you know how it happened? Was Brian involved with any gang..."

"No, Mom!" Spencer's blue eyes flashed. "Crud, you sound just like the cops! Brian didn't have *anything* to do with any gang! It was just some stupid, moronic mistake. Don't you people get it?" Then he stomped up the stairs as she watched speechlessly. She told herself that his anger wasn't really meant for her, he was just upset about Brian's death and she was the closest target. But it hurt just the same.

Somehow she made it through the evening. She cooked the fresh pasta, but didn't remember tasting it. Spencer had taken his plate into the family room where he sat silently in front of the TV as local news of the shooting flashed before their eyes in a three-minute blurb. Then he went to his room. She rattled around the kitchen, feeling like a stranger in her own home, nervously glancing out of the windows every few minutes, fearful that the shooters might return. Later as she sat alone in the darkened living room, she heard a car pull up. She jumped up and peered out the window to see the Jacksons' BMW pull into their driveway. Maggie dashed out the kitchen side door and across her driveway to meet Sandy as the haggard-looking woman pulled herself from the car.

The two of them hugged tightly for several long minutes, both crying freely. Then she offered to help in any way she could. Finally Sandy spoke. "I know that you, of all people, understand how I feel, Maggie. You know what it's like to lose someone too...but all I can think is that it's all so blasted unfair!"

"I know," said Maggie soothingly, her hand still on Sandy's shoulder. "I still struggle with that too. And it still doesn't make sense. But somehow I've learned to lean on God through all this. And quite honestly, I don't know what I'd do without him."

Sandy blew her nose. "Well, right now, I'm really, really mad at God!"

"It's okay, Sandy. I was angry too. Sometimes I still am. Just don't quit talking to him. Go ahead and tell God that you're mad—vent your feelings. Believe me, he can take it. God has big shoulders to cry on." They hugged again, and then Maggie helped them load some things into their car. They were going to a hotel—it was too painful to be in their home.

It was nearly midnight when she fell into bed exhausted, but sleep was far, far away. Her mind was pummeled with troubling questions. What if another drive-by occurred? Could Spencer possibly be involved with a gang? It seemed unlikely, but how could she be certain? And what about drugs? What would Phil do? And how was a single mom supposed to keep an eye on her kid when her job took her from home? On and on she went—one answerless question chasing the heels of the next.

Finally, she forced her mind to refocus. She *had* to trust God—anything else would drive her over the edge. She breathed deeply, willing herself to think of something, anything, to release her mind from her troubles. *Whatever is good, whatever is pure, whatever is lovely...* And for the second time that day a vision of Silver Lake drifted before her like a cool wisp of fresh air, peaceful, serene, bright blue sky, crystal clear water...ahh, she was almost asleep...

Suddenly, she sat up in bed. *That* was her answer—the newspaper job in Pine Mountain! She ran downstairs and turned on her computer, waiting impatiently for the screen to warm up, and then logged on and connected to the Net. She searched for the ad, hoping desperately that someone else hadn't already snatched the dream job away. But at last she found it—the ad was still there! She smiled as she read the benefits package again. Someone in Pine Mountain had a sense of humor.

She didn't get to bed until after three, but when her head hit the pillow her earlier sense of panic had abated. And for the first time since losing Phil, it felt like her life was actually on track. She decided to trust God to open or close this new door. And even if the door should open, she knew there might be some unseen challenges—she was no fool. But if it was the right thing, it would all work out. Like a child, she'd just taken her first step of faith. But it was God who would have to lead her on this journey.

Two

aggie spent Memorial Day weekend stuffing everything she could fit into the back of her Volvo wagon. The garage sale had been a huge success and the movers would pick up all the large furniture and boxes next week. It was no use expecting Spencer to help out at this stage. She just hoped he didn't cut out before he was safely buckled into the front seat of the car. And he'd probably leave a trail of black heel marks all the way up I-5 from the way he was dragging his feet right now.

Her coworkers had said they envied her—just taking off like that and escaping the rat race. Skip had heartily patted her on the back, saying he always knew she had it in her. But she saw flickers of doubt in the eyes of some, as if they wondered but were afraid to ask how she'd survive the isolation of the Oregon mountains, and wouldn't she miss the action and energy of the city? Those things worried her a little too. But so far, everything had worked out so perfectly that she felt certain it was God who was sending her and Spencer to Pine Mountain.

Clyde Barnes, the owner of the *Pine Cone*, Pine Mountain's weekly newspaper, had called her with a job offer just one day after she'd faxed her resume. He said he was getting too old to run the paper and wanted more time to go fishing in the numerous mountain lakes that surrounded the area. Then he'd connected her to his real estate agent friend, who had promptly emailed her information about several houses currently on the market. Maggie had instantly fallen in love with the quaint-looking farmhouse complete with *seven* bedrooms. The description said it was a perfect location for a bed and breakfast with full mountain views, several outbuildings, and a nearby stream. And the price was a steal— by far the best deal of the group. The idea of running a bed and breakfast had always intrigued her and now seemed like a potential way to supplement her income. The salary at the *Pine Cone* was modest to start with, although Mr. Barnes had promised that if circulation increased her salary would follow. But money wasn't crucial just yet. She still had Phil's stipend and insurance settlement, and the equity from her house covered the price of the farmhouse. Afraid that some other prospective buyer might snap up the real estate bargain, Maggie had purchased the farmhouse property sight-unseen. When her cash-offer was accepted, she was so excited that she called her mother in San Jose to share the good news.

"I sure hope you know what you're doing, honey," she said in that *you could be making a big mistake* voice.

"Don't worry, Mom, it's going to be great. I have a real sense of peace about it."

"Well, you better enjoy that peace while you've got it."

Maggie forced a laugh. "Why don't you come out and visit us for a couple weeks this summer. Then you can see the place for yourself."

"I just might do that. How's Spencer taking the move?"

She thought for a moment. "As well as can be expected..."

"You mean he's furious."

"Well, I don't know about *furious*, but he's acting like a typical fourteen year old who doesn't want to leave his friends behind—you know the spiel."

"How's he handling Brian's murder?"

"He's pretty closed-up about it. He keeps acting like nothing's wrong, like nothing even happened. Right now, I'd say our communication is at an all-time low."

"Did you get him into counseling like I suggested?"

"I tried, but he told me I was overreacting and then he skipped out on his appointments. Finally I just gave up."

"That's too bad. I think he needs to talk to someone."

"Well, maybe you can work him over when you come visit," teased Maggie. "No sense in letting that counseling degree go to waste."

"You know I *never* practice on family or friends."

She laughed. "So you say..."

"Besides..." Her mother's voice grew flat. "I'm retired now."

"How's it going—being retired and all? Lifestyles of the relaxed and leisurely?"

Her mother groaned. "I'm bored out of my mind, Maggie. I never should have done it. You know I've never gone in for things like golf or shuffleboard, and I'm hopeless at bridge. I'm halfway tempted to hang out my shingle again."

"Maybe you just need to give it more time, Mom. Learn how to have fun."

Her mother sniffed. "That means a lot coming from you, Ms. Workaholic."

Maggie bit her tongue. This was an open invitation for an argument. Raised by two workaholic parents, how could she possibly have grown into anything else? "Well, I'm changing my ways, Mom. And I think this move will help."

"Well, for your sake, I hope so. Tell Spencer to hang in there. I've got a book I'll send you about teens and grief. And you two make sure you stop by here on your way up to Oregon so I can do the grandmother thing."

ᴼᴸ

And now the day was finally here. Maggie backed the loaded car from the driveway, glancing at her son as she checked for traffic. His arms were folded tightly across his chest and his face was dark and stony, but at least he was in the car. Of course, she had hoped it would be different than this. She had imagined the two of them taking final looks around the place and sharing old memories—like when Phil had built the tree house, or put up the basketball hoop. Maybe even take a few snapshots. But now she was afraid to push her luck with him. Better just to get out of there as quickly as possible. Her eyes avoided the vacated Jackson house next-door. Unable to live in their home after losing Brian, they had moved to a gated community in Pasadena. Many other neighbors were talking about leaving as well. She swallowed the lump in her throat as she drove down Poppy Street for the last time. Would all their happy memories be wiped out by a few recent events? It hadn't always been like this. She remembered when Phil had found the newly built split-level house. It had been shortly after their third anniversary, just a few months before Spencer was born. Phil had wanted a real yard for the baby to play in. But it had taken every penny of their savings, plus a gift from his parents, just to scrape together the down payment. It had been their home for nearly fifteen years, fairly happy years too, and the only home Spencer had ever known.

"I know this isn't easy," she began as they entered the crowded freeway.

"'Isn't easy?'" he exploded. "That's quite the understatement, Mom! It stinks. It sucks. It's totally *unfair.*"

She blinked. "I'm sure it seems that way to you…"

"*Seems* that way? I'd say it *is* that way. I didn't have any choice in the matter. Who cares what I think anyway? I'm just a stupid kid." He turned his face toward the passenger door, his back squared against her like a brick wall.

"I *do* care what you think, Spence. And you're not a 'stupid kid.'" But it was too late. His headphones were in place and he was putting a disc into his portable CD player.

He cranked it so loud that she could almost make out the words—that is if the words had been intelligible. She shook her head and sighed. Funny how her parents used to complain about *her* music, and yet it was nothing compared to the trash kids listened to nowadays. She smiled grimly at her curmudgeon-like attitude when it came to today's music. Spencer had accused her of being raised by Ozzie and Harriet, which wasn't too far from the truth. But several months ago, she had surrendered in the battle over his music, hoping, in turn, to gain some ground in the battle for his heart. She drove on in silence, fighting against the hopeless feeling that, despite leaving L.A., she was still losing her son. Maybe not to a bullet like in her worst fears, but she was losing him just the same. For all she knew, this move could prove to be the final straw.

By late afternoon they made it to San Jose where they would visit her mother. As always, Maggie felt a sense of comfort to be in her childhood home again. She fought against the guilt that Spencer would never enjoy that same comfort. His childhood home was gone now and there was no turning back. But, she also told herself, their situation was different. His father was gone. There was nothing she could about that. Besides, who knew how many times she would get to visit here, perhaps this would be the last. The old house and large yard were a lot for her mother to keep up, and the old neighborhood was deteriorating noticeably. But her mother's kitchen was still cheery and bright, with homemade marinara sauce simmering on the stove and fresh linguini hanging nearby to dry, evidence of her mother's late-in-life attempt to resuscitate her old Italian roots.

Normally Spencer enjoyed his grandmother's attention and witty humor, but as if to punish his mother he refused to engage in any conversation, choosing instead to sulk in front of the TV all night. After a late dinner and leisurely walk through the old neighborhood, Maggie had excused herself to bed, partly to escape her moody son but also because she wanted to get an early start in the morning. She wanted to reach Oregon as soon as possible, hoping, for no rational reason, that the miles would somehow wear down Spencer's resistance.

As she got ready for bed in her old room, she was unprepared for the assault of memories tucked here and there. The faded yellow daisies on the wallpaper made her remember the long week in third grade when she'd been stuck in bed with a severe case of measles and had to wear dark glasses to protect her eyes from the light. And the familiar crack in her ceiling still reminded her of the sharp-nosed profile of her junior-high English teacher, old Miss Maisley, the first one who had ever told her she could write. Even as she looked out the window to admire the nearly full moon, she was reminded of the time she and Rebecca Bishop had climbed out this very window to meet with several friends out on the street—it had been Rebecca's idea and a bold move for Maggie. She chuckled at the memory and then sighed. She'd been exactly the same age as Spencer then. When had she grown old?

She pulled down the shade and turned abruptly from the window. Standing before the gilt-framed mirror, she tried to assess the toll the last two decades had taken. Her brows were pinched together in a perennial scowl that accentuated wrinkles that weren't actually there yet, but she suspected would follow if she continued to frown like that. She took a deep breath and willed herself to relax. That alone made her look a little younger. Then she turned on the table lamp and searched her dark, shoulder-length hair for any signs of gray, but found none. Her father had gone prematurely gray, but thankfully she took after her mother's side. She stood up straight and evaluated her overall image. She weighed only slightly more than she did in high-school, yet she looked decidedly frumpy. Maybe it was the clothes or perhaps the hair. Since Phil's death she had focused her attention on work and Spencer, letting her appearance go. Well, it wasn't too late to make some changes. Stand up straight, she told herself, shoulders back. Better. She smiled. Maybe she should smile more. Then she picked up a framed photo from high-school days. It was a candid shot of herself with her best friend Rebecca. They had entertained such big dreams back then. Suddenly she remembered the email from Rebecca yesterday. She hadn't had a chance to respond before leaving, but now she plugged her laptop into the phone line and climbed into bed. She quickly began to write.

RB,

I see that you're back from New York. I wish we could have gotten together before I left, but maybe you'll come up for a visit. Between you and me, I'm scared to death right now. I've never done anything like this. You've always been the brave one, traveling around the world, taking on new challenges…. And I've always played it safe. But where did it get me? So, now I'm taking a big step—a risk. I know it probably seems like nothing to you, but for me it's huge! And even though I'm frightened, I'm also excited. The truth is, right now I feel more alive than I've felt since losing Phil. Maybe I am doing the right thing. I'll let you know how it goes. Say a prayer for Spence. He is not making this easy.

mc

⌒

The next morning her mother stood in the driveway, her faded blue bathrobe blending with the pre-dawn light. "Drive carefully, Maggie," she said. "It's a holiday weekend, you know." Then she grabbed her grandson's jaw and gave it a friendly little shake. "And, *you*, keep your chin up, Spencer. You never know what's around the next corner."

"I'll try, Grandma," he said unexpectedly.

Maggie tried not to register her pleased surprise as she turned and winked at her mother, mouthing the word *thanks!* as Spencer climbed into the car.

"Don't forget your promise to come visit this summer," she said as she closed the door and started the engine.

Spencer slept all morning. For companionship, Maggie kept the radio playing softly, searching for new stations as old ones grew fuzzy with static as she drove out of range. It was some comfort having him along, but still she felt very alone. But then she remembered her earlier assurance that God had opened this door—that he was leading her. Everything would be okay once they got to Pine Mountain.

By afternoon, she was tired and road weary. But as she made the ascent into the Cascades her spirits revived as tall, majestic evergreens appeared along the highway, standing tall like giant green sentries set out to greet travelers. And when she finally spotted the white, snowcapped peaks set pristinely against the cloudless, incredibly blue sky, she felt strangely energized. She glanced over at Spencer. He had exchanged earphones for a science-fiction book, and now he sat hunched over with his eyes fixed on the page before him.

"Isn't it beautiful?" she ventured at a particularly breathtaking vista of mountains.

Spencer barely looked up from his paperback and grunted. "I s'pose."

Well, that was something. When they reached the top of the pass she noticed the ski area directly ahead. There were what appeared to be several new buildings and even more lifts than she remembered seeing as a kid.

"You know," she began carefully, "Pine Mountain is only about fifteen minutes from that ski resort, Spencer. Hadn't you mentioned something about wanting to learn how to snowboard?"

His eyes flickered just slightly as he lifted his gaze to the rounded mountain before them. "Maybe. But that doesn't look like much of a ski resort." He snickered. "Maybe it's the *last* resort."

Maggie forced a laugh, hoping to humor him. This was the most conversation they'd had in days and she wanted to keep it coming. "It looks like there's at least a half-dozen chairlifts on this side. That would be enough to keep me busy, of course. I'm not much of a skier. Wouldn't it be fun to go up there next winter?"

Spencer exhaled his displeasure loudly. "You really think we'll still be here by then?" Without waiting for her response, he turned his back to her and opened his book again.

She glanced back at the mountain and sighed. Doubts were creeping in again. What if Spencer didn't adjust to small town life? What if his rebellion only grew worse? She couldn't bear to lose him. She longed to reach over and ruffle his strawberry blond hair and tell him everything would be okay. But she couldn't bear another disparaging scowl from him. She focused her eyes on the road. They'd soon be in Pine Mountain—their new home. Things would surely get better then.

Three

Just past the ski area was a road sign indicating the Pine Mountain exit to the left and twelve miles to the town. This seemed odd since Maggie remembered the town being right smack on the main highway, handily located only minutes between the popular ski area and Silver Lake. Still, she obediently followed the sign and turned off the highway. Although beautifully lined with enormous Ponderosa Pines, this section of asphalt road was deeply rutted and sorely in need of repair. She slowed her speed to navigate around the numerous potholes, many of them large enough to damage a smaller car. Why in the world had Pine Mountain allowed this road to fall into such dire condition?

It was close to the dinner hour, and she suddenly remembered the old Pine Mountain Hotel's restaurant. Built like a Swiss chalet, the hotel resembled an old Alpine lodge with antique skis and woven rawhide snowshoes adorning its walls. A huge river-rock fireplace dominated the large dining room with white cloth-covered tables nestled all around. Maybe that would impress Spencer. She imagined the two of them sitting together in the nearly 100-year-old hotel, and she would tell him about how she used to come here as a kid and how her dad used to order the biggest steak in the house, so big it would hang over the edge of his plate. And how the baked potatoes were so creamy they almost melted in your mouth. Not to mention the marionberry cobbler á la mode. She smiled to herself as she dodged another pothole.

At last the town finally came into view and her heart began to beat a little faster. Their new home! She drove down Main Street, looking from the left to the right, trying to take it all in again. And it did look familiar, but at the same time something seemed different. No, something was wrong. She had no trouble finding a parking spot right in front of the Pine Mountain Hotel, for the street was nearly deserted of both cars and pedestrians. And when she looked up at the old hotel, she saw the sweet shuttered windows now boarded up and the flower boxes empty and in need of paint. A faded sign was nailed to the front door proclaiming the hotel *closed until further notice.*

"Nice place, Mom," said Spencer sarcastically as he looked up at the hotel. "This where we're staying tonight?"

Maggie frowned. "I don't understand. This place used to be the nerve-center of the town."

Spencer glanced around, then shrugged. "Looks like it still is...because if you ask me this town has about as much life in it as this hotel. It's all pretty dead."

She felt the anxiety slip over her like a tight-fitting garment, shrinking and constricting, making it difficult to breathe. What in the world had happened to Pine Mountain? Why had no one told her about this? Had she just made the biggest mistake of her life? She took a deep breath and shoved down her doubts. It was too soon to jump to conclusions. Besides, she must maintain a strong front for Spencer's sake.

"I'm hungry," she announced bravely as she locked the car and looked around. "And I'm going to find a place to eat."

Spencer joined her on the sidewalk, stretching lazily. "Good luck finding anything, Mom. It looks like everyone in this town has left town." His voice held a cynical note of triumph, as if he'd finally proven that he'd been right all along.

"I can see that," she snapped, her irritation bubbling to the surface. "But there must be something. There…" she pointed victoriously down the street. "Dolly's Diner." She began to walk in that direction.

"'Dolly's Diner,'" mimicked Spencer. "Sounds like something out of a Stephen King novel. I wonder what kind of delicacies they might serve in there…" He jogged up to catch her. "Hey, wait a minute. This *might* get interesting."

She smiled at him, slightly cheered by his curiosity, even if it was somewhat derisive. But when she opened the door to the diner, she was instantly assailed by the acrid smell of stale cigarette smoke and grease. She stepped back to the sidewalk, allowing the door to swing shut.

"Well, maybe there's another place," she said quietly, fighting the defeat in her voice.

Spencer groaned. "Or maybe we should just turn around right now, cut our losses, and go home."

She looked her son directly in the eye. "We go nowhere until we eat."

He pointed across the street. "Okay then, how about that hole in the wall?"

"Galloway's Deli," she read the sign with reserved hope. "I didn't notice it before, but it does seem neat and clean. Look, they even have pansies in their flower boxes. You can't go too wrong with a deli. Let's just hope they're still open."

Fortunately the door was unlocked. She opened it and was greeted by quiet music and a dozen or so tables covered in cheery gingham cloths.

"Good evening," said a short, plump, dark-haired woman from behind the counter. "Welcome to Pine Mountain."

"Is it that obvious that we're newcomers?" asked Maggie.

The woman chuckled. "Sorry. I guess I tend to notice who's new in town. Are you passing through, or visiting?"

"Actually, we've come to live here," she announced, hoping to sound more convincing than she felt.

"That remains to be determined," muttered Spencer from behind.

The woman smiled. "Then a double welcome to you." She eyed Maggie carefully. "Let me guess, you must be the new editor from Los Angeles. Clyde told us all about you."

"Yes, I'm Maggie Carpenter, and this is my son, Spencer."

"Pleasure to meet you both. I'm Rosa Galloway. Now, you must be hungry. What can I get for you?"

As they placed their orders, Maggie noticed the hours on their menu. "It says that you close at five..."

Rosa waved her hand. "Oh, don't worry about that. When you run your own business, you call the shots. I was finishing up some baking and forgot to flip the closed sign on the door. But I don't mind staying a little later—especially for our new editor."

"Thanks, we really appreciate it."

Soon after they were seated, a pretty, dark-haired girl came with a pitcher of ice water. "Hi, I'm Sierra," she said. "My mom said to be friendly and introduce myself because you guys are new in town. So, welcome to Pine Mountain."

"Thanks. I'm Maggie and this is my son, Spencer."

"How old are you, Spencer?" asked Sierra as she filled his glass.

"Fourteen." Spencer eyed the friendly girl with suspicion.

"Me too," said Sierra brightly. "I'll be a freshman this fall. How about you?"

Spencer nodded glumly. "Yeah, I'll be a freshman."

"Cool." She arranged their utensils and napkins on the table. "I can't wait to go to high school. From what I hear it's not too bad."

"Really?" Spencer's eyes exposed a glint of interest.

"Yeah. And they even have a snowboarding-team. Do you snowboard?"

"No, but I've been wanting to learn. I can ski, but I've never tried snowboarding." Spencer's voice had perked up, but Maggie tried to appear nonchalant as she sipped her water and pretended to study the art on the wall.

"I just started snowboarding a couple years ago, and I absolutely love it. Hey, I'd be happy to give you a free lesson next fall."

Spencer nodded. "Thanks. That'd be cool."

"Who knows, maybe we can both get on the snowboarding team."

"I probably wouldn't be good enough."

"You never know," said Sierra. "Since you can ski already, you might take to boarding real quick. I did. And once you get the balancing part figured out, you just gotta have nerve."

He smiled ever so slightly. "Sounds cool."

She grinned. "It is. I better go help Mom. Nice meeting you two. See you around, Spencer?"

"Sure." Spencer watched the girl go back behind the counter. Then he glanced sheepishly back to Maggie, as if embarrassed that he'd found something to appreciate about this town.

"Sierra seems nice," said Maggie. An understatement, since she was restraining herself from jumping up, hugging the girl, and shouting hallelujah.

He just shrugged and looked blankly out the window. She followed his gaze to see some picnic tables arranged neatly in a garden area out back. It seemed that this deli had more going for it than initially met the eye.

"Here you go," announced Rosa as she set their plates down. "Enjoy."

Maggie ate her soup and sandwich quickly. The food was delicious, but she felt guilty for keeping Rosa and her daughter here after hours. To her surprise, Spencer's plate was empty even before she finished her last bite.

OUACHITA TECHNICAL COLLEGE

"Goodness, you're fast eaters," said Rosa as she refilled their water glasses. "Leave any room for dessert?"

"Aren't you ready to close now?" asked Maggie.

Rosa waved her hand. "I told you not to worry about that. Like I said, I make the rules here. Now," she turned to Spencer, "how about some marionberry cobbler with ice cream?"

"You have marionberry cobbler?" asked Maggie in disbelief. "I used to get that over at the Pine Mountain Hotel when I was a little girl."

"So did a lot of folks. For that reason, I try and keep the tradition alive—at least while I can."

Maggie and Spencer both decided to have the cobbler and Rosa turned to the kitchen and called out, "Two cobblers á la mode, Sierra."

"When did the hotel close?" asked Maggie as Rosa topped off her coffee.

"About five years ago. It held out longer than most, but finally the owners couldn't take it anymore. They went bankrupt and moved back to Portland."

She could no longer contain her curiosity. "What's happening here, Rosa? Why are so many businesses closed?"

Rosa pressed her lips together and slowly shook her head. "It all began about eight years ago. You see, the state rerouted the main highway past Pine Mountain—just cut us off completely. And without the tourist traffic passing through here on a regular basis, the town has slowly died—is dying," she corrected herself.

Maggie swallowed. "But can't anyone do anything about it?"

Rosa shrugged. "Some have tried, but they usually give up and eventually they just leave. We're barely holding on ourselves. If it wasn't for the loyalty of the locals I'd have been wiped out by now. But folks get tired of home-cooking occasionally, and Dolly's isn't everybody's cup of tea."

"No, I guess not..." Maggie was trying to process all that Rosa had just said. Eight years ago the interstate had bypassed this town and in effect delivered a death blow. It seemed that she had left everything to run a newspaper in what was slowly becoming a ghost town.

"Here you go," announced Sierra as she plunked two heaping ceramic bowls of cobbler and ice cream before them. "Mom makes the best cobbler in town."

Rosa laughed. "That's not saying a whole lot, honey."

"Okay then," said Sierra as the two returned to the kitchen. "How about the best cobbler in the state?"

The dessert was excellent, but Maggie had difficulty swallowing over the lump that was steadily growing in her throat. How could she have risked everything without checking out the facts better? She watched silently as Spencer finished his cobbler, scraping his bowl clean. Then she rose, laid a generous tip on the table, and moved mechanically toward the counter.

"Thanks, Rosa," she said with a forced smile. "That was delicious."

"See you around then?" asked Rosa with a raised brow.

"I guess so," said Maggie flatly. "I don't seem to have much choice at the moment."

"Give it some time, Maggie." Rosa reached over and warmly patted her hand. "I know you must be surprised at the state of things around here. But I hope you won't give up on us just yet."

Four

aggie drove in shocked silence, waiting for
Spencer to launch into some sort of adolescent
I told you so lecture. Thankfully he did not.
She had decided to go directly to their new house. Just a mile
north of town, it would give them enough distance to forget
about Pine Mountain's troubles—at least for a while. She
would deal with that later. Right now she was so tired that
she only wanted to get out of the car and rest, and think
about nothing.

She easily spotted the house from the road. Identical to
its photo stood a tall, white, two-and-a-half story Queen
Anne-style farmhouse. She turned the car into the long
gravel driveway, then paused for a moment to savor her first
impressions. She could already imagine a glossy brochure for
the bed and breakfast featuring the house shot from just this
angle. Situated like a graceful lady upon a carpet of lush
green, it was surrounded by delicate aspens and backdropped by snowcapped peaks against a clear, blue sky. A
large, wrap-around porch framed in lilac bushes stretched
lazily around the house, promising restful evenings relaxing
in wicker rockers, breathing clean mountain air, and sipping
iced tea.

"*This is it!*" she spoke with emotion. At least one thing was turning out right. "Isn't it beautiful, Spencer?"

He sat up straighter, looking on with interest as she continued to drive down the gravel driveway. She thought she noticed his eyes light up ever so slightly.

"Sure is big."

"It has *seven* bedrooms," she proclaimed proudly as she turned off the engine.

"What are we going to do with all *that?*"

She hadn't mentioned her idea of a bed and breakfast to Spencer yet. She wasn't sure that he'd been ready for that, and it wasn't something she had even decided upon. "I don't know exactly what we'll do with it, Spence. Maybe we'll just have room for lots of visitors."

He brightened. "Like some of my friends from back home?"

"Sure." She climbed out of the car. "Why not?"

Spencer was already heading for the front porch, and she dug in her purse to find the keys—

"Yeow!" he cried suddenly. In alarm, she looked up to see her son's left leg buried thigh-high in the porch.

She ran to the steps. "What happened? Are you okay?"

"I'm fine, but this porch is rotten." Spencer pulled his leg out and held up a broken board that had obviously seen better days. He pulled on the board next to it and the soft wood crumbled in his hands.

"Stop," she pleaded, "you're tearing the porch apart."

"Mom!" He waved a piece of board in her face. "It's all rotten! It'll all need to be torn out anyway."

"Oh, dear..." She leaned weakly against the handrail, and then felt it sway slightly beneath her weight. "Oh, no..." She stepped away quickly.

"Mom," began Spencer quietly. "Do you really know what you've gotten us into?"

She swallowed. "Maybe it's better inside."

He rolled his eyes. "Let's check it out. But be careful on the porch."

She gingerly stepped onto the porch, carefully going around the gaping hole. She slipped the brass key into the large ornate door. "This looks like the original beveled glass," she said, pointing to the window in the door. "It's still in one piece."

The door swung open and she peeked inside. It was dark and smelled old and musty, but she stepped in, treading lightly. The wood floor squeaked beneath her feet and for a moment she wondered if it too might give way. Directly before her was a large curving staircase, and to the right was a set of glass-paned double-doors. Carefully, she opened them.

"Kinda spooky looking in here, if you ask me," said Spencer from behind her.

"Let's open some of these old drapes." She stepped into the dark room, went over to the window, and gave the cord a tug. The next thing she knew the heavy, dust-covered drapery fell down upon her—rod and all! Visions of spiders and creepy things assaulted her as she fought to escape the bulky weight of the velvet drapery.

"Here, Mom," yelled Spencer. "Let me help you."

Finally free of the drapery, she took a deep breath and dusted herself off, trying desperately to remain calm and wishing for a better sense of humor. "Thanks, Spence. I wasn't expecting that."

With more light coming into the room now, they could see what had probably once been a library or den. Thick wood panels and bulky bookshelves covered most of the walls. The wood's finish was so darkened by age that she couldn't begin to guess what it was. Spencer discovered a large sliding door on the back wall.

"Shall we see where this goes?" he asked.

"Sure, why not?" Truthfully, she longed to go outside and breathe some fresh, dust-free air, but since Spencer was game, she thought she better continue too.

He pushed hard to slide the solid door open until a loud thud sounded and the door became wedged at an angle, leaving an opening about a foot wide. "Looks like this needs some work too," he said as he slipped through the space. Maggie followed him, not wanting to be left behind. She held her breath as Spencer opened the drapes in this room. Fortunately the rod stayed attached to the wall.

"I bet this was the dining room," observed Maggie, pointing to a large cabinet built into the wainscoting. "That's a sideboard."

"Look how worn down the floor is where chairs must've scraped," said Spencer as he moved his foot over the warped floor. "This place needs a lot of work, Mom."

"I can see that now…" She moved over to a set of glass doors that opened out to what must've once been a garden area, but the exterior steps were long gone and the drop-off was several feet below them. She swallowed hard. Without some major renovation this house was not only an eyesore, it was probably a little unsafe.

Spencer pushed open a swinging door that led to a hallway that passed behind the back of the stairs. "There's the kitchen," he pointed out, as he held another swinging door open for her to inspect.

She peeked inside. It was archaic, with an old wood-burning cook-stove and a huge, stained porcelain sink. The only thing that appeared to have been updated was the flooring and it was linoleum that looked to have been laid back in the forties. Absolutely nothing in it looked usable. She closed the door and shuddered.

"Doesn't it just make you want to go in there and whip us up a nice cheese soufflé?" teased Spencer.

Maggie groaned, unable to comment as they continued their downstairs tour. They discovered a pair of small connected parlors and a bathroom with rust-stained fixtures and a warped floor.

They moved quickly through the upstairs bedrooms and baths. These rooms were only slightly better than the ones below. But it seemed that almost everything was in its original state, and all in need of some kind of repairs—and to

Maggie some places seemed beyond repair. As they went down the creaking, curving staircase, she wondered if the whole house might suddenly collapse around their ears and bury them both alive.

"Let's go outside," she suggested quickly.

Once there, she took a deep breath, eager to fill her lungs with clean air again. Spencer stood out on the driveway looking up at the house. She could not bear to look at it. So pretty on the outside, a nightmare on the inside. She should have known better. The price had seemed too good to be true, and as an investigative reporter she should have known what that meant. Why hadn't she checked into things more carefully? How could she have been so naïve? She had thrown away their financial security, her successful career, their family home all for a dead-end job in a ghost town and a house that should've been condemned years ago. How could she have been so reckless and foolish?

She collapsed on the front steps, buried her head in her hands, and sobbed uncontrollably for several long minutes. It was the most crying she had done since Phil's death, and for awhile she nearly forgot that she wasn't alone. But then she felt a gentle hand resting upon her shoulder.

"Don't cry, Mom," Spencer spoke softly. "It's going to be okay."

She looked up at her son and blinked. "I…I'm sorry. I…I don't know what to do, Spence. I can't believe I've gotten us into this mess. I'm so sorry…"

"It's not so bad, Mom."

She stared at him in wonder. "*'Not so bad?'*" she repeated. "It's a nightmare, Spencer."

He pressed his lips together thoughtfully, the same way his dad used to do when he was trying to figure out something. "Remember how I saved all Dad's tools from the garage sale?"

Maggie nodded, unsure of what that had to do with anything.

"Well, I used to hang out with Dad a lot when he was fixing things up around the house. And he taught me how to use all his tools. And I helped him build the tree house too, remember?"

Maggie nodded again, wiping her nose on a Kleenex.

"Well, I think I could fix up a lot of these things."

"Are you serious, Spencer?"

He nodded proudly. "Of course, I'll need some help with some of the bigger things, but there's a lot of small things that I think I could fix with the right materials."

Maggie wasn't so sure, but she was so touched by his new attitude that she didn't voice her doubts. "So, are you saying that you want to stay here, Spencer?"

He shrugged. "Not exactly. But I s'pose we could try it for a while. It might be kind of fun during summer vacation. And if it doesn't work out, maybe we could go back home again."

"Sure, Spence. I think that's a good way to approach things." She looked back at the disappointing house. "It looked so perfect on the outside. I never guessed it would be such a mess. But I should've known..."

"Anyone can make a mistake, Mom." Spencer grinned. "And besides, I think this house has some really good potential."

"Maybe you're right. With careful restoration, it might even have some historical significance—the realtor said it's one of the oldest houses in the area. But I don't know if it's safe for us to stay in it—in its present condition. I think I should get it checked out by a professional first."

Spencer glanced back behind the house. "What are those other buildings?"

"There's supposed to be a barn and a carriage house and some sheds."

"Why don't we check them out before it gets dark?"

"I guess it can't hurt to look." She glanced at her watch, wondering where they would spend the night. The Pine Mountain Hotel certainly wasn't an option, and she hadn't noticed any other places in town. And she had no intention of spending the night in that house of horrors. She would rather sleep under the stars. Or perhaps the barn, on a nice pile of straw.

She followed behind her son as he confidently strode towards the outbuildings. Suddenly he seemed taller and older than before. She liked this mature side of him, and it was a relief to let someone else lead for a change. The barn was clean and neat and in fairly good shape. Other than signs of mice, it wouldn't be a bad place to spend a night if they swept out the loft and took a lantern up there. The next building was divided into thirds. It appeared that one section had housed a garden shed, with ancient rakes and shovels still hanging on the wall. It also appeared as if some family of critters had made a home in a corner. Maggie quickly moved on. The mid-section of the shed had lots of shelves, apparently for storage; and the third part was a woodshed, still half-filled with split wood. The sun was getting low in the sky when they came to the final outbuilding—the carriage house. And its door was locked. Since Spencer had taken charge of this tour, Maggie ceremoniously handed him the ring of keys sent by the realtor. He tried several keys until one finally worked, then he opened the door and peered inside. Maggie waited on the step, not eager to intrude on a family of opossums or possibly skunks. She shuddered.

"Well, look what we have here," announced Spencer as he motioned her through the opened door.

Hesitantly, she stepped inside. Dimly lit by the last rays of the setting sun, she stared about the room in wonder. No longer a carriage house, this building was finished inside. Remodeled into what appeared to be a neat, little house, it seemed to be in good repair. The high vaulted ceiling gave the illusion of more space, and as they raised the blinds, Maggie could see that the unobstructed mountain view to the west was amazing, especially now as the sun transformed some stray, wispy clouds into a peachy pink. The front room appeared to suffice as a living and dining area with a kitchen off to one side. The compact kitchen was well-designed with solid pine cabinets and granite countertops complete with modern appliances. Throughout the house were pine plank floors, giving the whole area a pleasant, golden glow, and a small wood-burning stove promised warmth on a cool night. In the back of the building was a bedroom, and small bathroom. It seemed fine for a single person, but two would be cramped. Just then Spencer scaled a set of ladder-like stairs and leaned over the heavy log railing above her.

"This is a loft," he exclaimed. "About twelve foot square, I'd guess."

"Great," said Maggie. "Maybe we can use it as a bedroom."

"I claim this territory as my own," he declared, then added, "if that's okay with you, Mom."

She nodded, then looked at everything again in amazed wonder. From the pine floors to the casement windows, it was incredible. "I can't believe this place," she finally said.

"What?" Spencer looked down at her with a goofy grin.

"This little house—it's like a miracle."

"It's just a house, Mom."

"I know. But I'm so thankful it's here. I don't know what we'd have done..."

"You shouldn't worry so much, Mom. Things usually work out, you know."

She just looked up at him and shook her head in amazement.

"I'll go unload the car. You should probably just take it easy. You seem kind of stressed out right now. Can I have the keys to move it over here?"

She nodded dumbly and handed him the keys, not even concerned that he had only moved the car from the driveway a few times before. She stood in front of the window and looked out to the west where the sun had now dipped below the snowcapped peaks. She stared out the window as the sky steadily grew dark. Then as she saw the headlights of the Volvo slowly coming her way, she wondered if the electricity in this building would possibly work. She hadn't thought to call ahead and have anything turned on. Again, she chided herself for her lack of planning. But Phil had always been the one to take care of things like this. Hesitantly, she flipped a switch by the door. To her surprise the porch light came on. She turned on more lights, then went into the kitchen and tried the tap. The water was turned on too! Out of curiosity, she opened the refrigerator door and was completely amazed to see neat provisions thoughtfully arranged on the top rack. A carton of nice brown eggs, a stick of butter, a loaf of whole-wheat bread, a jar of homemade raspberry jam, a carton of orange juice, and a small jug of milk. Someone was watching out for her! But the only one who had known she was coming this weekend was Clyde Barnes. Could he have taken care of these things for her? At first, she felt deep gratitude, but then suddenly remembered that it was Clyde Barnes who'd gotten her into this whole mess in the first place. He had conveniently failed to mention that Pine Mountain was a town slowly dying, or even that she had purchased a decrepit white elephant from his realtor buddy. Now she remembered how he had skillfully evaded some of her questions, instead going on and on about the clean mountain air, the beautiful rivers and lakes, skiing in winter, hiking in summer... He had not once given her any inclination as to the reality of life up here.

Well, Mr. Barnes was going to get a big, fat dose of reality tomorrow. First thing in the morning, she'd see to that!

Five

aggie awoke suddenly in the middle of the night. Disoriented, she crawled out of the sleeping bag on the floor and stumbled to her feet. Then it hit her, she was in Pine Mountain, Oregon. As she tiptoed across the wood-plank floor and made her way to the front door, her only source of light was the nearly full moon shining brightly through the window. She opened the door slightly and peered outside, looking for something although she didn't know what. Something had disturbed her sleep. She listened intently for the sound of an intruder or animal, but heard nothing. *Nothing.* She had never heard such silence in her life—not since she was a child staying with her family at Silver Lake. She sighed deeply, then took a deep breath of the cool evening air and thanked God.

The next morning she awoke refreshed and relaxed. She pulled on jeans and a sweatshirt and began to dig quietly through the boxes scattered across the floor until she found the one containing some necessary kitchen essentials. Soon her coffee maker was gurgling happily and she went out to the front step to get her morning paper. She laughed when she saw the empty stoop. What had she been thinking? This was Pine Mountain! The *Pine Cone* only came once a week.

But surely there must be some other local or state newspaper that delivered daily. She'd have to check into that. And she needed a phone hooked up, maybe two lines for her fax and computer. And what about cable TV? She'd better make a list. And she better not forget to—

Just then she heard the lonely cry of a hawk. She remembered how Phil would always stop and listen when he heard that long, forlorn screech. And he would make her pause and look too; always expecting her to appreciate the bird of prey that sailed so gracefully across the sky in the same way that he did. Phil had been a good one to slow her down and make her take notice of her surroundings.

She paused and did so now. She watched the hawk circle slowly overhead, finally disappearing into the top of a tall pine on the edge of the meadow. She stood on the step for a long time, breathing deeply and soaking in her surroundings. Wouldn't Phil have loved this. He would be so happy for her. Suddenly she remembered how irritated she had felt last night, how angry she was at Clyde Barnes for enticing her to come to Pine Mountain under false pretenses. But then what were his pretenses? He had boasted of blue sky, tall pine trees, clean mountain air. He had simply told the truth. Sure, he might have left out a few minor details, but was she sorry to be here?

She suppressed her earlier desire to make lists and get busy. Instead she poured herself a cup of coffee, found a fleecy blanket, and went back outside to enjoy her first morning in the mountains. She sat down on the stoop and studied the snow-covered peaks to the west. They looked bright and fresh in the morning light. She wondered if their clean snowy jackets would last throughout the summer, or would they melt away? Before long she spotted a doe and two tiny spotted fawns nibbling on the lower branches of the aspen trees next to the big farmhouse. She longed to wake Spencer and show him this sight and share the wonder, but wisely decided to let him sleep. Later that morning she wrote another email to Rebecca.

RB,

The natural beauty around here is spectacular. I wish you could see it. I don't know what I'd do without it right now, because I think I've made a huge mistake. Pine Mountain is not what I'd hoped. The town seems dead and I don't know what to do. But at least Spence is being a good sport. It's strange—I'm frustrated, frightened, tired, and at the same time excited, hopeful, and invigorated. It must be the mountains! Hope they don't impair my judgment completely. If you sense me becoming somewhat deranged and feel the need to make an intervention, please do. Until then, pray!

mc

∽

They drove into town just before noon. Maggie was anxious to meet her new employer and see the newspaper office, and Spencer had suggested they eat lunch at the deli again. Maggie controlled the urge to tease him about only wanting to see Sierra.

The town looked as dismal today as it had yesterday. She had hoped that she'd overblown the bleakness of it in her imagination, but it seemed, if anything, her imagination had been overly optimistic. The sign outside the city limits boasted a population of 2,276, smaller than she'd expected at first, but now she wondered where all those people were actually hiding. Certainly not in town. The streets, as before, were nearly deserted with only a couple of cars to be seen along Main Street. Most of the shops were closed, many with boarded up windows. Yesterday's feelings of anxiety began to flood her again. How could a town this size even support a newspaper? Who would buy any advertising? Dolly's Diner?

"Do you want to come with me to meet Mr. Barnes?" asked Maggie as she parked the car on the side-street in front of the newspaper office.

"Nah, I think I'll go look around."

She wondered what he could possibly want to look at. "Okay. Come on back by here when you're done, or else I'll just look for you. Shouldn't be too hard to find someone in..."

"...in this one horse town." Spencer finished for her. He grinned mischievously, then took off toward Main Street.

Maggie locked the car and adjusted her jacket. She hadn't wanted to overdress today as she suspected clothes in Pine Mountain tended to be casual, but at the same time she wanted to make a good first impression. She had finally settled on a natural linen blazer and matching skirt and a pair of neat woven leather pumps. She felt apprehensive as she walked toward the office. *The* Pine Cone, *Pine Mountain's Weekly News* proclaimed the wooden sign. The office had an old-fashioned front porch, complete with a wooden rocker. In an old apple crate next to the door was what appeared to be this week's paper. She picked one up, quickly glancing at the banner and layout. But the date of the paper was a couple months old.

"Hello there!" boomed a voice from inside as the door abruptly swung open.

Startled, Maggie dropped the paper on the porch, then quickly stooped to pick it up again. When she stood, a crusty old man stood before her holding a cardboard box and wearing a lopsided grin. It looked like he hadn't shaved for several days, and he wore baggy black work-pants held up by a pair of frayed red suspenders. Under these was a yellowed thermal shirt—not the fashionable kind, but the kind old men used to wear as long underwear. On his head was a faded fishing hat, complete with a selection of bright-colored flies.

"Welcome to Pine Mountain, young lady," he said loudly, as if he might have a hearing problem.

"Why...thank you. I'm Maggie Carpenter. I'm here to see Mr. Barnes..."

"Of course you are! And you're as welcome as the rain, Maggie Carpenter. And my, don't you look nice—just like a city girl from Caly-fornia." He chuckled as he set the box down, then extended his hand. "I'm Clyde, and I'm mighty glad to meet you."

"You...you're *Mr. Barnes*?" Maggie tried not to appear as shocked as she felt.

"You better call me Clyde, Maggie. I don't go in for that Mr. stuff. Now, come on in and see the place. I wasn't 'specting you to come to town today. I figured you and the boy'd be getting all set up in your new place."

"Well, our moving van doesn't get here until tomorrow, so I thought I'd come into town and see..."

"Glad you did. I've been looking forward to this—counting the days even."

Her brows lifted. "Counting the days?"

"Well, you see it's fishing season, and since I've been short-handed I haven't been out like I'd like to be."

"Oh, I see. How many people work here?"

"Well..." He grew thoughtful for a moment. "Just you and me right now."

"Oh." She looked around the cluttered little office in dismay.

"Course, I have several people in town who like to write articles from time to time. And I used to have Abigail McPhearson to do the office work, but she thought she was getting too old. And my nephew Gavin mostly ran the paper, but he cleared out last winter and I've been shorthanded ever since." He sighed. "'Bout time I got me some decent help."

"I see..." Maggie suddenly envisioned herself running this paper entirely on her own. "Do you plan on hiring anyone else?"

"Well now, little lady, I thought I'd leave all that up to you. I reckon you'll want someone to help with the phone and the filing. And maybe a part-timer to help with the distribution. Hey, maybe your boy'd like some work."

Maggie smiled. In spite of herself, this Clyde character was growing on her. "My son's name is Spencer. And he might like having some part-time work."

"Great. I have a good feeling about you, Maggie. I think you're just what the doctor ordered."

He gave her a quick tour of the long narrow building, which consisted of the cluttered front reception area, a fairly stark editor's office, a smaller office, and a grimy bathroom. In the back was a large room that housed a small, antiquated printing press and other various machines.

"Everything in the front half is your domain, Maggie, but *this* back here is my territory," declared Clyde proudly. "I lay out the paper, run the press, and oversee distribution."

"That's quite a job."

"You bet it is. And it's been one heck of a job to do it all on my own these past few months. There's been weeks when I haven't even been able to get the paper out." He shook his head sadly. "Just kills me when that happens."

"What is your circulation?"

Clyde rubbed his bristly chin. "Well, I print 500 copies. About half those stay in town and the rest get delivered."

"Who delivers them?"

He smiled sheepishly. "Yours truly."

She sighed. "I can see why you're so glad to see me."

"When can you start?"

"First I have a few questions."

"Shoot away, Maggie."

"Can we sit down and talk?"

"Why sure. How about if we go into *your* office." He led her back to the front of the building and into the editor's office. "This used to be Gavin's office. It looks pretty bare in here since he took most of his stuff with him. You feel free to furnish it however you like—just send the bill to me. There's a big office furniture store over in Byron."

"Where's Byron?"

"About twenty minutes from here. It's a good-sized town. Population of about 40,000 and growing fast. Folks 'round here do most of their shopping in Byron."

"You mean because it's so limited here in Pine Mountain." She studied his face.

He frowned slightly as he nodded. "Didn't used to be like that. Used to be you could find most anything you needed 'round here. But maybe that'll change."

"I hope so." She glanced around the dingy office for a place to sit.

"And while you're getting things for your office you might as well go ahead and spruce up the reception area too. Gavin always said he was going to do that..."

"Now, you say that Gavin is your nephew?" She spotted a couple of folding metal chairs against the wall.

"That's right. But we had a little falling out. I don't care much to talk about that." He pulled the chairs out and nodded for her to sit down.

"Okay, we won't talk about *that*," she said as she sat. Crossing her legs, she leaned forward, almost as if she were conducting her own interview. "But what I do want to talk about is what exactly is happening to this town? It looks like it's dying a slow and painful death."

Clyde nodded sadly. "Well, there's no denying that it's been hit with some hard times, Maggie. But I think if the right person came along—someone with youth and enthusiasm, someone with know-how and common sense—I think this town could be turned around."

She lifted one brow skeptically. "Do you really think that's possible?"

"Why sure it is. There's still lots of good folk here. And it's beautiful country—no place like it on earth. And believe you me, I've been around some to know."

"I can't disagree with you there, Clyde. It is beautiful here."

"See!" He pointed his finger like an exclamation mark. "And I've always believed that this newspaper could make a difference. That's why I bought the whole thing and brought Gavin out here back when the town first started to go downhill. I'd hoped that Gavin could make a difference..."

"But he didn't?"

"Like I said, I don't much like to talk about Gavin. The thing is, Maggie, *you* could make a difference. I just know you've got that kind of enthusiasm and drive..."

"How do you know that?" She leaned forward and peered into his faded blue eyes, searching for any sign of insincerity. She had no desire to be strung along by a smooth-talking old codger. "You've only had a few phone conversations with me. And we've barely met. Now tell me, how do you really know that I could do those things?"

He smiled smugly and tilted his chair back on two legs. "I just know, Maggie. You see, I have an innate sense about these things."

She thought about it for a moment. He seemed a little overly confident but at the same time genuine. "But what about Gavin? Didn't you have an innate sense about him..."

Clyde stood abruptly, noisily scraping the chair across the floor. He folded his arms stubbornly across his chest and looked her square in the eyes. "I *said* I don't want to talk about Gavin. And just for the record, I never did have that kind of a sense about him. He came to me with fancy promises and big expectations. And it just didn't work out. I hope this is the last time we have to talk about him."

Looking up at him, she saw the pain in his eyes. "I'm sorry. I know how family relationships in business can go sour, Clyde. But you must understand that I need to know as much as possible in order to make my decision..."

"Make your decision?" The old man's face clouded over like a little boy who'd just dropped his ice cream in the dirt. "But I thought you'd already made your decision, Maggie."

"Well, I thought I had too. But when I got here and saw the condition of things, I wasn't so sure anymore. It was quite a shock finding the town like this. And then when I saw the house…"

"You don't like the house?" His brow creased. "Now, what the devil's wrong with the house?"

"I'll admit that it's beautiful on the outside," she explained. "But have you ever seen the inside? Why, it's a wreck! The place is absolutely falling to pieces…"

"But it can be fixed, can't it? And you got it for a real bargain…"

"A *bargain*? Do you have any idea what it will take to restore that place?"

He shook his head.

"Me neither. But I'm a single mom, and I have to support my son and myself."

"Now, Maggie," soothed Clyde. "I think that house just needs a little TLC…"

"Or a bunch of TNT," she suddenly exploded. "I just can't believe that I made such a huge mistake…"

He looked crestfallen. "You think buying that house was a mistake?"

She shrugged. "I don't think the house is even habitable."

"But what about the carriage house? Can't you stay there until it gets fixed?"

"The carriage house is the only reason I'm still here." She sighed deeply.

He was pacing now, rubbing his chin, as if somehow this was all his fault.

"I'm sorry, Clyde. There's no point in taking all this out on you. It's that realtor that I should go after. Although I must admit, the carriage house is really quite nice. But it was a shock to find the big house is such disrepair."

"Maybe you just need some time," he suggested uncomfortably. "And maybe the repairs on the big house won't be so bad after all…"

"Maybe. By the way, thanks for the provisions. I assume they were from you."

He waved his hand. "I had Abigail run those things over."

"The lady who used to do the office work?"

"Yep. She's a good ol' gal."

"But you say that she's too old to work now?"

"Well, that's what *she* says. But then she and Gavin didn't get on too well, and now that he's gone..." He grew thoughtful as he hooked a thumb under a suspender. "And now that you're here...maybe we could get ol' Abigail to reconsider—that is if you were interested. Like I said before, Maggie, you're in charge of this paper. I expect you to make the decisions."

"I'd like to meet her."

"Good." He pulled a pocket-watch out of his pants pocket and flipped it open. "So, does that take care of your questions?"

She blinked. "I guess so, at least for now..."

"Fine, 'cause if I hurry I might still get in some bass fishing before it gets too hot out." Clyde tossed her a key. "Stay as long as you like. Make sure you lock up. Used to be no one locked anything in this town. But we've had some problems..."

And then he was gone. Maggie rose from the chair and looked out the dingy window behind her. Apparently Clyde saw no need for janitorial services. Well, she wasn't above using some of her own elbow grease. It might even prove a good way to work out some frustration. She turned around and studied the dimensions of her new office. It was many times larger than her old cubicle back at the *Times*. But then she remembered the circulation number for this newspaper and had to laugh out loud.

"Five hundred papers!" she exclaimed to herself in disbelief. "To think I came all the way up here to be the editor of five hundred papers."

Six

The deli was busier today, with several customers already seated and eating lunch. But Maggie couldn't help but notice that the majority of gingham-covered tables remained empty, their vases of fresh flowers waiting expectantly for admirers to come.

"You're still here!" exclaimed Rosa with a bright smile as Maggie and Spencer stepped up to the counter. "I was hoping we hadn't scared you off."

"We're going to give it a shot and see how things go," said Maggie as she scanned the chalkboard menu.

"Hey, Spencer," called Sierra as she carried an order to a table.

"Hey," answered Spencer with a shy grin.

Maggie winked at Rosa, then ordered the special for lunch. "By the way, Rosa, is there a furniture store somewhere nearby? I need some things for my office at the paper, and I thought it might be fun not to go the traditional office furniture route."

Rosa's eyes lit up. "I don't know if it's your style, Maggie, but a friend of ours runs Whitewater Works. It's a furniture store right here in Pine Mountain. The pieces are a little rustic but very nicely made."

"I saw that shop," said Spencer. "There was some cool looking stuff in there."

"It's down at the other end of town," said Rosa as she handed them their sodas. "Just a block beyond the newspaper office on the north side of Main Street."

"Thanks," said Maggie. "I'll check it out."

Sierra served them their food. "I have a break at one-thirty, Spencer," she said, as if they were old friends. "In case you're still in town and want to hang with me for awhile."

Spencer looked at his mother. "Is it okay?"

"Fine with me. I can walk around town and check out the local digs."

After lunch, Maggie went to the furniture store that Rosa had recommended. She noticed several rustic looking pieces in the window. Though they had a rugged appearance, the craftsmanship appeared to be very fine. She went inside and looked around. Each piece was beautifully and uniquely made. It was obvious that much time and care had gone into them, and yet the prices were surprisingly reasonable. These same pieces would go for much more in one of the many designer shops in southern California. Still, Maggie wasn't convinced she wanted rustic furniture for her office.

"May I help you?"

She turned around to see a tall man standing before her. His dark, straight hair was neatly tied back, and his high cheekbones and smooth features suggested Native American descent. The gaze from his nearly black eyes was surprisingly intense, catching her off-guard, as if he was reading her thoughts and knew she'd been admiring his looks. She felt her cheeks grow uncomfortably warm and she quickly glanced away, and refocused her attention on the fir bookshelf before her. She ran her hand over its satiny finish.

"Uh, yes," she stammered self-consciously. "I'm interested in some furniture for an office."

He nodded, but remained silent as if waiting for her to continue.

"And well, I don't really go in for this rustic furniture…" She stopped. "I mean it's well made and all, but I, uh…"

"You're not really the rustic type," he finished for her. She looked back up at him. Now it seemed as if he were assessing *her* appearance, and she grew uncomfortably aware of how Clyde had mentioned that she looked like a California girl, or something to that effect. Suddenly she felt all corporate and out of place in her tailored linen suit. With his faded denim shirt topped by a leather vest, this man seemed right at home in a place like Pine Mountain.

"So, what sort of style are you looking for?" he asked, folding his arms loosely across his chest and leaning back onto a massive pine table.

"Well, I really do like the rustic style, but I don't know if it would be appropriate for an office."

"I guess that depends on the office and the person. Is it for your office?"

She eyed him curiously. "Do you even carry office furniture?"

One side of his mouth curved into a half smile, almost as if he found her slightly amusing. "I do have a couple of desks in the back of the shop. But they're pretty much this same style. That's what this shop is all about." He made no move to show her anything, as if waiting for her to give up and leave.

Maggie frowned, not ready to give up. "Well, I guess I could look at them."

He gestured toward the rear of the store. "Right this way."

She followed him, noticing now that he wore knee-high fringed moccasins with his jeans tucked neatly inside. She smiled to herself. This was definitely not the sort of person you'd see walking down the streets of Southern California, that is unless you were in Hollywood and someone happened to be filming a Daniel Boone movie.

He went to the back of the store and stopped in front of a large desk. It was slightly different in that the drawers and face of this piece were adorned in a design of twigs and what appeared to be birch bark. Rustic, yet with an unexpected natural elegance. Maggie ran her hand over the top of the desk. Like everything else in the shop, its finish was as smooth as glass. She touched the ornamental pieces to see if they were securely attached. To her surprise there were no rough edges and a thin coat of varnish protected their surface. She experimentally pulled out a drawer. It slid perfectly, and the inside was lined with rose-colored cedar.

"I've only seen cedar used for the storage of clothing," she commented. "I'm surprised that a manufacturer would waste cedar on a desk."

"Waste?" His dark eyes flashed.

"Well, it seems a little extravagant for a desk."

"Smell the wood," he commanded in a quiet voice.

She leaned over and sniffed the pungent, fresh aroma. "Yes, it is lovely, but..."

"You think that's a waste?"

She stood back up and looked at him curiously. "Maybe not a waste. But unnecessary, perhaps..."

He nodded. "I see. Perhaps you might find something more suited to your needs at another sort of furniture store. There is a large commercial outlet over in..."

"I'm not saying I don't like this piece," interrupted Maggie, suddenly feeling the need to defend her right to purchase it if she pleased. "In fact," she turned to look at the unusual desk again, "I think it might be just perfect."

He looked at her doubtfully. "I thought you weren't the rustic..."

"Are you trying to talk me out of it?"

His mouth smiled, but his eyes remained sober. "No. Believe me, I have no desire to run off what few customers do come through this town."

"I'm sure your boss will appreciate that."

His brows raised slightly, and suddenly she regretted her assumption. Perhaps he was the owner of this shop.

"I probably should introduce myself," she said quickly, hoping to recover from her mistake, if she had made one. "I've only just moved to Pine Mountain. I'm the new editor of the *Pine Cone*. My name is Maggie Carpenter." She extended her hand.

He shook her hand formally. "Pleased to meet you. I'm Jed Whitewater."

"And so," she said with realization, "this must be your store."

He glanced at his watch. "Yes. Kate usually works in the shop, but I fill in now and then as needed."

"Of course, that makes sense. And what do you do with the rest of your time?" She knew she was prying, but it came with being a reporter. And what she really wanted to know was...who is Kate?

"I make furniture."

"You made all this furniture?"

He nodded. "Yes, and as you can see, it's getting crowded in here. I need to move some of it."

She looked back at all the furniture filling the shop and shook her head in amazement. "You are one very talented man, Mr. Whitewater."

"Please, call me Jed."

"Well, I definitely want this desk," said Maggie decisively. "And if you're as good a salesman as craftsman, you ought to try and sell me a few more things. I've got an empty office and a reception area to fill. Any suggestions?"

Before long they found several pieces to compliment the desk, and then a few more to use in the reception area. Suddenly Maggie began envisioning the office in a whole new light. She would use natural elements to enhance the rustic decor, a Navajo rug, a basket of pine cones by the door... suddenly the possibilities seemed endless.

"This is great," said Maggie as they walked over to the counter. "I can't wait to see it all together..."

"I'm back, Jed," sang a woman's voice from the rear of the store.

"There you are, Kate," said Jed as an attractive blond woman appeared. She was casually dressed in faded jeans and a navy vest worn over a plain, white T-shirt, but she could've been on the cover of a fashion magazine. She temptingly waved a small brown bag in front of Jed.

"I brought you some lunch." She flashed a brilliant smile his way, then glanced over to Maggie and added, "Sorry, it took me so long at the dentist, Jed. Want me to finish up this transaction for you?"

"No, that's okay. I'll handle it." Jed set the bag on the counter. "By the way, Kate, this is Maggie Carpenter. She's the new editor of the *Pine Cone.*" He looked back at Maggie. "And this is Kate Murray, my right-hand gal."

Maggie wondered what being a right-hand gal entailed. She saw no sign of wedding bands on either of them, but knew that meant nothing these days. What surprised her most was that she was even curious.

"Welcome to Pine Mountain, Maggie," said Kate warmly, reaching out to firmly shake Maggie's hand. "I hope you like it here."

"Thanks, it's certainly a beautiful place to live."

"Do you hike or ski or anything?" asked Kate eagerly, although her eyes looked doubtful. Kate's tall, athletic, suntanned appearance suggested she was an outdoor enthusiast. And for the second time that day, Maggie grew uncomfortably aware of how very out of place she seemed in a town like Pine Mountain.

"I do ski occasionally. I haven't hiked in years. But I'd like to get back into doing some of those things."

"Then you've come to the right place." Kate turned to Jed. "All right, I guess I'll go unpack those boxes of hardware that just came in."

He focused his attention back on Maggie. "So, is that going to be everything for you?"

She glanced once again at the small pine table and four ladder-back chairs that she'd been admiring off and on since she'd entered the store. The set would go well in the carriage house, much more suitable than her large, ornate oak dining set. "One more thing," she said suddenly, pointing to the table. "I think I'll take that dining set too. Would you please put it on a separate bill?"

"Be glad to." Jed went over to get the tags. "Do you want these delivered to the *Pine Cone* too?"

"No. I'll need them delivered to my home." She gave him the location and began to write out the check.

"You're kidding." Jed looked at her curiously. "You mean you're the one who bought the old Barnes place?"

"*Barnes* place?" she repeated. "You mean, as in *Clyde Barnes?*"

"Exactly. Clyde's folks built that place 'round the turn of the century."

She stared at him incredulously. "That was Clyde's house?"

"Well, he hasn't lived there for ages. He has a real nice cabin out on Silver Lake. But he grew up in that homestead as a boy. His younger brother's family lived in the house for years after the parents passed on, but the property has always belonged to Clyde."

"Oh dear," she said as she recalled her harsh criticism earlier. "I had no idea it was Clyde's house. I hope I didn't offend him."

"How's that?"

She grimaced. "Well, I complained about the condition of the house. I basically told him that the place was a wreck."

Jed chuckled. "Is it?"

"Let's just say it needs a *lot* of work. If it wasn't for the carriage house, I think I'd be on my way back to California right now."

"I see." He handed her the two receipts. "What are you going to do about it?"

She sighed. "I'm not completely sure. The funny thing is, my fourteen-year-old son, who dragged his heels all the way from L.A., has taken a sudden interest in trying to fix up the old place. It has sort of given me hope..."

He leaned forward against the counter with what seemed unusual interest. "So, does your kid know anything about remodeling?"

Maggie laughed lightly. "Well, no. Not really. But he's got all his dad's tools, and he thinks he does."

"And where's his dad?"

She looked down at her checkbook. "He's dead," she said briefly, in the same moment wishing she'd put it more delicately. Even after two years, she still found it hard to deal with these questions. She disliked people's discomfort with her answers and she always tried to move quickly to another subject.

"I'm sorry," was all he said.

She looked back up at Jed. His eyes seemed to understand her loss, and she wondered if perhaps he had lost someone too. "It's been a couple of years now," she said surprising herself. "I know I should be beyond it, but sometimes it seems..." She stopped herself. Why was she telling him all this? The man was a virtual stranger.

"Seems like he should still be around?"

She cocked her head slightly. Who was this strange furniture-making man in the funny-looking moccasins anyway? But she only said, "Yes, that pretty much describes it."

The bell on the front door jingled and they both turned to see.

"Hey, Mom," called Spencer.

"Hey, you," called Maggie, relieved to detour their conversation. "Come and meet Mr. Whitewater."

Spencer walked up to the counter and Maggie put a proud arm around her son's shoulders and introduced them. As they shook hands Maggie explained that Jed had made all the furniture in the store. Spencer was suitably impressed.

"And I hear that you're handy with a hammer too," commented Jed as he walked them to the front door.

"Huh?" Spencer's face grew puzzled.

"Well, aren't you planning to do some repairs on the old Barnes house?"

"Oh, you mean where we live? Yeah, sure. I thought I might fix up some things."

"If you need a hand, feel free to give me a call," offered Jed.

Maggie turned and studied his face. Was this a sincere offer, or just an off-the-cuff remark?

"I mean it," he said. "I've had some experience with restorations. I wouldn't mind taking a look and giving you some advice—if you like, that is."

"That'd be great," said Maggie. "Maybe when you deliver the dining set, you could walk through and tell me what you think of the place."

"Be glad to." Jed opened the door for them. "Nice to meet you both. And once again, welcome to Pine Mountain."

Seven

So, what do you think of the town, Spence?" asked Maggie, almost afraid to hear his answer.

"It's okay, I guess, for a one-horse town. Sierra showed me a shop that sells snowboarding stuff. She knows the guy who runs it. It didn't seem like he had much to choose from, but he says he can get 'most anything for a decent price from catalogs. Plus he's got some rental boards, but when he wasn't listening Sierra told me the rental boards looked pretty lame."

Maggie eyed her son cautiously. "So, do you think we'll still be here by the time snow flies?"

He shrugged. "You never know, Mom."

"Do you want to see the inside of the newspaper office?" she asked as they walked toward the car.

"I guess so, but it sure doesn't look like much from the outside."

She laughed. "It's not much on the inside either. But I need to use the phone to check on the moving van and to get our phone hooked up."

Maggie made some calls from her barren office while Spencer nosed around. As she waited on hold with the phone company, she tried to imagine her new furniture all set up in here.

"All done," she finally called to Spencer. "What do you think of the place?"

He made a grim face. "I don't mean to offend you, Mom, but it's pretty dumpy."

"I know. I'm hoping to change that. I've already ordered new furniture, and I want to get some other things to perk it up. Which gives me an idea, Spence. Want to make a deal?"

He frowned. "Sounds like it involves work."

She smiled slyly. "But what if the payment is a snowboard?"

His face brightened, then dimmed slightly as she launched into a detailed plan for cleaning and clearing out the front half of the newspaper office. But to her pleased surprise he agreed, and before long they made a detailed list, rounded up boxes and cleaning supplies, and Spencer went right to work.

"I'm going to run a bunch of errands, and then I'll be back to pick you up around five," called Maggie. "Have fun!"

He groaned dramatically, but she knew he had visions of snowboards swooshing through his head. What he didn't know was that she would've gladly purchased him a board anyway, just to entice him to give Pine Mountain a fair shake. But it'd be even better if he felt he had helped to earn it himself. Phil had always talked about how kids needed to invest their energy into things, rather than having things just handed to them. It wasn't always easy though, and in the past two years her demanding career and grief over her loss had made it simpler to just give things to Spencer. Perhaps that would begin to change now.

She was surprised to find a few more businesses in town than she had realized, but many of them were forlorn little shops with poor inventory. And the ever-present faded for-sale sign sat in many front windows, itself a proclamation of defeat. She went into several shops, taking time to introduce herself to the locals, and when she could find something she could use, she purchased it. For the most part, she felt welcomed. Many were hopeful at the prospects of a new newspaper editor. But some of the shopkeepers seemed disheartened and apathetic. It was clear that they had given up on Pine Mountain and couldn't understand why anyone would choose to relocate here.

Cal, the owner of the secondhand store, was especially vocal. "Don't know why anyone in their right mind would leave a good job down at the *Los Angeles Times* to come up here. Can't you see this place ain't much more than a ghost town? Better get out of here while you can, young lady."

"I'm surprised that you'd continue to stay here if you feel that way," said Maggie. She glanced around the musty, grimy, cluttered shop. Even if there was anything she needed here, she'd never find it amidst the chaos, and Cal didn't budge from the old recliner behind the counter where a little black and white TV blared.

He pointed to the for-sale sign in his window. "If I could get a decent offer on this place, I'd be outta here in a heartbeat. But every penny I have is stuck in this shop. And who wants to buy property in a hole-in-the-wall town like this?"

She nodded sympathetically. "Yes, I see your problem, Cal. Tell you what, if I hear of anyone wanting some business property, I'll be sure to send them your way."

"Well now, I'd appreciate that. Maybe some of your fancy Los Angeles friends might like to buy me out." His eyes lit up. "I'd give 'em a real good deal on the whole kit-n-caboodle."

Maggie grinned. She could just imagine the faces of her friends if they could see this shop full of garage sale leftovers and Salvation Army rejects. "Thanks for you time, Cal." She waved and retreated back out to the street, eager to breathe the fresh, clean air again. She had noticed an antique shop on the other end of town, not far from Jed Whitewater's store. She didn't know if it would be any better than the secondhand store, but decided to give it a try.

To her surprise, Clara Lou's Antiques was a pleasant little shop. Classical music played softly, and a large crystal bowl of potpourri by the front door greeted customers with a sweet fragrance. Maggie introduced herself to a grandmotherly sort of person who turned out to be the owner of the store.

"Well, I'm so glad you've joined our little community," said Clara. "And I hope you'll be happy here. We moved over here because Lou loves to hunt and fish. And thanks to his retirement we don't have to worry about whether or not business is good." She waved her hand around the cheerful shop. "I do this just for the fun of it."

Maggie smiled at the tiny white-haired woman. "Lucky for you. You seem to have a good selection here. Maybe you can help me. I'm looking for some pieces to use as decorative accents at the *Pine Cone*. I bought some rustic furniture from Whitewater Works..."

"Honey, you've come to the right place," exclaimed Clara. "Let me show you."

It wasn't long before Clara had rounded up a good selection of baskets, including some Indian pieces, some earthenware pots to use for plants, a couple of Navajo rugs, and other various old pieces to use as accents. She even pulled out an old wooden wheelbarrow.

"You could put the weekly edition in this and keep it in the reception area," suggested Clara.

"What a great idea!"

"When Abigail was still working there, I tried to get her to buy it for that purpose, but she was afraid that Gavin would object. That man was always such a sourpuss."

"Is Abigail a friend of yours?"

Clara smiled. "Next to Lou, she's my best friend. She's the only reason we discovered Pine Mountain. She and her husband moved here back in the sixties. Lou and I would come to visit them. Finally, we decided that we wanted to make it our home too."

"I can understand why. It's a beautiful place." Maggie examined a wicker fishing creel that looked like it could be adapted into a mailbox for her office.

"Abigail's husband passed away a few years back." Clara sadly shook her head. "Working at the paper was all that kept her going after he was gone."

"Do you think she'd like to come back?"

Clara's eyes lit up. "Well, I don't know for sure. But she just might."

"Would you tell her that I'd like to meet with her—that is if she's interested. I can't promise anything, but at least I'd like to talk with her."

"I'll tell her." Clara reached out and clasped Maggie's hand, giving it a tender squeeze. "I think you're just what this town needs—a little bit of life and spirit. I hope everything works out for you, dear."

Maggie carefully tucked her new-found treasures in her car and then decided to hurry over to the post office in order to rent a mailbox before closing time. She'd been disappointed to learn there was no rural route by her house and that no daily newspapers were delivered in that area. Inconvenience seemed to be the price one paid for living in nature's wonderland. Hopefully, it would be worth it.

She suspected the man behind the counter to be the postmaster. His grim face seemed to match the framed photo behind him proclaiming *Greg Snider, Postmaster*, but the large, slightly balding man had the social skills of a longshoreman. He didn't even greet her. And when she introduced herself and made a request for a post office box, he just grunted and shoved a form at her. And then he stared, tapping his fingers impatiently, as she quickly filled in the form. She glanced at the clock, thinking perhaps she had kept him past closing time, yet it was barely past four.

"Here," she said, quickly handing the form back. She fumbled in her purse for cash, not wanting to waste his precious time writing out a check, then handed him a twenty. "I'll pay for six months' rent today."

"You really think you'll be here that long?" He pushed a thinning strand of hair off his forehead and handed her the change.

"I hope so." She forced a smile. "I think Pine Mountain's a wonderful place."

"Let's hear what you think of it come the first winter storm."

"I'm looking forward to winter."

He rolled his eyes. "I don't even know why Clyde insists on keeping that paper going." He plunked a mailbox key on the counter. "Nobody reads it anyway."

Maggie stared at him for a long moment, their eyes locked in stalemate. Why was he so antagonistic? A variety of sarcastic remarks flitted through her head, but she controlled herself and simply said, "Well, maybe they'll start reading it now."

He slapped a closed sign on the counter and then walked away. She glanced at the clock. It was only four-ten and the hours posted said the office closed at five. Oh well, it wasn't her problem that the man was rude and lazy. It was just too bad he was the postmaster. Did he cast his gloomy shadow on everyone who came in there, or did he reserve it for newcomers like herself? It was becoming clear to her that not everyone in Pine Mountain was a happy camper. It was rather sad, because the town's setting had such great potential. As she walked down the street, she marveled that the snow-capped mountains could actually be seen from town. Already, she had begun to care about Pine Mountain and its future. She just hoped that Clyde was right about her being the kind of person who could make a difference.

Suddenly a flashing blue light caught Maggie's eye and she looked over to see the sheriff's car parked right in front of the *Pine Cone* office. Memories of drive-by shootings zipped unwanted through her mind as she raced down the street. She knew it was ridiculous. This was Pine Mountain. Still, her heart pounded with fear as she imagined Spencer harmed in any way. What if he had climbed on something and fallen? She'd come to Pine Mountain to escape any more tragedies—how could something have gone wrong so soon?

"What's going on?" she demanded breathlessly when she spotted the sheriff walking cautiously up to the front door, his right hand hovering over his gun holster.

"Got a burglary," he answered gruffly. "You stay back, ma'am."

"My son's in..."

Just then the front door burst open and Spencer lunged forward with Clyde right behind him with a hand clasped tightly around Spencer's upper arm.

"Spencer!" cried Maggie, pushing past the officer to reach her son. "What in the world's going on here?"

Spencer's blue eyes sparked with anger. "This crazy old coot thinks that I broke into the newspaper office!"

"Clyde!" cried Maggie. "This is my son Spencer!"

Clyde released Spencer, and Maggie threw a protective arm around her son's shoulders. "Sorry about this, Spence. Are you okay?"

He shrugged, then narrowed his eyes toward Clyde.

"I caught him carrying some boxes out back!" snapped Clyde, his face still flushed with excitement. "Looked to me like he was up to no good."

"I asked Spencer to do some cleaning and to clear some boxes out for me," explained Maggie, still feeling a little shaken.

"Well, I've had problems in the past." Clyde glanced uncomfortably at the sheriff. "And I just figured it was more of the same. Sorry, Warner, I guess it was a false alarm this time."

The sheriff peered at Spencer, then back at Maggie. "This your new editor, Clyde?"

She took a deep breath, then, without waiting for Clyde's introduction, extended her hand, determined to regain a sense of dignity. "Yes. I'm Maggie Carpenter. And this is my son, Spencer. As you can see, he's *not* a thief. He was only helping me with some *much-needed* cleaning." She threw a sharp glance at Clyde.

"Glad to meet you both." He touched the tip of his cap. "I'm Sheriff Warner. Sorry 'bout the mix-up, ma'am. I'll be on my way now."

Maggie thanked him, then looked back at Clyde. The old man smiled sheepishly, then turned to Spencer and said, "Heck of a way to meet my new editor's son. I'm real sorry about jumping you like that, boy. But, well, you see I've had some problems in the past. And I just thought you were one of them..."

Spencer looked at Clyde doubtfully, then finally shrugged and said, "It's okay. I s'pose it did look suspicious to you since we'd never met before."

Maggie was so proud she wanted to hug her son, but instead said calmly, "It's partly my fault for not introducing you two. I'm sorry."

Apologies were repeated, and then she informed Clyde about the furniture purchases she'd made.

He frowned. "You bought stuff from Jed Whitewater?"

"Well, yes. Is that a problem? He makes some very nice things..."

"You're going to bring a bunch of that Indian trash in here?"

Maggie glanced at Spencer, hoping for support, then realized this was her battle to fight. She stood up straight and looked Clyde in the eye. Might as well have it out right now. "First of all, Clyde," she spoke in a firm voice, "it's *not* a bunch of Indian trash. It's a very well-made style of rustic furniture. And I think it will look perfect in the *Pine Cone*. Furthermore, I thought you told me I was in charge of the front offices and reception area. And if you're worried about the cost, I will pay for it myself."

"I'm not complaining about the money, Maggie. I've been called many things, but a tightwad is not one of them. I just don't understand why you'd even want a bunch of that Indian..."

"Native American," she corrected.

Clyde put his hands on his hips and glared at her. "Now, I s'pose you're gonna give me a two-bit lecture on the latest politically correct jargon!"

In spite of herself, she had to smile. Clyde—politically correct—was it even possible? But she could try. "Well, I've found that in the media business, it's least offensive to use the current P.C. terms."

"You mean if you can keep up with the current..."

"We're getting away from the point, Clyde," she said. "We were talking about the office decor. And I think we had better get things clarified from the start. As I recall, you said that I have complete control of the front half of the building. Have you changed your mind?"

He groaned and shook his head. "No. I just don't want the place looking like we're going to have a powwow."

She studied him carefully. "You know, Clyde, you're going to have to trust me with a lot of big things when it comes to running this paper. Office decor is a pretty small part of the big picture. If you don't trust me, maybe we should get it out into the open right now."

"I trust you, Maggie. And I'm a man of my word." He sighed deeply, almost as if in resignation. "You go ahead and do as you think best. I'll trust your judgment on this."

She eyed him skeptically. "'On this?'"

"Yes, and on other matters, too. But I can't promise that I won't give you my opinion from time to time."

"I would hope that you would, Clyde."

"But you're the one running this paper from now on, young lady. And I'm counting on you to make a difference in this town."

She swallowed. "I hope I can, but I'm already starting to feel it won't be easy."

"Good things don't usually come easy, Maggie."

"So I've heard."

He turned back to Spencer, who had been listening intently the whole time. "You've got yourself quite a mama, young man. You know that?"

Spencer looked at Maggie, then grinned knowingly. "She's not so bad, if you know how to *work* her that is."

Clyde chuckled. "Well, I'd be obliged if you'd share some tips on just how you do that, son."

Eight

That night, Maggie sat on the floor of the carriage house with her laptop and wrote a brief email to Rebecca.

RB,

Well, I'm either a fool or a dreamer, I'm not sure which, but for the time being I'll stay here. The old guy who owns the paper thinks that I've come to save his town—ha! I can just imagine you laughing at me right now. Me, the one who likes to quietly write behind the scenes, now about to take on an impossible mission like this! But I must admit I like the challenge, and it's amazing how much this old guy seems to believe in me. Anyway, we've agreed not to publish the paper for a couple of weeks so I can get to know the town better, not that there's much to know. I thought I might start working on an editorial tonight, maybe do a little reminiscing about how I remember Pine Mountain in its former glory days and how I believe it could be restored… The question is, do I really believe it? It is so incredibly dismal. But, hey, miracles can still happen—right? Keep praying, old friend. And please don't be overwhelmed by all my little emails. It's good therapy for me.

mc

"When does the moving van get here?" called Spencer from his lofty perch above.

Maggie stretched and looked at her watch. "Tomorrow. Do you mind sticking around here while I go to town to supervise the furniture delivery at the *Pine Cone*?"

"Guess not."

"Thanks, Spence. You've been a great help."

He made a grunting noise of acknowledgment, then flipped off his light. "Night, Mom."

"Good night." She turned off her computer, then went to the kitchen and poured the last of the decaf into her mug. Grabbing a blanket, she quietly slipped outside and sat down on the front step. The cool air washed over her face as she slowly turned her head from side to side to relieve the stiffness in her neck, a result of writing for too long in an uncomfortable position. At the *Times* they had often received lectures for not practicing good ergonomics. What a luxury it would be when their furnishings arrived and she could set up her desk area. She rubbed a particularly sore spot on her right shoulder, then suddenly remembered the feeling when Phil would massage her neck after a long day at the computer. She sighed. He seemed so far, far away now. Back in their old home in California there had been constant reminders of him everywhere she looked. From the brick walk he'd put in the front yard to the fruit trees he'd planted in back. Each time she sat on the tri-level deck, his carpentry masterpiece, she had thought of him. It had been a real source of comfort—sometimes she almost forgot that he was gone, pretending he was only at work. It had been a silly little game, but it had helped to pass those first few difficult months. Now here she was, in a different town and in a different house, and suddenly it seemed like all traces of Phil were completely erased from her life. She swallowed hard. What disturbed her most was that she couldn't even see his face in her mind right now. And all the photos were packed away, riding across the country in a moving van. She looked up at the stars shining brightly overhead, so close it felt as though she could touch them. The stars were closer in Pine Mountain, but it seemed that Phil was moving farther and farther away. Perhaps it was time to let him go. She felt the lump grow in her throat, and she wondered how she would ever completely be able to do that.

Even on the day when the sixteen-year-old's bullet had stolen him from her, even then she had not *let* him go. Instead, she had clung to him more tightly than ever before. In bitterness and anger, she had clung, unwilling to part with that which was hers. Then later she became angry at him for abandoning her. Why had he insisted upon being a hero? Jumping in to protect another, and in that same instant leaving his own family vulnerable and unprotected. But anger brought no relief to her hopeless grief, and she had quickly discovered that only God could hold her together. Without God she would have shattered into a million pieces and gone spinning uncontrollably throughout the universe. And then Spencer would have been all alone. So she had ceased clinging to Phil, and instead learned to cling to God. Now she realized with sudden clarity that Phil had been moving further and further away from her until it felt he'd become only a memory. And as painful as it was, she knew that it was right.

Something about the still night and brilliant stars made it easier to face this reality. For the first time since Phil's death, she felt a deep sense of gratitude just to be alive. She also sensed that the road before her wasn't going to be easy, but that God would lead. Once again, she prayed for strength. She'd never considered herself a particularly strong person, in fact she had never wanted to be. But it seemed more than ever that strength would be needed. Raising a teenager and running a newspaper would require it. She prayed for the town of Pine Mountain and all its residents. She didn't know God's plan for this town, but she wanted to be part of it, and she wanted to make a difference.

For a long time, she sat in silent contentment. Glad to be alive, and glad to be in Pine Mountain. She thought of Jed Whitewater and their conversation earlier today. For a brief moment, it had seemed as if he had gazed right into her soul. And then within that same moment they were nothing more than two strangers from two very different worlds. She thought about Kate, and wondered once again about what kind of relationship those two shared. It didn't take a genius to guess. Kate was a beauty, and the way she had flashed that smile at Jed seemed to say it all. Suddenly Maggie was assaulted by a wave of loneliness. She wrapped the blanket more tightly around her.

"I am not alone," she said quietly. "I have my son. I have my God. I am *not* alone."

ᴐ—

The next day, she stopped by the deli. "Morning, Rosa," she called cheerfully. "Got any coffee?"

"Hello, Maggie," said Rosa. "Just brewed a fresh pot of Starbucks."

"You use Starbucks?"

"You bet. We might live in the sticks, but we can still drink big city coffee."

Maggie laughed. "Well, I'll tell you, I'd give up big city coffee in heartbeat just for the commute time of living in the sticks. It took me *three minutes* to get to town this morning. I love it!"

Rosa handed her a cup of coffee. "I've got some blueberry muffins just out of the oven," she said temptingly.

"Sounds great. I'm going over to the office to wait for my new furniture to arrive. Jed is delivering it this morning."

"Good for you! I'm glad you took my advice. Doesn't he do beautiful work?"

Maggie nodded. "I also found a few other things to add as decorative touches. I can't wait to see it all together."

"Are you going to hire any help?"

"I think so. Clyde didn't seem to have a problem with that." She glanced around to see if anyone else was listening, but the only other customers were a couple tucked away in the corner. "You know, Rosa, I can't help but wonder how the paper gets by financially. I know the subscribers can't support it, and I didn't see enough ads to keep it going..."

Rosa waved her hand. "Oh, you don't need to worry about that, Maggie. Clyde has more money than he knows what to do with—that is," she lowered her voice, "unless that scoundrel of a nephew has cleaned him out."

"Gavin?"

Rosa nodded. "Has Clyde told you much?"

"No. He doesn't like to talk about him."

"I can understand why." Rosa put the muffin into a bag and handed it to Maggie. "Say, we're taking the boat out to the lake tomorrow after work, having a little picnic. Spencer gets on so well with Sierra, why don't you two join us?"

Maggie smiled. "That would be fun. I've been wanting to show Spencer the lake. I haven't seen it since I was a kid."

"Good. Meet us at the main dock around six."

⌒

Maggie was impressed with how much Spencer had accomplished before he'd been accosted by Clyde. Yesterday she hadn't even noticed that her office had a wood floor, but today it glowed. And the window sparkled. Looking out she realized that it faced Pine Street and that she could see the boarded-up backside of the old Pine Mountain Hotel. Too bad someone wasn't interested in restoring that place. It would be such a shot in the arm for this town. She turned her attention back to her office, imagining where she would have Jed place the new pieces. Only the old five-drawer wooden file cabinet remained, wedged into a corner and too heavy to move. She began to peruse through the dusty faded files that looked as if they hadn't been touched in decades. Good history, but little help for the present. She wondered if

Gavin had kept any sort of records, or had he taken everything with him? No matter, she didn't mind starting fresh.

She went out to the reception area where Spencer had stacked the office machinery on the large front counter. She hadn't taken time to check on the quality of the electronic equipment before, but was surprised to see that everything looked fairly new and was top of the line. It almost appeared as if it had never been used.

"Hello there, Maggie," called Clyde as he came through the front door.

"Good morning, Clyde." She turned around and was surprised once again by his crusty appearance. She thought maybe yesterday had been a fluke, that perhaps she'd caught him on an off day. But it seemed that Clyde's garb of choice was stained shirts, work jeans, and frayed red suspenders. She smiled, glad that she'd worn jeans and a T-shirt today. She felt more like a Pine Mountainer.

"Hey, I thought you were going to take a few days to get yourself adjusted. I don't want you tuckering out before you've even begun."

"Well, my mother has always accused me of being a workaholic, but I'm trying to reform my ways. Actually, I only stopped by to supervise the new furniture delivery."

He nodded grimly. "Jed bringing that stuff by today?"

"Yes," she said firmly. "And if that's going to be a problem..."

"Not at all." He held up his hands in submission. "This is your show, Maggie. Run it how you like. All I ask is that it be a big success."

She frowned at him. "You don't expect much, do you?"

He laughed. "Just miracles, is all."

"Then you had better start praying."

"What makes you think I'm not." He winked at her. "Now, don't mind me. I just came to pick up a couple of things and to check the answering machine for news leads and whatnot. Then I'll be out of your hair."

"Say, Clyde," began Maggie curiously, "these computers and printers and things look brand new."

A shadow crossed his face. "Yep. They are."

"You didn't have to go to all that trouble for me. I certainly didn't expect everything to be state of the art around here, and these look really nice."

"Well, if I hadn't gotten these you'd have been stuck using a pencil and two-bit tablet. Don't think you'd have liked that too much."

"You mean you didn't have *any* computers or printers when Gavin ran the paper?"

He sighed deeply. "Oh yeah, I had computers all right. But they sort of upped and disappeared when Gavin left."

"Oh, I see. I'm sorry, Clyde."

"Me too. Now, let's not talk about it anymore. It gets my indigestion going."

She smiled. "Well, if it makes you feel any better, I appreciate this equipment and will do my best to utilize it well."

"I know you will, Maggie."

She watched as he walked slowly toward his domain in the back. His step was slow but strong. She wondered how old he was. Her first impression was that he was ancient, but now she wasn't so sure. He seemed to be in good health, able to go fishing and work on the paper. Still, he seemed awfully old, far beyond the traditional retirement age. Rosa had said that Clyde's philanthropy kept the paper afloat. If that was true, what would become of the paper if something happened to him? Maggie sighed. Best not to worry about such things now. Better to focus her energies on making the paper as self-supporting as possible.

"Hello in there?"

She looked up to see Jed Whitewater peering through the door. "Come in," she called.

He propped open the door and waved to Kate, who was standing out on the sidewalk. "If you're ready, we'll start bringing it in."

"Of course," said Maggie. "Can I help?"

He shook his head. "Thanks, but we'll be fine. We're used to doing this."

She was surprised at the disappointment she felt when she saw Kate helping him. She realized that she'd hoped he would come alone and that he'd need her help to put the furniture into place. As it was, she tried to keep out of their way, simply pointing to where each piece should go. Within minutes they were finished.

"Can we drop that table set by your house today?" asked Jed.

"Sure," said Maggie. "I plan to be home all afternoon."

"See you later then."

Maggie studied the new furniture in her office, and even experimented with some of the antique accents she had acquired yesterday. The overall effect was much better than she had expected. Then she set up her phone, fax, and desktop computer, taking a minute to check her email. Rebecca had finally responded.

MC,

Sorry I've been so busy that I haven't answered your fascinating little notes. I'm just in shock that you've really done this, Maggie! When are you coming home? No, that wasn't fair—just selfish on my part. The truth is, I'm very excited about your new little venture. I think you've done the right thing. And if not, you can always start over. You know how many times I've reinvented my life—each time more interesting than the last. I must admit, your new life sounds quite charming in a Garrison Keiller sort of way, and the challenges will probably be good for you. I may even be a little bit envious. But I don't think I'd last a week in a town that size—no big corporate firm to sue the pants off of. :) Keep me informed, and hang in there, kiddo!

RB

Maggie smiled to herself as she exited the Internet. Rebecca, in her three-hundred-dollar suits and alligator shoes, would make quite a spectacle on the unpretentious streets of Pine Mountain. She jotted down a quick list of a few more things she needed to complete her office, then glanced at her watch and realized it was time to go home and check on Spencer and the moving van. It still amazed her that she could get to and from home in mere minutes. It had taken longer than that just to enter the freeway back in L.A. She put the windows down as she drove—no more putrid exhaust fumes or overheated traffic jams. And the scenic view was unbelievable. Rebecca and her other friends in L.A. would be so envious. Of course, they'd also roll over laughing if they realized how she'd come up here to run a paper the size of the *Pine Cone*—which was actually more the size of a pine nut!

She spotted Spencer out in the front yard as she pulled into the driveway, but something large and brown and wiggling was jumping at him. As she climbed out of the car she realized it was a dog.

"Hey, Mom!" called Spencer. "Look at this." He threw a stick and the dog dashed after it and brought it right back. Spencer leaned over and patted the dog. "Isn't he great?"

Maggie curiously studied the large animal. "He looks like a chocolate lab. Where did he come from?"

"I don't know. He was just out here barking this morning. And he doesn't have a collar or anything. I gave him a piece of cheese, and now he thinks he's my best friend." Spencer was grinning. "Can I keep him, Mom?"

Maggie laughed. "You remind me of when you were six and brought home that cocker spaniel, remember?"

Spencer rolled his eyes. "This is different, Mom. I didn't kidnap *this* dog."

"I know. But I'm sure a dog like this belongs to someone. And his owners are probably frantic."

Spencer frowned. "Or maybe they were mean to him and he ran away to find a better home." He leaned over and scratched the dog's ear, and was rewarded with a sloppy wet tongue across his cheek.

"I have no problem with having a dog, Spence. But we need to do the responsible thing and see if we can locate this guy's owners."

Spencer groaned.

"Honey, think about it. If you had lost your dog, what would you want someone to do?"

"But our phone's not even hooked up."

"We can go to town."

"What about the moving van?"

"Okay, I'll go to town. And while I'm at it I'll bring us back some lunch. Which reminds me, Rosa invited us to join them at the lake tomorrow."

"Great."

Maggie patted the dog on the head. "He is a beauty, Spencer. But that makes me even more sure he has owners."

"Maybe they want to sell him."

She smiled as she walked back to the car. In some ways, Spencer was still so naïve and vulnerable. She knew that would change in time. But for now she would savor the moment. Too bad he couldn't keep the dog, but maybe they could find another one.

Nine

*T*o tell you the truth, Mom," began Maggie, "we've only been here a few days and I've acquired an antiquated house that's about to crumble, a boss who looks like he just crawled out of the hills, and now Spencer thinks we should adopt a runaway dog." Maggie couldn't bring herself to even mention the disappointing status of the town itself.

Her mother laughed on the other end. "Oh, my. Sounds as if your life is full of exciting challenges. I think I'm jealous."

"Come on out and see," suggested Maggie dryly. "I'm sure there's enough challenges to go around. I'll even introduce you to my new boss—although I doubt he's your type, and I'm sure he's old enough to be my great-grandfather."

"I always did like older men. Speaking of men, how's my grandson?"

Maggie filled her mother in on Spencer's adjustment to Pine Mountain and how Sierra had helped out. "...and tomorrow we're going out to the lake with the girl's parents."

"It sounds delightful, Maggie. I'm so happy for you. Keep in touch, and good luck finding the owner of that dog."

Maggie hung up, then called the local radio and newspaper in Byron, informing the appropriate sources of the found chocolate lab. She left the *Pine Cone* phone number for responses, then called a couple of vets to see if any were familiar with the dog. Finally she made and placed several signs in town, bought some dog food at the market, then picked up lunches to go and went home, halfway expecting the big, brown dog to be gone.

But he was still there. He trotted up to meet her, tail wagging fiercely, tongue lolling out of his wet, pink mouth.

"Hi there, boy," she said as she patted him. His coat was smooth and shiny. "I'll bet somebody is missing you right now. But I've done everything I can think of, so I guess you'll just have to hang out with us for awhile until your master comes to get you."

Maggie spread a blanket out on the grass and they ate lunch outside. The dog was content to wolf down a large pan of dog food, then he flopped down at Spencer's side and slept peacefully. Spencer petted the dog as he slept, fondly caressing a silky ear.

"I sure wish I could keep him, Mom."

"I know, honey, but don't get your hopes up. It's probably just a matter of time…" Just then she saw a truck come down the road and turn into the driveway.

Spencer's face fell. "Do you think that's his owner?" The dog was awake now and barking furiously at the old red truck that had parked in the driveway.

Maggie stood up. "No. I think that's Jed Whitewater's truck. He's bringing a table and some chairs over." She peered at the truck, noticing that Jed was alone—no Kate.

"Hello there," he called as he climbed from the truck. "Is your dog friendly?"

"Actually he's not ours," yelled Maggie over the loud barking.

"It's okay, boy," soothed Spencer. "That's just Jed, and he won't hurt you." As if he understood, the dog quit barking and trotted over to investigate. Soon his tail was wagging happily as Jed leaned over to pet him.

"Do you recognize him?" asked Maggie.

"Is that a rhetorical question?" said Jed. "Or am I supposed to know him."

Maggie laughed. "Well, he seems to be lost, and he wound up here. I thought you might recognize him as someone's pet in town."

Jed knelt down and looked more closely at the dog, then shook his head. "Greg Snider has a black lab, but I don't know anyone who has a chocolate."

"You mean the postmaster?"

"Yeah, why?"

"Oh, nothing... I just met him the other day. I don't think he likes people coming in before closing."

Jed stood up and smiled. "Greg can be a little cranky sometimes. But underneath it all, he's okay." He turned back to the dog. "You know, sometimes folks from the city have been known to dump their pets around here, hoping to get them good homes out in the country..."

"Do you really think so?" asked Spencer eagerly. "I'd like to keep him."

Maggie frowned. "I can't believe anyone would dump a dog like this."

"He is a handsome guy," agreed Jed. "Maybe he's just lost."

"Do you need some help with that table?" she asked.

Jed glanced at Spencer. "Sure, why don't you give me a hand, Spencer."

She watched as the two of them easily unloaded the table and chairs, carrying them into the carriage house.

"It looks perfect," she said. "You do great work, Jed."

"Thanks. And that means a lot coming from someone who didn't really like rustic furniture to begin with."

She didn't know if he was teasing or not, but decided not to take the bait. Besides she had something more pressing on her mind. "Jed, you probably don't have time to go through the main house, do you?"

"As a matter of fact, I do. I was hoping you'd ask. I haven't been in that house since I was a kid."

"You've been in it before?" asked Maggie as the three of them walked over to the house.

Jed laughed cynically. "Well, just barely. You see Gavin and I are the same age, and when we were in second grade, Gavin had a birthday party. He brought these fancy invitations to school and passed them out to all the boys in class. Everyone but me, that is."

"Oh," said Maggie, suddenly aware again of Jed's Native American heritage and the problems he might have faced growing up in a small community like Pine Mountain.

"Well, the teacher got real mad at Gavin, and called his mom. And the next day, Gavin handed me an invitation too. Like a fool, I decided to come. My dad warned me not to. And as it turned out, my dad was right."

They were stepping onto the porch now, carefully navigating around the broken boards. Maggie didn't know what to say.

"What happened at the party?" asked Spencer innocently.

Jed had knelt down to check the remaining boards on the porch, but he paused to look up at Spencer. "Well, it's a long story. If you're really interested, I'll tell you the rest of it some other day."

The three of them spent about an hour going through the whole house. Spencer and Maggie listened intently as Jed explained what needed to be done to restore and renovate the various rooms. He gave Spencer a list of suggestions that he could begin to do on his own, and then he offered to help on some of the larger projects.

"It's really not as bad as it appears at first glance," said Jed. "Most of this house is in excellent condition. You can attribute that to our dry climate. But without work, it will slowly deteriorate just the same."

"So, maybe I don't need to hire a general contractor?" asked Maggie.

"That's up to you, but I wouldn't bother with one. Have you met Sam, Rosa's husband, yet? He's a plumber—a good one. I'd have him take a look at the plumbing. And then you should ask Clyde about when the last electrical work was done. My guess is that it was rewired after the war. If so, it should be fine."

"Thanks for all your help, Jed." Maggie stepped out on the porch. "I was having nightmares that the whole place was going to fall down in a windstorm."

Spencer laughed. "That's probably because the porch is such a mess."

Jed poked around on the porch some more. "Yeah, you'll have to replace a few boards. But most of it is still solid."

Spencer went off to throw a stick for the dog, and Maggie spoke quietly to Jed. "Do you really think Spencer can tackle some of these things? I like his enthusiasm, but I'm afraid he might be in over his head."

"He'll definitely need some help. But I'd be willing to come out a couple days a week to give him some tips and get him going."

"Really? Can you spare the time? I'd be so grateful! Of course, I'll pay you." She felt like she was sputtering and it embarrassed her. She was normally much more controlled than this, but something about Jed made her feel like she was fourteen again.

"I'd enjoy doing it." He ran his hand over the porch railing. "Fixing up historical houses ranks right up there with making furniture as far as I'm concerned."

"Great," said Maggie. "You've come to the right place then."

He glanced at his watch. "I better go. I promised Kate I'd be back by three."

Just as Jed's truck pulled onto the road, a big moving van appeared and stopped to turn in the driveway, with another one not far behind. Maggie ran into the house to get the list she had made for Spencer detailing where each piece should go. Most of their larger furnishings would have to be stored in the barn until the big house was ready for occupancy.

It took several hours to empty both trucks, and when the movers drove away it seemed that nothing was in the right place. Maggie flopped down on a large cardboard box still sitting outside and sighed deeply.

"I'm hungry," said Spencer, "and there's nothing to eat in the house."

Maggie groaned. "Where's pizza delivery when you really need it?"

"That's the problem with these one-horse towns," said Spencer.

"Ain't it the truth. Tell you what, Spence, let's get the rest of these boxes into the barn, and then we'll drive over to Byron and see what we can spook up. Maybe even take in a flick."

"They have movie theaters in Byron?"

Maggie laughed. "I would imagine so. Clyde said that the town has a population of about 40,000. Surely they'd have a movie theater and a McDonald's there."

Spencer picked up a box. "What're we waiting for?"

They made it to Byron just in time to do a little shopping, then grab some burgers before the last showing of a newly released action-adventure film that Spencer had been wanting to see and was surprised to find playing in Byron. Maggie leaned back in the seat and actually fell asleep halfway through the noisy movie.

"Thanks," said Spencer as they exited the theater.

Maggie yawned. "Sure. Thanks for all your help today." She looked around as she drove through the town. It seemed strange to see businesses, city lights, traffic moving, even stop-lights. She chuckled as the one in front of her turned red.

"What's so funny, Mom?"

"I was just thinking that *this* was a big town."

Spencer laughed.

"I guess it's all relative."

"At least they have a decent movie theater," he said optimistically, "and we didn't even have to wait in line to see a new release."

The light turned green and she continued down the main street, leaving town and heading down the dark highway. Even as she drove, she could see the stars shining brightly overhead. "You'd never see stars like those in L.A."

Spencer leaned forward and peered out. "Do we still have that old telescope that used to be Dad's when he was a kid?"

"I think so, but it's probably in the bottom of one of those boxes we stored in the barn today."

"I'll look for it this week."

As Maggie drove toward home, Spencer leaned back in his seat. Soon she could tell by his even breathing that he had dozed off. She smiled to herself in the darkness. A very real sense of well-being and contentment seemed to drape itself over her like a soft, warm comforter. Things were going to work out, she just knew it. But she told herself to remember this moment for those times when life got tough, or she was tempted to give up. And she knew those times would probably come. But for tonight she would savor the peace.

Ten

aggie and Spencer dedicated all day Saturday to unpacking boxes and trying to put their household together. The telephone was connected just before noon, and Maggie checked for messages at the *Pine Cone*, curious if anyone had responded to her "found dog" announcements. There was a message from a Pine Mountain woman who had trapped a raccoon in her trash can and wanted someone from the paper to come out and take a photo, but no one seemed to be missing a dog. The friendly lab still seemed perfectly at home with them, and Maggie could see that Spencer was growing more attached to him by the moment. She dreaded the phone call that would take the dog away. Perhaps they would accept an offer to buy the lab, although this sweet animal must be like a member of someone's family and she doubted they'd part with him for any price.

By late afternoon, the phone still had not rung, but the chaos of unpacking had lessened somewhat. A sense of order had slowly begun to emerge, but they were still a long way from being finished.

"Quitting time," announced Maggie, as she pushed a damp strand of hair from her forehead. "Going to the lake is sounding pretty good to me right now."

"Yeah," agreed Spencer. "I thought you said it never gets real hot around here."

"I heard on the radio that this was unseasonably warm for June, and the weatherman said we'd better enjoy it."

"I'm ready!" said Spencer. "Just as soon as I take a quick shower."

Maggie smiled at his back as he headed to the bathroom. Since when did her son take a shower just to go to the lake? Of course, there was only one reason for this new interest in hygiene—and she would also be at the lake, hopefully not donning the kind of bikini that Maggie used to wear at that age. And while this was all somewhat amusing, it also worried her a little. She hadn't spent much time discussing what her mother had called "the facts of life" with Spencer. Phil had always taken care of this area, and if Maggie even broached the subject Spencer simply made wisecracks and said that he already knew all that stuff anyway. But did he really? What if she had missed something? Probably the important thing would be to keep the communication lines open. Surely, that's what her mother would say.

Silver Lake, while still naturally beautiful, looked different. The lake was still big and blue, surrounded by tall pines and with mountain peaks cresting majestically in the horizon. But the dock was newer and bigger, with a new camp-store situated nearby. And the old camping area had been updated and enlarged, complete with lots of cement and blacktop. There was even a large cinder-block bathroom complete with shower facilities, and over on the north shore were some newly built log cabins. Everything seemed fairly well-planned and neatly done, but it saddened Maggie to see the changes. The quaint Silver Lake of her happy childhood memories no longer existed.

"This place has changed," said Maggie as she parked the car in the gravel lot.

"Looks fine to me," said Spencer as he grabbed his towel.

"Hello there!" called Rosa. She was toting a picnic basket, and behind her came a large, burly-looking man packing a big ice chest. "This is my husband, Sam."

He nodded to them. "You must be Maggie and Spencer. I've been hearing a lot about you two lately."

"Hey, Spencer!" called Sierra, waving from a big white boat that was tied to the dock. To Maggie's relief, the pretty girl was wearing an over-sized T-shirt over her swimsuit.

Spencer waved back then turned back to her father. "Do you need any help with that?"

Sam smiled. "Sure, grab a handle, Spencer." The two of them carried the chest over to the boat, and Maggie followed with Rosa.

"Spencer is such a polite boy," said Rosa.

"Actually," confessed Maggie, "I think your daughter brings out the best in him."

Rosa laughed. "Good. I hope that continues."

"This place has changed a lot since I was a kid."

"Yes. I've only lived in the area since Sierra was a toddler, but it's changed a lot since then." Rosa pointed to the cabins across the lake. "Those are only a couple years old. They're rentals, but the developer also has plans to build some more that will be sold as summer homes."

"Nice. But I sure hope they don't overdevelop this area. It's such a beautiful place, I'd hate to see it spoiled."

"You're not the only one. There's a group in town, headed by Greg Snider, that is adamantly opposed to any more development of the lake. In fact, sometimes it seems as if the people involved are opposed to development of any kind."

"That's too bad, because it seems that growth is inevitable. People are drawn to these naturally beautiful locations. And so many other parts of the country are getting overcrowded..."

"You mean like California?" Rosa looked up at Maggie from beneath her sunglasses.

Maggie laughed as they stopped in front of the boat, waiting to board. "Yes, the rumors are true. We, Californians, are planning to take over Oregon."

Sam took the picnic basket from Rosa and set it inside the boat. "You know, we used to have a governor who had a slogan for Californians, something like 'Come visit Oregon, just don't stay.'"

"Watch yourself, Sam," Rosa warned good-naturedly. "Don't forget that you married a California girl."

Sam helped the two women board the boat. "I didn't mean I was against Californians, I was just recalling the anti-California campaign from the sixties. We had another one, 'keep Oregon green, bring money.'"

Maggie laughed. "Maybe we could adopt that one for Pine Mountain."

"Yes," agreed Rosa, "I could use some of those kind of greens for the deli."

They took a spin around the lake, then Sierra pulled out an object that looked a little like a small surfboard with foot straps. She explained it was a wakeboard, sort of like water-skiing, then hopped in the water and showed them how it was done. Spencer watched with admiration as she skillfully balanced and maneuvered the board across the wake behind the fast-moving boat. When her turn ended she gave him some quick instruction, and then he jumped in the water. After numerous falls and almosts, Spencer finally got up and managed to ride the wake for a full circle around the lake before he hit a wave that plunged him headfirst into the water. He came up sputtering but wearing a huge grin.

"That was great!" he said as Sierra helped pull him back onto the boat.

"I don't know about the rest of you, but I'm starved," said Sam. "Want to take a dinner break, then get in a couple more runs before dark?"

Everyone agreed, and Sam guided the boat across the lake.

"You did great," said Sierra as Spencer toweled himself dry. "I bet you'll be good at snowboarding too."

"Hope so," said Spencer as he pulled his T-shirt over his head.

Sam tied the boat to the shore, then pulled out a fishing pole and immediately tossed a line into the lake. "Gotta fish while I have the chance," he said.

Maggie helped Rosa set up the picnic dinner while the kids took off down a nearby trail. "Don't be gone long," called Rosa.

Maggie spread the tablecloth over the table and Rosa began to unload the food. "I hope you guys like Mexican food," she said almost apologetically.

"We love it!" exclaimed Maggie as she examined a large baking dish. "Those enchiladas look delicious. You shouldn't have gone to so much work, Rosa."

Rosa waved her hand in dismissal. "I love to cook like this. All day long it's soup and sandwiches, but *this* feels more like real food to me. It's how my mother cooked."

"Why don't you cook like this in your restaurant?" asked Maggie as she munched an obviously homemade tortilla chip.

"That was my original plan when we moved to Pine Mountain. But I had to fight against some discrimination problems, so I decided to forget the Mexican cuisine and avoid all the stereotypes that go with it."

Maggie was caught off guard again. "You mean people in Pine Mountain were prejudiced against your Hispanic heritage?"

Rosa laughed. "You sound so surprised. Don't you know there are some very narrow-minded people in our town? But somehow running a traditional deli has made folks more accepting of my Mexican roots. It's weird. Especially when I think how my parents, for years, ran a very successful Mexican restaurant down in San Diego."

OUACHITA TECHNICAL COLLEGE

"Too bad," said Maggie. "I think a Mexican restaurant in Pine Mountain would be delightful."

"I'd always hoped that if the town grew enough, I might be able to start one up. But right now it's a challenge just keeping the little deli going."

"How did you and Sam meet?" asked Maggie, abruptly changing the subject. Then she laughed. "Rosa, you'll have to excuse me—always the news reporter wanting to know everything about everyone…"

"It's all right. You're probably wondering how my big gringo husband hooked up with a Mexican girl."

"Actually, it's not that uncommon in California."

"Maybe not now, but believe me, it was sure frowned upon twenty-five years ago when we first met."

"You've been together that long?" Maggie took another chip.

"Yes. Sam's from this area originally, but we met when he was stationed down in San Diego—in the Navy. He came into my parents' restaurant one day and was totally smitten." She laughed lightly. "I was younger and thinner back then. Anyway, both of our families had objections to the engagement, so we just eloped to Las Vegas. To be honest, my parents never did fully accept our marriage. Sam's family has been a little kinder." She paused for a moment to call everyone to come eat, then turned back to Maggie. "But it's amazing. It seems the adversity has only made us stronger. And I should mention that, besides Sierra, we have two older boys. Scott just graduated from college with his B.A., and Max enlisted in the Air Force last fall."

By now everyone had gathered around the table. To Maggie's surprise, Sam said a short prayer, and then they all loaded their plates with the delicious food.

"These enchiladas are absolutely scrumptious, Rosa," said Maggie after her first bite. "If you ever do open that Mexican restaurant, it's sure to be a huge success."

"Yeah," agreed Spencer enthusiastically, "I've never had food *this* good."

Maggie scowled dramatically at her son.

"Sorry, Mom," said Spencer with lifted brows.

She laughed. "It's okay. I should be glad that I raised such an honest kid."

After eating, they packed up the food, then returned to the lake. Spencer and Sierra took turns on the wakeboard until the sun began to dip behind the mountains. With everyone back on the boat, Sam turned on the running lights and took them for one last loop around the dusky blue lake. On the far side were a few more cabins, older and spaced further apart. Rosa pointed to a log cabin not too far from the water's edge. A small dock with a fishing boat bobbing alongside it reached like a dark finger into the quiet lake. "That's where Clyde Barnes lives," she said.

Maggie looked at the golden light pouring from the paned windows in front of the cabin. "It looks like a peaceful place to live. Does he live alone?"

"He has for as long as I can remember," said Rosa. "Sam could fill you in better. Clyde and Sam's dad are good fishing buddies. Clyde was married once, but his wife suffered poor health. They never had any children, and his wife passed away back in the fifties, I believe. He never married again."

"Oh," said Maggie. "I didn't know. How sad..."

"Don't feel too sorry for old Clyde," said Sam. "He lives the life most other guys can only dream of. Fishing, hunting—why, you name it and Clyde has done it. He's mined for gold in the Sierra Nevadas and hunted for opals in Australia. He's even gone big game hunting in Africa."

"And I heard that his family made their money from logging their own land," said Maggie. "Is that right?"

"Yep," said Sam. "Clyde still owns several hundred timbered acres—and that's after he sold a good-sized chunk to pay off his brother's wife."

"'Pay off his brother's wife?'" repeated Maggie with interest.

"Yes," said Rosa in a quiet voice, as if someone might be eavesdropping on their conversation out in the middle of the lake. "As the story goes, Clyde had a brother named Wesley..." She paused. "Sam why don't you tell the story, you know it better than I do."

Sam cleared his throat as the boat cut through the quiet water. "Well, let's see. I think Wesley was about fifteen years younger than Clyde—kind of a surprise for Clyde's parents. Anyway, Wesley had been too young to fight in World War II, but Clyde had gone and returned home a big hero with all sorts of medals and ribbons. Pine Mountain even had a special parade for him. So, when the Korean War came along, Wesley signed right up, leaving his wife and newborn son behind. Everyone said he wanted to come home with more medals than his older brother—kind of a competition."

"But Wesley never made it back," finished Rosa.

"That's right. And the wife, her name was Betty, blamed Clyde for Wesley's death. My dad said it just about killed Clyde to lose his baby brother like that. And then it was only shortly after that when Clyde's wife died too. For years, Clyde worked his family's timberland. He completely supported Betty and Gavin. And when his elderly parents passed away and left all their property to him, Clyde allowed Betty and Gavin to stay on as long as they liked in the homestead. But when Gavin was in high school, Betty got fed up and decided to move back east, where she was originally from. Some folks say she'd been hoping that Clyde would marry her." Sam laughed. "But I don't know who would've wanted to marry *that* woman. She was the snootiest thing in Pine Mountain. Always walking around dressed like she was a queen and better than the rest of us. She had a real superiority complex. That probably explains some of Gavin's problems."

The boat was nearing the dock as Sam continued. "Anyway, my dad said that before Betty left, she demanded that Clyde split the property with her. She felt that half of it was rightly Wesley's and should go to her and Gavin. So, as much as he hated to give it up, Clyde sold off a bunch of timberland—more 'n half, I'd guess. Then he gave the proceeds to Betty." Sam jumped off the boat and began tying it down in the slip. He chuckled. "Actually, I think Clyde probably thought it was well worth it just to get rid of that uppity woman."

Maggie stepped off the boat onto the darkened dock. "That's quite a story. Thanks for sharing it with me, Sam."

"The only reason I did is because you're working for Clyde now, and I don't expect he'd fill you in on all his history. A lot of that stuff isn't common knowledge, except with old-timers, and I trust you'll respect Clyde's privacy. But since I know Clyde can come across as a grumpy old codger sometimes, I hope this will help you to be more understanding of him. He's really a good guy, Maggie."

"I know he is. And just for the record, I kind of like old codgers."

Rosa laughed. "Good for you."

"Hey, Spencer," called Maggie. "Time to head for home." Spencer and Sierra had been so engrossed in their own conversation in the back of the boat that she felt certain they'd not heard a word of Sam's story about Clyde and his brother.

"Thanks for everything," said Spencer.

"Yeah," agreed Maggie. "It was a wonderful evening."

"We'll do it again soon," said Sam. "We keep the boat on the lake so we can shoot up here anytime and play around."

"Next time, you have to let me help with the food, Rosa," said Maggie. "It won't be as tasty as yours, but it'll give you a break."

Rosa smiled at her. "It's a deal."

Eleven

By the end of the following week, Maggie decided to spend some time in the office. Spencer had helped her put their household together and all that remained to be done was to organize the leftover boxes and furnishings that would be stored in the barn. Spencer agreed to sort and condense everything and then carefully mark all the boxes, and hopefully he would unearth some important missing items while doing so. For this, Maggie still dangled the snowboard carrot, plus a season pass, in front of his nose. And fortunately for her, the incentive still worked, but she wondered if her bright son didn't suspect her twofold purpose.

On her way to work, she stopped by the hardware store and picked up a dog collar. It had been over a week now, and no one had called to claim their mystery dog. To their surprise, the dog could actually scale the ladder-like stairs up to the loft, and Spencer had been allowing the dog to sleep with him. And he'd started calling him "Buddy." Maggie was torn. Glad as she was that Spencer had gained such a nice companion, she was equally worried that the owners would show up soon and take the dog away.

"Hello, Maggie," called Clyde as he stepped into her office. He nodded approvingly around the room. "You know, this is looking right nice in here. I think I like your new furniture."

"Really?" She smiled. "Have you changed your mind about these things, or are you just being agreeable in your old age?"

He examined her desk more closely. "I guess I never gave it a real chance. I'd only seen Jed Whitewater's furniture from the store window, and I thought it looked kind of trashy. But up close, I can see it's very well made. And I like the way you've arranged everything. See, it proves my point."

"And that would be?"

"That you're a real smart cookie." Clyde grinned. "Just what this town needs."

"I hope so." She frowned. "You know, I've been going through files and things, and there seems to be a lot of missing pieces. I feel like I'm starting from ground zero." She rattled off a list of things that she couldn't find.

"Sorry 'bout that. But just consider yourself a pioneer. You get to rebuild this paper the best way you see fit—kind of entrepreneur-like."

"I guess that's one way to look at it. I just hope I'm up to the task."

"You're going to be fine, Maggie. Just don't worry about it too much. Things have a way of falling into place." He looked at the new dog collar sitting on her desk. "Are you thinking about getting a dog?"

"Actually, we sort of already have one. A dog just showed up one day, and he seems to have adopted us."

Clyde chuckled. "Happens all the time 'round here. City folks drive out and dump their unwanted animals, thinking they'll find a better home out here. Too bad too, 'cause most of 'em probably just end up becoming coyote food."

She grimaced at the thought. "Jed mentioned the abandoned pet theory too, but I don't think so, Clyde. This dog looks like a valuable animal to me. I can't believe someone would just dump him. I've called everyone I can think of to find his owners, but so far no one has responded. And the dog didn't have a collar or tag."

"What kind of dog is it?"

"A real pretty chocolate lab. Not too old."

Clyde dropped the dog collar on her desk. "A *brown* Labrador Retriever?"

"Yes. Any idea who he might belong to?"

"Gavin has a brown lab." His voice flattened. "But I only saw the dog once and he was still a pup. Gavin never brought the dog into town with him."

"Does Gavin still live around here?"

Clyde shook his head without speaking.

"Has he been around to visit lately?"

"Not that I know of." He folded his arms across his chest, his brow creased with concern.

Maggie picked up the dog collar and turned it around in her hand. "Well, then it's probably just a coincidence."

"Maybe." He pulled out his pocket-watch. "Well, I'll leave you to it." He started out the door, then paused. "If I remember correctly, Gavin's dog's name was Bart. Seemed like a tough name for what seemed like a real sweet dog. But you might try that name on him."

She blinked in surprise, then nodded. "Okay."

After Clyde left, she continued to sort through files. Finally, in frustration, she called up Clara from the antique shop and asked for Abigail McPhearson's phone number.

"Oh, I'm so glad you called, Maggie," said Clara. "I told Abigail all about you, and she got real excited. You be sure and give her a call now."

She thanked Clara, then dialed Abigail's number. The woman sounded eager to talk, and Maggie invited her to stop by the office after lunch, then locked up and headed over to the deli.

Sierra was working the counter today, and Maggie chatted briefly with her then sat down to eat her sandwich. Just as she finished, Rosa appeared with a cup of coffee.

"Looks like you've been doing some baking," she commented, pointing to the flour on Rosa's apron.

"Yes, it's a baking day. Been at it all morning." Rosa pulled out a chair. "Mind if I take a break with you?"

"No, I'd love it."

"I keep forgetting that I've been meaning to invite you and Spencer to go to church with us on Sunday." Rosa took a sip of coffee.

"Oh?" said Maggie. "Yes, I've been wondering if there's a good church around."

"Well, that's just it," explained Rosa. "It's a different sort of church. Not for everyone. But we like it."

"What denomination?"

"Not really any. It's led by Jed Whitewater."

"Jed Whitewater?"

"Yes. You see, we all used to belong to a church in town, but the pastor had some problems, and the church sort of stopped. But Jed had this idea for a church in the woods..."

"Jed is a pastor?" Somehow this just didn't make sense.

"Not exactly a pastor. More like a leader. I know it sounds strange, but it's not a cult or anything. I just wanted to invite you, if you and Spencer would like to come..."

Maggie glanced over at Sierra. "Well, if Sierra is there, I'm sure Spencer will be interested." They both laughed. "And to tell you the truth, Rosa, I think it sounds very interesting. Jed Whitewater...leading a church in the woods..."

"Well, we like it." Rosa set her cup down. "Say, did you hear that there's a new business coming to town?"

"No, I guess my reporter's nose is getting a little out of practice. Actually, I've spent most of the week at home trying to unpack and get our house together. Tell me everything, what's up?"

"A young woman is leasing the old shoe store on Main Street. Sierra just met her yesterday. She's from the Portland area and is opening some sort of clothing store. Apparently the skiing drew her here and, according to Sierra, she thinks Pine Mountain is 'simply divine.'" Rosa laughed. "Hope she's not disappointed."

"Do you know her name?"

"Chloe...something or other."

"I'll have to go meet her. I've been thinking the paper needs a business section to let people know what's going on in town. I'll start with her."

"That's a good idea. Sam suggested it to Gavin once, but he didn't seem to think it was necessary. But then he was never very interested in seeing any growth either."

"From what I can see, Gavin was a bit of a minimalist when it came to newspaper publishing."

Rosa laughed. "That's a nice way of putting it. Well, I think it's time to take the bread out of the oven."

Maggie walked by the old shoe store on her way back to the newspaper office. She peeked in the window to see inside, and sure enough it looked as if someone had brought in clothing racks and shelves, but no one seemed to be there right now. She would make a point to stop in later and chat with the woman. Just the thought of someone starting a new business in town gave her hope. Maybe things could change.

As she rounded the corner, she noticed a gray-haired woman rocking in the old rocker on the front porch of the *Pine Cone*. She had on a bright, almost Hawaiian-looking, floral print dress, and in her lap rested a shiny red handbag.

"Hello," called Maggie. "Can I help you?"

"I'm Abigail McPhearson," said the smiling woman, rising quickly from the rocker. Maggie felt surprised to see her tall, sturdy frame. This was no fragile, little old lady. When standing next to tiny Clara, they must look like Mutt and Jeff. Abigail extended a large hand, giving Maggie's a firm shake.

"Good to meet you, Abigail. I'm Maggie. Am I late?"

Abigail laughed. "No, honey, I'm just early. I guess I was eager to meet you."

"Well, come on in." She unlocked the door and led Abigail inside.

"Oh my!" said Abigail as she looked around the lobby. "You've certainly made some changes around here!"

Maggie peered at the woman curiously. She knew that Abigail used to spend a lot of time in here. It was quite likely that the woman would feel possessive, perhaps even territorial. What if she completely despised Maggie's changes? "So," she began tentatively, "what do you think?"

Abigail walked slowly around, quietly examining every single piece of furniture and decoration, right down to the antique wheelbarrow next to the front door. Finally she spoke. "I just love it! Whether you hire me or not, Maggie Carpenter, I'm certainly glad you're here. I think Clyde did right in hiring you. And I hope you'll stick around awhile."

Maggie liked this straightforward woman. But, not forgetting professionalism, she decided that a proper interview was in order. So they sat down in her office and she quickly proceeded through her short list of questions, then finally said, "Abigail, how soon can you start?"

Abigail grinned broadly. "Is Monday morning too soon?"

"Monday is great," said Maggie as the two women stood and shook hands. "I'm having difficulty figuring out the processes that Gavin may have used here, and I hope you can help to straighten me out on a few things."

"You bet I will, honey." Abigail's face was beaming as she picked up her bright handbag. "I can't wait to tell Clara the good news."

After Abigail left, Maggie continued to putter around the office. She made a list of things to do, feeling much more at ease just to know that the capable Abigail would be here to help next week. She'd have Abigail focus on organizing the advertising files to start with, then move on to other things later. The phone rang and she picked it up, thinking it might be Spencer calling to see if she was on her way home yet, but no one spoke on the other end. She shrugged, then hung up.

Just as well, it was time to leave anyway. Her goal had been to establish and maintain normal working hours at the paper right from the start, and eventually she hoped to do some of her writing from home and be more available to Spencer if necessary. She wasn't sure that it made any difference to him at this age, but she still remembered the lonely feeling of coming home to an empty house after school. She wanted to spare him that if she possibly could.

∼

The chocolate lab was stretched out upon the front step of the carriage house just as if he belonged there. His head perked up to watch as she climbed from the car. Already he was familiar with her vehicle and no longer barked when she pulled into the driveway. He seemed like such a good dog, and like Spencer, she wished they could keep him indefinitely. But suddenly she recalled Clyde's words about Gavin having a chocolate lab. Still, it seemed impossible that Gavin's dog would be in Pine Mountain when Gavin had relocated to Portland months ago. Portland was more than a three-hour drive from here. Just the same, and to relieve her concerns, she decided to try out the name that Clyde had mentioned as she walked toward the carriage house.

"Bart!" she called, just loudly enough for the dog to hear. The dog stood, ears perked, then dashed straight to her, tail wagging happily behind him. "Oh, I'll bet you'd come to any old name," she said as she stroked his sleek head. But, it troubled her. What if this *was* Gavin's dog?

"Why'd you call him Bart, Mom?" asked Spencer as he popped out of the house balancing a sloppy looking peanut-butter sandwich in one hand and large glass of milk in the other. He caught a dollop of jam with his tongue just before it fell, then broke off a corner of the sandwich and fed it to the dog.

"Clyde told me that his nephew, Gavin, the one who used to run the paper, has a chocolate lab named Bart."

Spencer's face fell. "Do you think this is his dog?"

"I don't know, Spence." She kneeled down to fasten the red collar around the dog's neck. "Gavin lives a long ways away, and this dog is so friendly that he might just come to any name you call him."

"But he came when you said 'Bart.' And I've tried calling him by lots of other names and he's never responded like that. I know, Mom, let's do a test. You go over there by that tree and call him by a bunch of different names, and then call him by Bart."

They tried Spencer's test, and while the dog would look at her as she tried other names, he never left Spencer's side. But when she said "Bart" his ears perked up again and he trotted over. Clearly, the dog thought his name was Bart.

Spencer groaned. "See, Mom. His name *is* Bart. He probably does belong to stupid old Gavin."

"I'm sorry, honey. We knew all along that he belonged to somebody. He's too nice to be a stray. But just because he responds to the name Bart doesn't necessarily mean he's Gavin's dog." Yet even as she said them, she didn't quite believe her own words. "How about if I phone Clyde and ask some questions?"

She called Clyde and quickly explained how the dog had responded to the name Bart. "I can accept that he might belong to Gavin, Clyde," she continued. "But I just don't understand why he turned up here. It makes absolutely no sense."

"Well, I don't know how or why he wound up in Pine Mountain, but I can guess why he parked himself at your place, Maggie." Clyde cleared his throat. "You see, Gavin used to live there. I let him stay on in the carriage house while he worked at the paper."

"Oh." She looked around her carriage house in dismay. It bothered her that the infamous Gavin Barnes had once inhabited her space. "Is that why it's fixed up so nicely?"

"Yes. I had that done for Gavin a few years back...he didn't think the big house was—uh—livable and the carriage house seemed a good option for a bachelor."

"I see..."

"I don't have his phone number, and I don't really know how to reach him. I think his mother lives in Florida, but I haven't heard from her for years."

"So what should I do about the dog, Clyde? You know it'll get tougher every day because Spencer's really becoming attached to him—we both are. He's a sweet dog."

Clyde grunted. "Well, if I had it my way, I'd say let the boy keep him. The only time I ever saw Gavin with the dog, I didn't much like the way he treated him. Never did think you need to beat an animal to get it to mind."

"He beat Bart?"

"The dog was barking at me, not mean-like, but just 'cause I was a stranger. Well, Gavin upped and gave him a hard smack with his fist, right on top of the head. Seemed unnecessary if you ask me."

"Poor dog." She sighed. "But how do you think the dog got to Pine Mountain, Clyde? Could he have walked all the way from Portland?"

Clyde laughed. "Almost 200 miles and over the mountains? Did he look all emaciated with bloody paws?"

"No, he looks just fine. But *how* did he get here?" She paused for a moment—years of reporting had taught her to dig deeper than just surface facts. "Gavin must've been in Pine Mountain for some reason, and perhaps the dog ran off and became separated from him... Obviously he slipped his collar, then somehow made his way back here where he used to live—thought he'd come home, poor dog."

"Sounds more'n likely. Although you'd think Gavin would figure to look over at your place for his dog. But then maybe he doesn't really care about the animal."

"Then perhaps he'd like to sell him to a good home."

"Maybe... In the meantime, I think you should just hang on to him." Clyde's voice grew firmer. "And if, or when, Gavin shows his face 'round here, you keep the dog with you and send my nephew over to talk with me. I've got a bone or two to pick with him anyway. Who knows, we might even work up some sort of agreement that involves rearranging the ownership of the dog."

She smiled. "Thanks, Clyde. I don't want to cause any trouble, but if the dog needs a good home, we're more than willing to give him one."

"I know you are, Maggie. In the meantime, I wouldn't worry about it. I doubt we'll be seeing much of Gavin. And you tell Spencer that ol' Uncle Clyde is going to do everything he can to see that you two get to keep that dog."

She hung up the phone and told Spencer what Clyde had said.

"I guess Clyde's not such a bad old coot after all," said Spencer as he affectionately scratched the dog's thick neck. "Maybe we'll get to keep you after all, Bart."

That evening, Maggie took her laptop outside, and sat on the porch to write an email to her friend Rebecca.

RB,

There seems to be some sort of mystery between my new boss and his nephew, Gavin. I know it's none of my business, but I wonder what it is. Gavin used to run the newspaper, and, from what I can see, did a pretty lousy job of it. Apparently, he was avidly against any kind of development (not unlike our eccentric postmaster) but this seems strange in a newspaperman. But something happened to make Gavin leave, and I'm really not sure who is to blame. I know there's bad blood between Gavin and Clyde, and I'd like to assume it's all Gavin's fault, but how can I be certain? The strange thing is that I, in essence, am taking Gavin's place, and now it seems we have even acquired Gavin's dog! Isn't that too weird? The good news is that I've hired a capable assistant. Maybe I can pick her brain about Gavin because she knew him, although from what I've heard they didn't get along at all. Ah, the plot in Pine Mountain thickens. :) More later.

mc

Twelve

Maggie and Spencer rode into town on Saturday to get some repair supplies at the hardware store and pick up their mail. Bart rode along in the rear, looking out the back window, his tail pounding happily against the floorboards. It was clear this dog enjoyed riding.

Spencer had put together a list of materials recommended by Jed. The two of them planned to begin work on the house the following week. Jed had suggested that Maggie open an account at the hardware store so that Spencer could pick up various items as needed. Maggie, unfamiliar with hardware stores in general, found this quaint old store charming although somewhat intimidating. Spencer seemed right at home asking questions and poking around the dusty shelves, but Maggie felt she was on foreign turf. After quickly filling out the forms to open an account, she left Spencer behind to peruse the goods and select his supplies while she took Bart to pick up the mail. The dog heeled nicely as they walked down the street. It seemed someone had worked with him before. Maybe Gavin. And yet, from all she'd heard about this man, it seemed unlikely.

Maggie tied Bart's leash to a pole outside of the post office, and he sat down quietly as if he knew how to wait.

"You're a good boy," she said, stroking his head. "I'll be right back…"

"Where'd you get that dog?"

She looked up in surprise to see Greg Snider hovering over her. So far she'd managed to come and go from the post office for nearly a week without bumping into the irritable postmaster. Still, she remembered how Jed had defended Greg, and she was determined to find this man's good side. Forcing a polite smile to her lips she quickly explained that the dog had actually found them.

Greg kneeled down and examined the dog more closely, then stood and looked Maggie squarely in the eye. "This is Gavin Barnes' dog," he said in what seemed an unnecessarily accusing tone.

"Clyde suspected that he might be," said Maggie, trying to keep her voice even. She took a step back. "Are you a friend of Gavin's?"

Greg nodded, eyes narrowed with obvious suspicion. "First you get Gavin's job. And now you've got his dog too?"

"Like I said, he just showed up." Maggie fingered the mailbox key in her hand. "We're taking care of him for now. He's a good dog."

Greg tilted his head to one side. "Well, have you even told Gavin that you've got his dog?"

Just then a petite, platinum blond woman walked up and stood right next to Greg. In her purple spandex biking shorts and a matching lycra top, she reminded Maggie of a Laker Girl wannabe. Surely this was not a local resident.

"I'll bet you're the new newspaper editor," said the woman in a perky voice, which was perfectly attuned to her appearance.

"Yes, I'm Maggie Carpenter." She smiled at the woman, relieved for any kind of distraction from Greg's hostile inquisition.

"I'm Cherise Snider," she chirped as she grinned posses-
sively up at Greg, "I'm married to the postmaster."

"Pleased to meet you, Cherise." Maggie took a half-step
toward the post office. "If you'll excuse me... I was just
picking up my mail."

"Yeah, the post office is such a cool place to see
everyone," said Cherise cheerfully, as if to prolong the
encounter. Then her brows lifted as if she had an idea. "Say,
Maggie, you may not be aware that I run the Pine Mountain
Fitness Center. Since you're new in town, I'd like to offer you
a real good deal. We have aerobics and weight training and
tanning..."

"Save it for later," snapped Greg.

Cherise just rolled her eyes at him and laughed. "Oh
yeah, Greg hates it when I go on about the fitness center."
She winked at Maggie. "But you come on in and we'll talk.
In fact, I think I need to run a special ad..."

"Come on, Cherise," commanded Greg, pulling her by
the arm. With her free hand, she waved at Maggie, still
smiling brightly and seemingly oblivious to the fact that she
was married to a tyrant.

Maggie stared in wonder. How could anyone bear to be
treated like that—and by their own spouse! But at least Greg
was out of sight now, and she could get her mail and leave.
She wondered if Greg really knew how to reach Gavin. If so,
she was certain that he would. She couldn't understand why
Greg was so hostile to her. Was he really so paranoid about
development? Or perhaps he was simply one of those men
who disliked seeing women in positions of power? She had
run into guys like that while working at the *Times*. But she
had always prided herself on being able to warm up even the
toughest interviewees. One time she'd gotten an L.A. city
councilman, known to be quite a chauvinist, to open up to
her and wound up breaking a big story because of it. Now,
she couldn't even get the postmaster of Pine Mountain to
speak civilly to her. Maybe she'd lost her touch.

Maggie pushed these thoughts from her mind as she and Bart walked back toward the hardware store. She noticed a young woman with long, curly red hair carrying a large box into the old shoe store—probably the new shop owner. Maggie crossed the street and peered past the open door.

"Hello?"

"Oh hi," called the woman as she carried the box to the back. "You can come on in, but I'm not open for business yet."

"I know and I don't want to bother you, but I'm the editor of the local paper—Maggie Carpenter. I just wanted to say hello."

The woman set the box down with a thud, then stood. Pushing her mane of hair back, she extended her hand. "I'm Chloe Applegate, and this is going to be a clothing store— called Chloe's Threads. I already have this really cool sign all made, but I need to get it put up."

"That sounds great," she said. "And welcome to Pine Mountain. I'm new myself, but I'm so glad you're here. I think this town could have a bright future."

"Me too!" said Chloe, her green eyes flashing with enthusiasm. "It's such a fantastic location, and so beautiful! When people on the outside learn about this place it's going to grow by leaps and bounds—I can just feel it. I think I'm really fortunate to get in on the ground floor like this."

Maggie smiled. "Well, Chloe, when you're not so busy, I'd like to come by and do an interview with you for the paper. I'm just starting it back up, and I've got lots of ideas about ways I can use it to help this town grow."

"That'd be great. I understand there's no Chamber of Commerce here, but I thought perhaps some of the folks might be interested in starting some sort of business associ- ation." Chloe nodded toward the front of the store. "I plan to paint the woodwork and put flower boxes outside. I'm hoping others might want to try and spruce their places up a little too."

"A business association is a super idea, Chloe. How about if we talk about that in your interview? Maybe I could even do a feature on it; or do a survey asking other business people how they feel about a business association."

"Sounds terrific. Want to stop by on Monday morning?"

"Sure. And I happen to know someone who might be able to help you put that sign up—if you need a hand, that is. I have a fourteen-year-old son who's pretty good with a hammer."

"You're kidding," said Chloe. "You have a teenager? Why, I thought you were about my age!"

Maggie laughed at the sweet compliment. "Thanks. I think you and I are going to get along just fine!"

"Great. Send your son over to see me," said Chloe. "Say, how is he with unpacking boxes?"

Maggie grinned. "Actually, he's had a lot of experience lately."

"Well, if he wants a temporary job, starting right now, I'd love some help."

"He's over at the hardware store," said Maggie. "I'll see if he's interested."

"Thanks so much!"

Spencer had already heard about Chloe from Sierra, and was pleased to get a paying job from someone besides his mom. When Maggie introduced them they seemed to hit it right off, so she left him there to spend the remainder of the day helping Chloe set up shop. In the meantime, Maggie decided to utilize the free afternoon to drive over to Byron to do a little shopping herself. After seeing Cherise's eye-popping outfit at the post office, Maggie was more determined than ever to get some suitable clothing for her new lifestyle in Pine Mountain. After unsuccessfully searching through numerous stores, Maggie finally discovered a classy little shop that had everything from walking shorts to khakis to hiking boots. A casual yet stylish saleswoman proved helpful as Maggie attempted to acquire some wardrobe basics that would suit both the climate and lifestyle in Pine Mountain.

Maggie purposely left a few holes, hoping that she might find these things at Chloe's new little shop when it opened. If not, she'd hop back over to Byron. It was oddly reassuring to know that this town, minutely small by L.A. standards, was only twenty minutes away.

As previously arranged, Maggie stopped by the shop to get Spencer at six. She was surprised to see Sierra also in Chloe's shop and helping out. "Hey, Maggie," called Sierra as she peeled some plastic sheeting off a pile of garments, then hung them on a rack. "You should see all the cool stuff Chloe has in here."

"I doubt that she's ready for customers yet," said Maggie as she eyed the piles of clothing still heaped in boxes.

"Not yet," said Chloe. "But with these two guys helping me, we got the truck completely emptied and a good start on getting things unpacked."

Maggie picked up a fleecy outdoors jacket. "This looks perfect for Pine Mountain. I'll be sure to come to your grand opening, Chloe."

"I can't wait," said Sierra as she held up an imported sweater. "Maggie, Mom told me to invite everyone over to our house for pizza tonight. Can you and Spencer come too?"

"Sure," said Maggie, noting the spark in her son's eyes. "Can I bring something?"

Sierra laughed. "I guess you still don't know my mom very well. You don't need to bring anything—just come and eat. She said it'll be ready around seven-ish."

Chloe glanced at her watch. "I guess we should start winding it down for the night." Maggie helped the three of them empty a few more boxes before they turned off the lights and locked up. Then the four of them walked over to the Galloways' house which was only a few blocks south of Main Street. It was pleasant walking through the quiet residential neighborhood that consisted of mostly older homes situated on large, treed lots. But a lot of the houses were vacant, and many were run-down. Another reminder that all was not well in Pine Mountain. Still, Maggie noted that a number of homes were occupied and well-kept with neatly landscaped yards. Finally, Sierra stopped in front of a buttery-yellow, two-story house complete with the proverbial white picket fence. Somehow it didn't surprise Maggie that this was where Rosa lived. It seemed perfectly suited to her sunny personality.

"I'm still amazed at how it looks like early spring here, and yet it's the middle of June," said Maggie as they walked beneath a rose arbor covered with soft pink blooms and then down a paved walk with flower-beds overflowing along the edges.

"Yeah, Mom gets real frustrated with her gardening in April and May. It isn't until June that everything starts to look good. But that's the price of living in the mountains."

"This house is straight out of a fairy tale," gushed Chloe as they approached the front door. "I expect to see Snow White peek out any minute!"

Sierra groaned. "Yeah, my mom is really into all this foofy kind of decorating. Just wait until you see the inside. She has dried flowers and lace and stuff everywhere."

Maggie laughed. "I take it that you have different taste in decor."

"You better believe it. If I ever have a place of my own it's going to be very sleek and modern—no foo-foo for me!"

"Come on in," called Sam through the open screen door. He led them into the living room, which Maggie noted was exactly as Sierra had described. And even though Maggie didn't go in for frilly decor either, she could appreciate how the soft floral prints and pastel colors reflected Rosa's feminine personality, and the overall effect was surprisingly inviting.

They ate in the backyard around a big picnic table covered in pale blue gingham cloth. And before long the conversation turned to the topic of a Pine Mountain business association.

"There used to be a businessmen's club," said Sam. "But it dwindled quickly after the highway cut off the town."

"Yes," said Rosa dreamily, "there was a time when everyone had such grand plans for the future of Pine Mountain..."

"It didn't take long before the loss of traffic made a lot of businesses go belly-up," continued Sam. "Folks were selling out right and left. Even now, those of us still here are hanging on by our toenails."

Chloe looked alarmed. "You guys are scaring me now."

"Sorry, honey," said Rosa as she passed the pizza to Spencer again. "But the truth is, it isn't easy to make a go of it in Pine Mountain. We business people really need to band together. A business association is an excellent idea."

"Yes," agreed Maggie, "with some focused energy we might be able to turn things around. Pine Mountain has so much going for it..."

"How about if we start organizing something right now!" exclaimed Sam. "No time like the present." He pulled a pen and pad from his shirt pocket. "We could start by listing all the businesses in town, and then invite them to a meeting."

"Good idea," said Chloe. "With the summer tourist season already upon us, there's no time to waste. We should set the meeting date right away."

The date was set and Sam quickly made a list of about twenty businesses. "I doubt that everyone will be interested, but at least we can invite them all. Now maybe we should work up an agenda or something."

"Maybe it would be best to invite input from the businesspeople first," suggested Maggie. "Perhaps we could use a big board where we can list everyone's goals and concerns and resources."

"That sounds good," said Rosa. "Would you consider acting as the chairperson, Maggie?"

"That's a real smart idea," said Sam. "Since Maggie's not actually running a business, folks wouldn't question her motives or anything."

Maggie's brows raised. "But I'm so new in town and…"

"But you've got good ideas, Maggie," urged Chloe, "and maybe being new allows you to bring in some fresh perspective."

It was unanimous. Maggie would chair the first gathering. She also agreed to make and distribute flyers announcing the upcoming meeting. She didn't mind this task since she wanted to get better acquainted with all the business people anyway, and the flyers would be printed at the newspaper's expense. Other details were quickly worked out, and everyone was eager to help.

"And we'll just see what happens," said Sam. "Nothing ventured, nothing gained."

"I just remembered something," said Rosa suddenly. "This lady came into the deli today. She gave me her business card. She was from Seattle and looking for a town where she could locate a bookstore and coffee house…"

"Oh, Mom!" exclaimed Sierra, "I hope you told her to do it here. A coffee house would be so cool!"

"Well, I had to be honest with her, Sierra. Pine Mountain has its problems as far as attracting the tourist trade. But I told her that I thought a business like that would be appreciated by the locals. Maggie, perhaps I could give you her card. She jotted down the number of the hotel where she's staying this week. Would you call her and invite her to our meeting?"

"Sure, if you think it's a good idea. But it's hard to know what to expect at the meeting, and I don't want to scare her away."

"I think if she saw that a bunch of us are committed to work together to turn this place around, she might be interested in joining in. She seems like a real go-getter. And she was certainly attracted to our low real estate prices and felt there was a lot of unrealized potential in Pine Mountain."

Maggie nodded. "I couldn't agree with her more!"

"Anybody home?" called a male voice from within the house.

"That sounds like Scotty!" exclaimed Rosa as she leaped from her chair. "He wasn't supposed to be here until next week."

"That's our oldest boy," explained Sam as he too rose from his seat. Sierra had already jumped up to greet her brother.

Maggie stayed at the table with Spencer and Chloe, enjoying the little family reunion from a distance. She studied the young man standing in the light of the kitchen. He was big like his dad, but had the dark, Latino good looks of his mother. He was quite a handsome young man, and it appeared as if young Chloe had noticed as well. After hugs and greetings were dispensed, Rosa introduced her son to those still outside.

"This is our son Scott," she said proudly. "He just graduated with his B.A. in journalism and was taking a little road trip with his buddies from school. We didn't expect to see him until next week. But we hope he'll stick around for a little while this summer."

"I'll stick around until I find a job," he added.

"What kind of work are you looking for?" asked Maggie curiously.

"Maggie runs the *Pine Cone* now," said Sam.

"But she used to work at the *Los Angeles Times*," injected Rosa importantly.

"You left the *Times* to come here?" Scott looked dumbfounded.

Maggie laughed. "When I was your age, I suppose I would've reacted exactly like that. But city living can be a real drain after awhile, and some things happened that made me ready for a change."

"You're talking *major* change!" said Scott. "You must feel like you landed on a completely different planet."

Maggie smiled indulgently. "I guess growing up here makes some people take it for granted, but for those of us less fortunate, Pine Mountain is a very desirable place to live."

"Here, here," said Chloe, lifting her Diet Coke in a mock toast.

Scott glanced at Chloe briefly, then turned back to Maggie as if she were slightly deranged. "Well, I guess Pine Mountain's okay if you like ghost towns."

"We were just discussing that," said his father. "We're working on a plan to see if we can bring some life back into the old place."

"Yeah," added Chloe. "I've only just come to Pine Mountain. And I'm not ready to give up without a good fight."

Scott studied her for a moment. "Are you saying that you actually came here on purpose? Of your own free will?"

Chloe stuck out her chin defiantly. "As a matter of fact, I did. And just for the record, I'm very happy to be here. But, the truth is, if I don't make good on Daddy's investment, I won't be able to show my face around home again for a long, long time."

"Good luck." Scott laughed sarcastically, then added more gently, "Believe me, you're going to need it."

"Thanks a lot." Chloe's finely arched brows drew together. "I think the least you can do after that remark, Scott Galloway—that is if you're still in town—is to come spend some money in my shop. I open next week. It's called Chloe's Threads, on Main Street."

"Girl clothes?"

"I have a few things for guys too."

"Her stuff is cool, Scott," said Sierra. "You'd like it. Really."

"Okay," he agreed, "I'll stop by and check it out." Then Scott turned his attention back to Maggie. "So, do you still know anyone back at the *Times*?"

"Sure, I know lots of people. Are you looking for a recommendation?"

"Well, now that you mention it..." Scott smiled appealingly.

She thought for a moment. "Tell you what, Scott. You come do some work for me at the *Pine Cone*, and I'll give you a recommendation based on your performance there. Does that sound like a deal?"

"*You bet!*" He reached out and vigorously shook her hand. "When do I start?"

"As soon as you like."

He glanced over at his parents. Both were smiling, and Maggie realized they probably thought she was only doing them a favor. But the truth was that she was thankful to find good help. Even if she had to do some initial training, with his journalism degree Scott was probably one of the best bets in Pine Mountain.

"How about Monday then?" said Scott.

"Sounds perfect. And on that happy note, I think it's time we headed for home."

Maggie and Spencer walked Chloe to the little cabin she had rented just a block from town. Then they walked to where Maggie had left her car parked in front of Chloe's shop. Main Street was dark and deserted now, with only a few stark street lights casting cold harsh shadows. The shops were dark, their front windows blackened holes, like unseeing eyes. Maggie shuddered. Pine Mountain looked deader than ever at night. Suddenly she questioned the dreams they had shared around Rosa's picnic table. Was there really any hope of reviving this forlorn little town? Were their expectations ridiculous?

Then suddenly, almost like a vision, Maggie imagined Main Street with old-fashioned iron lampposts glowing brightly with warm, golden light, and strings of white lights decorating the trees, just like one of her favorite shopping spots in Old Pasadena. Pine Mountain *did* have the potential to be charming! She just knew it. She paused in front of her car for a long moment, silently studying the shops again along the darkened street.

"Hey, Mom, what are you looking at?" asked Spencer as he waited on the other side of the car.

"Just imagining what could be." Maggie unlocked the doors. "I wonder if the business association should come up with some sort of town-theme for shop-owners to work around. Maybe something like the Pine Mountain Hotel. See how it has the look of an old fashioned ski lodge? Maybe all the shops could incorporate that same sort of look. Perhaps something like a Swiss Alpine village."

"I guess that would be kind of interesting."

"It makes sense with the skiing so nearby. Everyone could incorporate bits of Alpine-style architecture. It would be very quaint and old fashioned..."

"Mom," Spencer interrupted her. "I know you guys were having a good time making all your plans for this business association and everything, but it seems like you forgot one fairly important thing."

"What's that, Spence?"

"The old bottom line."

Maggie sighed. "You know, you're pretty smart for a kid."

Spencer laughed. "Been trained by the best. But really, Mom, everyone around here seems kinda down on their luck right now. Where would anyone come up with any money for the kind of things you guys want to see happen?"

"Actually, I've given that some thought, Spencer. I know of a few towns in California that were able to access some federal and state grant funds for certain types of urban renewal. I don't know too much about it, but I figure I can probably do some research on the Internet to come up with some answers."

"You know, you're pretty smart for a mom," said Spencer.

Maggie grinned. "Thanks. I just hope it all works out."

"Well, like Sam said, 'nothing ventured, nothing gained.' I guess it can't hurt to try. Besides, we can always go back to L.A."

She cast a sideways glance at her tall son. "Do you still hope we'll go back, Spence?"

"Not half as much as I used to."

That night, Maggie sent another email to her friend in L.A.

RB

Lots going on here. Almost gives one hope. We're trying to launch a business association, and believe it or not, they want me to head it up—at least to start with. I feel I'm in over my head, but must admit the challenge is appealing. And I do have a lot at stake here... I just hope I don't mess things up. These people are becoming dear to me. For the first time since childhood I'm feeling like I'm part of a community, and it feels good! Except there's this one person—the evil postmaster—who seems to hate me. Isn't that weird? At first I thought it was because he's very anti-development and probably thinks I want to turn this place into a little L.A. But then I found out that he's also a buddy of Gavin Barnes, so maybe he resents the fact that I have his friend's old job and, now it seems, his dog too. Boy, now that I think about it, I suppose the postmaster thinks he has lots of good reasons to resent me. But it does seem pretty childish. I suppose I should try to win him over. Tonight I'm too tired to even think about that. You should see the stars here, Rebecca. If one didn't believe in God, these stars, at the very least, would make them think...

mc

Thirteen

*M*aggie wondered what one wore to a church service in the woods. Certainly not hiking boots! The church they'd belonged to in California had been somewhat formal with impressive suits and designer dresses, but shortly after Phil's death Spencer had begun to call those people phonies, balking more and more until Maggie got tired of defending them, and then Spencer finally refused to go to church altogether. She was glad that he was willing to go today. For a moment she considered how much he had changed just in the short time since they had arrived in Pine Mountain. It seemed nothing short of miraculous, and she had already thanked God for it many times over. Of course, she knew better than to assume that the trials of teenage years were over, but at least now she had hope. She looked back into her narrow closet, finally deciding on a linen dress.

"Time to get ready for church," she called from downstairs as she filled the coffee pot with water in the kitchen. She watched in amusement as Bart climbed down the ladderlike steps from the loft, carefully setting one paw in front of the next as if he'd been doing it all his life. "You're such a smart doggy," she said as she opened the front door to let him out. As she watched him trot across the dewy grass, she wondered if Greg had already called Gavin with the news about the dog. If so, it was likely that they'd hear from him soon. It was not something she looked forward to, especially if he was anything like his acidic friend Greg.

"Mom," said Spencer as he poured himself a bowl of cereal. "I think you're a little too dressed up for *this* church. Sierra says that everyone just wears jeans, even her mom."

"Rosa wears jeans to church?" said Maggie.

"Uh-huh." Spencer took a big bite, then nodded. "You better go change."

She had never worn jeans to church, but decided to trust her son on this and quickly changed into her nicest jeans, tucking a cream silk blouse under her designer leather belt, then she slipped on a pair of smooth leather loafers, and stepped out and held out her arms expecting Spencer's approval.

Spencer looked up then just shook his head. "Mom, you still look *way* too fancy."

"Well, I never dreamed I'd be getting fashion advice from you!" Then she smiled sheepishly. "The really pitiful thing is that I actually need it." She went back for a third time, this time emerging with the same jeans, only now she had replaced the silk blouse with a polo shirt, and the loafers with canvas shoes.

Spencer finally nodded. "I guess that's okay."

As they were leaving, Maggie briefly explained to Spencer about the conversation with Greg at the post office and how she expected he would probably call Gavin about the dog. "Maybe we should leave Bart inside this morning. Just until we know what's up."

"Okay by me, Mom. I sure don't want to see him taken away."

Spencer played navigator while Maggie drove up a narrow, winding dirt road. "Are you sure we're not lost?" she asked as she dodged another big rock. "We're out in the middle of nowhere."

"This is exactly the way Sierra said to go."

"Well, if we get stuck, I'm making *you* walk back to town."

Spencer laughed. "That would leave *you* all alone out in the woods, Mom. Aren't you afraid a bear might get you?"

At last, they came to where a number of other vehicles were parked just off the road—all hefty four-wheel-drive rigs. "It figures," she muttered as she pulled off the road behind them. "Gotta have an SUV to survive around here."

"Really?" Spencer's eyes lit up. "That'd be cool."

"No, not *really*." Maggie waited for the dust outside to settle before she got out of the car. She spied a log structure directly ahead, neatly situated right on the edge of a ridge almost as if it had cropped up right out of the ground. Framed by tall pines on both sides and backdropped by a stunning view of snowcapped mountains, the scene looked like the cover to some glossy travel magazine.

"Wow," she breathed. "This is absolutely gorgeous up here, Spencer."

"Yeah, but we better hurry. I can hear music playing. I think we're late, Mom."

No usher greeted them as they slipped into the back of the building and quietly sat on a rough-hewn log bench that Maggie suspected had been made by Jed. In fact, the whole building seemed a likely result of his craftsmanship. It was a beautiful piece of rustic architecture that blended gracefully and naturally with its surroundings. The entire front wall was one gigantic window. Enormous panes of glass were framed by natural birch logs that fanned out into the shape of a tree—almost as if it had grown there with the glass panels tucked between the branches. And the view beyond the window was stunning. Nothing but mountain peaks and clear, blue sky. The view alone put her in a state of awe and worship and reverence. It took a few minutes to refocus her attention to the actual service up front where an older man, one she didn't recognize, was making some announcements. Then she noticed several musicians seated off to one side, including Jed and Sierra. It looked as if they were about to play. Jed began to quietly pick on a classical guitar, then a middle-aged woman came in on a mandolin, and finally Sierra bent her head and began to play a violin. No voices joined their little ensemble; it was only the pure classical strains of a beautifully arranged piece played under ideal acoustical conditions. And the result was ethereal and spiritually uplifting. Maggie felt tears well in her eyes as she listened, and she honestly wondered if this was like a small slice of heaven. When the piece ended she sighed deeply, then glanced at Spencer. He too seemed moved, leaning forward with wide eyes. Maggie longed for the trio to continue, but they seemed to be finished, each dispersing in different directions—Sierra to her family, the mandolinist to the man who had given the announcements, and Jed to the podium.

Jed, dressed no differently than any other day, including the fringed moccasin boots, waited until the other musicians were seated. Maggie used this break to survey the congregation sitting ahead of her. She estimated the headcount to be around twenty, maybe thirty at best. She recognized the older couple who ran the Gas-n-Go and Carol, the friendly checker, from Pine Mountain Mercantile. Even Chloe was here today, sitting, not surprisingly, next to Scott with the Galloways.

Jed cleared his throat and the church grew quiet as he began to speak. He acknowledged the musicians and welcomed the small group of listeners. He used no microphone, but his voice was clear and resonant. Maggie noticed Kate sitting in the front row, her head tilted slightly back as if she were looking right into Jed's face—

"And I see we have some visitors today," said Jed. Caught off guard, Maggie smiled nervously as he pointed to the back of the church, then continued. "Maggie and Spencer Carpenter, would you please stand..." They complied and Jed proceeded to introduce them and explain what had brought them to Pine Mountain.

After a brief prayer, the congregation sang a couple of hymns with Jed accompanying once again on guitar. Then Sam came forward and read a portion of Scripture, the parable of the prodigal son. Jed returned to the podium and began to expound on this familiar parable. He explained that his own story was not unlike the prodigal son; telling how he, against his father's wishes, had left home at an early age to go into the military, then he attended college on a GI bill, and then after many years of struggling to find himself, he finally found God. That had only been five years ago.

"And so you see, I'm just a fledgling believer. And I know there are those who feel I need more experience under my belt before I try to fill a pulpit. To that I can only answer that I believe God has called me to this, at least for now. And when God calls you, what can you do? More importantly, I think everyone must ask themselves—'what is God calling me to do?' And then you must do it—and do it with your whole heart." Maggie noticed several heads nodding in enthusiastic agreement. If this had been a southern church they might have shouted "amen." But all was quiet and controlled. And peaceful.

Jed prayed again. Not wordy or long-winded, but the prayer seemed sincere and from the heart. Then everyone began to rise from their seats and move around. Church was over. Less than one hour and church was over!

Spencer grinned as he checked his watch. "I *like* this church, Mom."

She smiled at him and nodded. "I do too."

They stayed and visited with those they knew, and met some of the ones they didn't. Finally the little crowd began to break up.

"A bunch of us are going out to the lake today," said Rosa. "Want to come along?"

"You bet," said Spencer, looking eagerly at Maggie.

"Sure, why not," she answered. "Except for one thing, Rosa. You must let me bring some food or something."

Rosa's brows knit together, then she held a finger in the air. "I know. Why don't you pick up some soda and chips, and how about a bag of ice while you're at it?"

"Great," agreed Maggie with a grin. "Spencer must've told you about my culinary skills. Anything else?"

"No, I've already got a lot of stuff ready to go. Scotty even helped me make a huge potato salad this morning. We'll see you at the lake about one-thirty."

～

Maggie decided to take Bart with them. She didn't mention that the motivation was the nagging fear that Gavin might show up at any given moment and take back his dog. Besides, Bart was well-mannered and she thought he would enjoy the outing.

A lot of people from the church were there, including Jed and Kate. Lunch turned out to be a potluck affair, and after tying the dog in the shade of a tree, Maggie sat with Carol from the market. Carol explained that she had two school-aged boys who would have loved to be here today but, because of a shared custody arrangement, they were spending their summer with her ex-husband and his new, barely-out-of-high-school-aged, wife.

"Not only that," complained Carol. "But my ex lives in the city and his wife works, so the boys are in child-care most of the time, and when they're not I'm sure they're parked in front of video games. It's just so unfair that they have to spend summers there."

Maggie's heart went out to her, but she wasn't sure how to offer comfort. "Do your boys like to ski in the wintertime?" she asked hopefully.

Carol's face brightened. "Yes, we just took it up last year, and they absolutely loved it. But this year my nine-year-old is begging for a snowboard." They talked about boys and snowboards until people began to clear away the picnic and it was time to load up the boats. Spencer and Sierra were already planted in the back of her dad's boat, and Carol joined the Mitchells from the Gas-n-Go. Maggie suspected there were more people than there was room in the boats, and with Scott here, plus Chloe adopting the Galloways, Maggie figured their boat would be pretty full.

"Rosa, I think I'll stick around shore," said Maggie, hoping to alleviate any pressure that she join them. "Actually, I'd really like to take the dog for a walk and look around some."

"Are you sure?" asked Rosa.

"Positive." Maggie smiled convincingly.

"Okay, then. See you later."

Maggie watched from a distance as they began to load the boats. Part of her felt slightly left out, but it was her own choice. And she had never been that fond of motorboats anyway. It sounded much more peaceful to walk Bart around the numerous trails, and recall times from childhood spent on this very lake.

For awhile, she followed Bart along a trail that circled the perimeter of the sparkling blue lake, and as they walked she drank in the quiet peace of light reflecting off water, the soft lapping waves along the sandy shore, and the pungent, warm-pitch aroma of pine needles soaking up the sun. Suddenly, it seemed as if nothing about this place had changed. "Delicious," she said out loud. Bart looked over his shoulder at her with curious golden eyes, his pink tongue lolling out the side of his mouth. "Are you thirsty, old boy?" she asked, leading him down to the shore where he could drink from the lake. He took a long drink, then waded into the water and laid right down in it. After that they walked back to the dock area.

By the time she reached the camp store, she understood Bart's thirst. She tied him in the shade and went inside for a bottle of water. Inside the store was dark and cool, just as it had been in her childhood memory. And the shelves were crowded with everything from fishing lures to marshmallows. Maybe the store hadn't changed all that much either.

It was just perspective. She bought her water and stepped back outside.

"Hi there," called Jed. "I was looking for you."

"For me?" Maggie squinted at him in the bright sun, pushing a damp strand of hair off her forehead as she took a cool drink of water.

Jed smiled attractively. "Yes. Rosa said you'd stayed behind with the dog. The boats were a little crowded so I stayed back too. I thought you might like some company."

Maggie glanced around uncomfortably. Where was the beautiful Kate? She'd seen them sitting together at lunchtime, and for all practical purposes they seemed like a couple. "I just took a walk with the dog," she explained for no apparent reason, then took another swig of water. "It's getting pretty hot out here."

"We could rent a canoe if you like," offered Jed. "It's cooler out on the lake."

"That actually sounds like fun," said Maggie with renewed interest. "I haven't been in a canoe since I was a kid—and it was on this very lake." Then she remembered Bart. "But what about the dog?"

"He might like it too," said Jed. "You bring him and I'll get us a canoe."

Jed held the canoe steady while she carefully got in, stepping one foot at a time into the center, then slowly moving toward the front. Then she gently coaxed Bart into the middle, telling him to sit quietly, which he did. When Jed climbed in, he pushed off from the dock in one graceful motion and sat down and began to paddle.

"You look like you've done this before," said Maggie with admiration.

"Didn't you know it's in the blood?"

She looked puzzled, then realized he was referring to his Native American roots. "Does that *really* make a difference?"

He chuckled. "Not really. I had a cousin who couldn't even keep a rowboat afloat."

She laughed, then glanced around for another paddle. "Don't you want me to help paddle?"

"No, if you don't mind, I like doing it myself. I think it's smoother when only one person paddles."

"Fine with me." She leaned back comfortably against the life-preserver cushion. "Although, just for the record, I *do* know how to paddle a canoe."

The canoe sliced quietly across the calm end of the lake where the limited speed sign was posted. Bart stretched out on the bottom of the boat as if to absorb the coolness of the water sliding beneath them. Maggie heard the distant rumble of boat motors and the muted voices of children splashing in the roped-off swimming area on the other side. But those sounds were detached and far away, not loud enough to disturb the peace. Conversation seemed unnecessary. Both of them seemed content to simply enjoy their pleasant surroundings. At one point Jed stopped paddling and silently pointed up into the sky. Maggie peered up in time to spy a large bird of prey hovering straight over the center of the lake. Only when it began to dive did she notice the white head.

"A bald eagle?" she asked in surprise.

Jed nodded, and they both watched as the bird's open claws skimmed the surface of the water, dipped down, then emerged with a small, wiggling, silver fish. Maggie watched in wonder. She had only seen such a thing on the nature channel. "Amazing!" she breathed.

"You know an eagle won't go after a fish that's too big," said Jed quietly, almost reverently.

"Why not?"

"It's difficult for the eagle to release the fish once he's in flight. So if the fish is too heavy it can weight the bird down and even pull him back into the water. I actually saw an eagle go down once. It never came back up."

"You're kidding—it drowned? I've never heard of that."

He nodded solemnly. "So even the eagles, who can fly so high, need to accept their limitations."

"I guess that's like what my mom used to say about not biting off more than you can chew."

He smiled. "Good advice. Do you always listen to your mother?"

"Almost never."

"I hope you haven't bitten off more than you can chew with this town, Maggie."

She looked at him in surprise. "What do you mean?"

"Oh, you know. The word's getting around that Maggie Carpenter is going to save Pine Mountain."

She shook her head. "Wow, I guess what they say about the rumor mills in small towns is really true."

"You better believe it. And like a mill they can grind you up and spit you back out."

"Has that happened to you?"

"It happens to everyone. Just wait until you start printing that paper, you'll see how it works. Just remember that in time most things will blow over."

She thought for a moment. His comment about "saving the town" disturbed her a little. Although she had to admit it was partly true—she would love to save Pine Mountain—at the same time she also knew it would take the whole town to do it. Did he think she planned to do it all on her own? She glanced at him again. He was still looking up at the sky.

"Jed, you know what you said today about knowing what God has called you to do and then doing it?"

His eyes lit. "Yes. I really meant that."

"Well, it may sound weird, and believe me I don't go around telling everyone this, but I honestly think that God has *called* me to Pine Mountain. I'm not completely sure why, or even exactly what I'm supposed to accomplish, if anything. But I did feel called."

"Good for you, Maggie. Then this should be quite an adventure." Suddenly, as if changing gears, he began to paddle again. But she wasn't ready for this conversation to end just yet. She had opened up to him about feeling called to Pine Mountain, and now she felt brushed aside. Jed's attention seemed more focused on the lake than her.

"I like your church," she said, hoping to regenerate their previous dialogue. She watched as he paddled, waiting for his response. But his face suddenly looked strangely blank, almost as if a curtain had been pulled shut. She couldn't begin to guess what he was thinking beneath the smooth countenance.

Finally he spoke, slowly as if he was explaining something very complex. "I do not consider it *my* church, Maggie. I like to think that it belongs to God."

She looked at him mutely, feeling very much like a child who'd just been corrected for speaking out of turn. He continued to paddle in silence, and she leaned back again, determined to simply focus her attention on the beautiful lake and the sky. Why concern herself with trying to figure out Jed Whitewater anyway? Especially when she had such a knack for putting her foot in her mouth around him. Probably just as well, since their relationship seemed destined to remain nothing more than a casual business acquaintance. She glanced at him from behind the protection of her sunglasses. It was kind of him to take her out in the canoe, and that may have been motivated by his pastoral concern for her; the poor newcomer left behind on the shore. Well, she didn't need his pity—

Just then the canoe began to lean to the left and she noticed that Bart was standing up and straining over the edge. A pair of ducks were floating nearby, and he looked uncomfortably interested.

"Sit down, Bart," she commanded as she reached over to grasp his collar. But before she could contain him, the dog lunged for the ducks, and the canoe tipped them all into the chilly lake. Maggie sputtered to the surface, spotting Jed just a few feet away. Bart was already halfway to the shore. The ducks were nowhere to be seen.

"Can you swim?"

"Yes."

"Okay, then let's upright the canoe."

They worked together to turn the canoe right side up in the water. It was still two-thirds full of water, but at least it floated. They retrieved the life jackets and paddles and placed them inside, and together they towed it to a nearby sunny beach. Jed pulled the waterlogged canoe halfway onto the shore and laid the soggy equipment on a nearby rock to dry. Bart was already on the shore, sitting proudly as if he'd just pulled off a great stunt.

"You bad dog," scolded Maggie, shaking a finger in Bart's oblivious face. Then she turned to Jed in embarrassment. "I am so terribly sorry about all this..."

"It's okay. I needed a cool dip." Jed looked at her, then began to chuckle.

Maggie grinned self-consciously. "I bet I look pretty bad."

"No, that's not it," laughed Jed. "It's just...you should've seen your face when you were in the water. It looked like the city girl got her dunking. I kept suppressing the urge to say: Welcome to Pine Mountain, Maggie Carpenter."

Maggie began to giggle, and soon they were both laughing almost uncontrollably. Just then one of the ski boats stopped not far from their beach, motor idling.

"Everything okay here?" called Fred Mitchell, owner of the Gas-n-Go.

"We're fine," yelled Maggie. "Just needed to cool off." She smiled brightly, then suddenly noticed that Kate was one of the passengers onboard. Kate had on a sleek black bathing suit and her hair was wet as if she'd just been skiing. But at the moment, her pretty face looked more than a little concerned as she stared at the two of them, clearly puzzled by what she saw.

"Are you all right, Jed?" she called.

"Sure. Just a little dunking is all. The dog went after some ducks."

"Okay, then," called Fred as he turned the boat away from shore. "It's almost quitting time. We'll see you back at the dock in a little while." He gunned the engine and headed off toward the center of the lake.

"That boat didn't look very crowded," said Maggie. She examined Jed with a raised brow. "I thought you said it was full."

Jed shrugged sheepishly. "Well, the truth is, I don't much enjoy motorized boats. They're too fast and noisy for my taste."

She nodded. "I know just what you mean. It's not really my cup of tea either, but I put up with it for Spencer's sake."

"You're a good woman, Maggie."

She looked at him in surprise. Was he teasing? But his face seemed sincere, and he continued. "Sorry if I sounded a little testy out there about the church thing. I don't know why I feel so defensive about it, but I do. If you get to know me better, you'll realize that I can be a little abrupt. I guess I don't have the most polished social skills. Kate says I can be a real brute sometimes."

"Oh," said Maggie, surprised at this sudden openness. "I suppose there's nothing wrong with telling something like it is, as long as you don't hurt anyone in the process. I know I've found that to be challenging when I'm trying to report on a difficult story."

"I'm glad you understand." He glanced at his watch. "I suppose we better start bailing out the canoe if we want to get back in time to meet the others."

Maggie thought perhaps she didn't care when or if they got back. But she kept this to herself. In the meantime, she focused her attention on helping him bail. It was the least she could do since it was her fault they'd been dunked. She glanced over at Bart, now lying happily in the warm sun. *Good dog,* she thought with a smile.

Fourteen

The following week, Maggie visited every business in town, dispersing flyers and inviting all the business people to the meeting that would be held Saturday night. Though some were a little suspicious of her participation, others were excited at the prospect of organizing an association to promote their town. Cherise Snider appeared genuinely enthusiastic about the association despite her husband's antidevelopment convictions and, as earlier promised, offered Maggie a reduced rate on her first month's membership at the fitness club. Maggie said she'd get back to her on it. Then she stopped by Clara Lou's Antiques. Apparently, Abigail had already told Clara about the planned meeting, and Clara said she'd be there with bells on. Maggie thanked her and gave her several flyers to post around town, just as reminders.

Maggie sensed that while a strong core of positive business owners were willing to work hard to make Pine Mountain flourish and grow, they were not the majority. Most of the business people seemed complacent if not downright pessimistic. Many had resigned themselves to barely surviving with no hopes for a brighter future, ever. And no matter what Maggie said, there were those who didn't believe things would ever change in Pine Mountain, and they had years of struggling decline to back this up with. If they were lucky they'd be able to pay their bills, just barely. And if not, they'd soon leave town like those who had gone before them, hopefully before winter set in. But Maggie continued her mission undaunted. Their apathy was understandable. Her challenge was to give them a reason to hope.

She even slipped into the post office to tack a flyer on the bulletin board, hoping that since it was the lunch hour she might avoid seeing Greg Snider. But before the tack was even in place, Greg was standing behind her, peering over her shoulder. He read the flyer out loud in a sarcastic voice, then added. "I don't know what makes you think you can come in here and change this town, *Ms.* Carpenter. But it won't be long until you find out that folks 'round here have their own ideas about these things. And they know how to run their own town."

Maggie turned and looked him squarely in the eye. "This is a public bulletin board, is it not?"

He nodded dourly.

She turned on her heel. "Well, thank you, then. I just wanted to make sure that all the business people in town were fully aware of the meeting." She didn't know what made that man so disagreeable, but she was determined not to let him get the best of her. She had to maintain a positive attitude if she planned to encourage others. And she still had a few more businesses to visit—the ones she'd put off for last. She'd purposely delayed going into Dolly's Diner because it was so smoky and greasy smelling. And then there was still the Eagle, the bar next-door to Dolly's. For some reason, she supposed those two establishments would be antagonistic towards the association. But even if they weren't interested, Maggie couldn't afford to snub anyone in town. She stopped at Dolly's first. To her surprise, more than half of the diner's tables were filled. But it was the lunchhour and, as her mother often said, there was no accounting for taste. Maggie hoped to use this unexpected busyness as an excuse to keep her visit brief.

"Hi, there, honey," called a tall, thin woman from behind the counter. "Go ahead and take a seat right there, and I'll be with you in a flash." Something about the woman's long neck, pulled-back dark hair, and small face reminded Maggie of Olive Oyl from the old Popeye cartoons. But when she saw the woman's name tag, she realized that this was in fact Dolly, the owner. Maggie had to smile, thinking how she'd imagined Dolly as a rough-talking, chain-smoking, buxom blond! As a reporter she knew better than to make such assumptions, and *that* was exactly why!

She waited by the cash register, prepared to quickly explain her mission, then thought better of it. Perhaps it wouldn't hurt to take a seat and order a small meal. After all, she was running the *Pine Cone* now and this was probably as good a place as any to gather local news. She slid into a red plastic booth and picked up the vinyl-covered menu, trying to ignore the thin coat of grease that seemed to be everywhere. The smell of cigarette smoke and fried food was strong, but probably not any worse than in other small-town diners across the country. In many ways, Maggie had led an insulated life in southern California. Perhaps it was time to step out and stretch herself a little more. Funny, that she should realize this just when she'd settled into what she had expected to be a very protected little town.

"All rightie, then," said Dolly. "What can I get for ya?" She adjusted a small pair of wire-rimmed glasses, then pulled out her order pad and pencil.

Maggie smiled brightly. "First, I want to introduce myself..."

Dolly laughed. "Oh, I know who you are, honey. You're Maggie Carpenter, the new editor of the *Pine Cone*. Everybody knows that." Then Dolly frowned. "But why haven't you been in here yet? It's been nearly two weeks, honey. Don't you believe in eating out?"

Maggie thought quickly. "Well, we try to eat more natural foods. You know how obsessive Californians can be about health." She laughed.

Dolly chuckled, then spoke in a conspirator's whisper. "I know *exactly* what you mean. If it weren't for my regular customers, I'd change my menu a little. I never eat most of the stuff we serve here." She nodded toward the kitchen. "But my old man, Jinx, just loves to fry food. He's from the south, you know, and it's the way his mama always cooked. And since I don't really like to cook much, I just try and put up with it."

Maggie handed Dolly a flyer and quickly explained about the meeting, then asked her what she recommended for lunch.

"Well, considering what you said about being health conscious, I'd suggest a bowl of my soup of the day. It's Spring Vegetable. I make it myself, and I don't mind saying that it's not half bad."

"Thanks," said Maggie replacing the menu. "That sounds perfect."

When Dolly returned with soup and crackers, she nodded back toward the kitchen again. "I told Jinx about the meeting and he says we'll come."

After lunch, Maggie went next door to the Eagle Tavern. After her eyes adjusted to the dimness, she realized that it was a rather nice looking bar. Clean and neat, its walls were decorated with all sorts of hunting trophies: elk, deer, moose, even a gigantic polar bear skin. "Looks like someone here likes to hunt," said Maggie to the back of a large man emptying a dishwasher behind the counter.

He turned around with a grin. "That'd be me." Then he peered at her more closely. "Hey, are you that new editor from the *Los Angeles Times*?"

Maggie smiled. "That'd be me."

"Well, I'm Rich Stuart. Welcome to the Eagle."

"Thanks." She handed him a flyer and explained about the upcoming meeting.

He frowned slightly. "Hope you're not going to a lot of trouble for nothing."

"What do you mean?"

"Well, I've been here a pretty long time. Probably longer than most. You know, it's funny, Maggie, people can run out of money for a lot of things, but they never seem to run out of money for a drink or two. I see 'em all from time to time."

She bit her lip and waited from him to continue.

"Anyway, the way I see it, Pine Mountain is pretty much washed up. I honestly don't think anything short of a miracle can save this town. Fact is, I'm surprised Clyde could lure someone like you to leave a good job to come to a place like this. I told him that even before you got here. We had quite a discussion over it." He studied her, as if looking for some sort of clue as to why she had come.

"I understand what you mean. In fact, I felt the same way after I got here and saw what Pine Mountain had become. But since I'm here, and in a way I'm stuck here because I bought property, I figure it can't hurt to give it my best shot. And you know what you said about a miracle— well," she held her chin up, "I happen to believe that miracles *can* happen. But sometimes they need a little help. And I guess I'm willing to help."

Rich nodded. It looked as if he was suppressing a smile. "Well, then you better go for it, little lady. I won't promise any help, personally, but who knows? I might stop by your meeting if the bar's not too busy on Saturday. Although that's usually my busiest night of the week."

"Thanks, Rich." She smiled brightly. "I hope to see you then."

When she stepped out of the bar, she was nearly blinded by the bright afternoon sun and walked right into another pedestrian. "Excuse me," she apologized. Then she looked up to see Jed standing before her.

"Are you okay?" He looked down at her with what seemed unnecessary concern.

"I'm fine. I just didn't see you there..."

"You've been in *the Eagle?*" He frowned up at the bar's neon sign behind her.

Maggie laughed nervously. "As a matter of fact, yes. Is that a problem?"

He look puzzled. "I just didn't think you were *that* type…"

"'That type' of what?" Maggie felt irritated. What exactly was he suggesting? Did he think she'd been in there belting down whiskeys with the good ol' boys?

Jed just shook his head. "Oh, I don't know. What you do is your business, Maggie."

"Are you saying it's wrong to step into a bar?" Even as she said it, Maggie wondered what the point of pursuing this conversation could possibly be. She should just shut up and move on. But for some reason she couldn't. Maybe it was her father's stubborn German heritage popping up at the wrong times, but she was often a sucker for a good fight.

"Maybe." He sniffed the air. "You smell like smoke, Maggie."

She stared at him as he stood before her, so clean and wholesome…yet so judgmental. "You consider yourself a pastor, Jed," said Maggie defiantly. "Do you happen to know where Jesus spent a fair amount of time?"

He sighed. "I know what you're getting at, but that's not it. I was just worried about you, about your reputation. You're new in town and…" He shrugged.

Maggie rolled her eyes. "I'm a big girl, Jed. You don't need to worry about me or my reputation." She shoved a flyer at him. "I'm just out distributing these flyers for our business meeting. I left one at your shop with Kate, but maybe you haven't had a chance to read it yet. I wanted to be sure that *every* business was invited!" Then she walked off. She knew it wasn't a very mature reaction on her part, and it surprised her that she felt so strongly, but it was too late to take it back now. Besides what right did he have to act worried about her anyway?

⌒

For the rest of the week, Maggie concentrated all her energies on the newspaper. Abigail was a true God-send. In just a few days, she had the place completely organized. Scott Galloway officially joined their team on Tuesday and she put him right to work contacting the local freelance writers to see if they had any stories worth considering. By midweek, they had several good leads, some paid advertisements, and Clyde seemed pleased with the progress. By the end of the week, the four of them were falling into something of a routine. And if all went according to plan, they would publish their first paper the following week. Scott turned out to be a computer whiz, and at their Thursday morning meeting he suggested they consider getting a new digital computer that could handle the complete layout of the paper electronically. Clyde told Scott to find out how much a system like that would cost and he would consider it.

"As long as we're moving into the twenty-first century, how about taking the *Pine Cone* online?" suggested Maggie.

"That's an excellent idea," said Scott. "What a way to spread the word about Pine Mountain. We might even draw in some poor unsuspecting tourists."

Abigail frowned at him. "For your information, young man, a lot of tourists would *love* Pine Mountain, if they only knew it was here."

Maggie nodded. "And that's my goal—to let folks know that it's here!"

"Go ahead with it, Maggie," said Clyde. "Put the paper on the Internet if you like. I may be old, but I've never been stodgy, and I'm sure not opposed to the latest technology."

"Would you look into that, Scott?" asked Maggie.

"Sure, whatever you say, boss." Scott was trying hard to please her. And even though she suspected his ulterior motive was to get a job at the *Times*, she didn't really mind. After all, she was the one who'd set him up in the first place. It was just a shame that she'd have to let him go someday.

Maggie spent most of Friday morning searching the Net and making phone calls for grant information. Before noon, she had discovered several excellent possibilities. One exceptionally good grant from the state lottery had an application deadline for the following week. She had the forms faxed to her, and decided to devote her weekend to writing up the most enticing proposal she could think of to get the grant committee to take notice of little Pine Mountain. If nothing else, she figured she could reuse her proposal for other grant applications. And she would use Saturday night's meeting to glean some helpful information for the direction the businesses would like to see the town go in.

"Abigail," began Maggie. "I made a list of questions and information that I'd like you to gather for me. Sort of a Pine Mountain profile: some historical stuff, statistics, etc."

"You bet." Abigail skimmed over the list. "When do you need it?"

"Is early next week too soon?" she asked hopefully.

"I'll have it done by Monday afternoon. How's that?"

Maggie grinned. "You are amazing, Abigail." Then she told her about the grant possibility, asking her to keep the information under her hat until more was known.

"See. You're just what this town needs."

"Well, like my grandma always said, let's not count our chickens before they hatch."

"Well, I don't know but I think I can hear them pecking at their shells." Just then the phone rang and Abigail picked it up. Her face grew perplexed as she listened. "Hang on there, Spencer," she said in voice that was obviously meant to be calming. "Your mom's right here." She handed the receiver to Maggie. "You better take this right now. He sounds pretty upset."

Maggie grabbed the receiver. "What's wrong, Spence?"

"Mom, *he's here!*" Spencer was whispering, but Maggie could hear the frantic urgency in his voice.

"*Who's* here?"

"Gavin Barnes. He's knocked on the door twice, but I didn't answer. Somehow I just know it's him. And now he's nosing all around the place. He knows we've got Bart..."

"How does he know?"

"Bart barked when he knocked. Mom, what should I do?"

"I'll come home, Spence. I'll be there in less than five minutes. Okay?"

"Thanks, Mom. I don't want him to take Bart."

She hung up and turned quickly to Abigail. "It's Gavin. He's at the house and he's looking for the dog. I've got to go help Spencer."

Abigail scowled. "I don't like the sound of this, Maggie. Maybe we should call the sheriff. Gavin can be quite difficult. Maybe I should come..."

She was already halfway out the door. "No. Just tell Clyde...right away." Maggie wished that Scott was there to join her, but he was taking photos of Chloe's shop this morning for the new business section. No telling when he'd be back. She drove home fast, unconcerned that she might catch the attention of the sheriff. She'd just have him follow her home and then explain that her son had an intruder on her property. Even as she speeded, she considered using her cell phone to dial 911, but feared that was overreacting. Maybe Gavin would be gone by the time she got there.

But he wasn't. A late-model, red Suburban was parked right in front of the carriage house. She pulled up fast and hopped out of her car. Angry now that this thug should come around here frightening her son, she was ready to face him head on.

She marched up to the carriage house and looked around, her cell phone clutched in her hand like a weapon, all ready to dial for help if necessary. Then she spotted him over by the barn. "Hey!" she yelled in a loud, tough voice. "What are you doing over there?"

"Hello there," yelled the man in a friendly answer, holding up his hands as if to show he was unarmed. "Don't shoot." Then he laughed at his own joke and slowly walked toward her. "Sorry to disturb you like this," he called. "I'm just looking for my dog."

Maggie stood her ground on the porch, arms folded across her chest. She felt the door open slightly behind her, then Spencer stuck his head out. "Stay in there," she hissed over her shoulder.

"I'm Gavin Barnes, Clyde's nephew. No doubt you've heard of me." He stepped up and extended his hand.

She was puzzled at this gesture. Here she was ready for a fight, and he wanted to be Mr. Congeniality. But she wasn't ready for friendliness and kept her arms folded tightly across her chest until his hand finally dropped to his side, and then she spoke. "I want to know exactly why you're snooping around my place, Mr. Barnes."

"Your place?"

"That's right, I'm the owner. Now what are you doing here?"

"You mean Clyde *sold* this place?"

She nodded briefly. "What do you want, Mr. Barnes?"

He scratched his head as if still processing the news of her ownership. "I'm looking for my dog. Do you have him?"

Maggie studied Gavin for a long moment. He was an attractive man with wavy blond hair. Probably in his forties. His casual outdoor clothing looked like it had come straight from an L.L. Bean catalog, and his perfect smile looked like it had charmed its share of women. Well, it wouldn't charm her.

"We found a dog a couple weeks back. He seemed lost or abandoned. I placed all sorts of ads. No one answered."

"A chocolate lab?"

She nodded, lips pressed firmly together. "My son has become quite attached to him."

"You have a son?"

His interest surprised her, and it bothered her that he wasn't playing his villain role the way she had anticipated. It seemed he was determined to be nice and make this difficult. "My son has been taking care of your...uh, I mean the lost dog. And, as I said, he's grown quite attached."

Gavin sighed and nodded. "I see..."

Maggie grew hopeful. Maybe she was playing this all wrong. Maybe the thing to do was to warm up to him, win him over, and then offer to buy the dog from him. She stepped down from the porch and extended her hand. "I'm sorry, Gavin. I have been very rude. But my son called me at the office, freaked out over some intruder. And so, as you can see, I was a little worked up."

"It's understandable." He smiled again.

"I'm Maggie Carpenter. You've probably heard that I'm the new editor of the *Pine Cone*..." She stopped herself, not wanting to dredge up more unhappiness.

"Yes, I've heard. And I'm sure you've heard a lot about me too. My uncle's pretty ticked off at me right now."

"Actually, Clyde doesn't speak of you much at all."

"Well, I really screwed up. I still want to make things right with him, but I'm not sure how."

"Well, maybe it just needs time," offered Maggie, then she remembered what Clyde had said. "Although, I do think Clyde wants to talk to you. He mentioned to me that if I ever saw you around here that I should send you his way."

"I'll bet he did." Gavin's voice took on an edge that she hadn't noticed earlier. She studied him again, curious about the untold story she knew lay beneath this charming exterior.

"About this dog," she began again. "If by some chance he is your dog, Gavin, would you be willing to sell him?"

Gavin rubbed his chin thoughtfully. "I might be persuaded."

"Persuaded?" She waited for an explanation.

He nodded. "How about if you have dinner with me tonight..."

"Wait a minute." She held up her hands. "I'm not..."

"Hold on, hold on." Gavin grinned. "I'm not suggesting anything more than just dinner and conversation. And after that I'll let you make me a fair offer for the dog."

She thought for a long moment. The reporter in her was interested in hearing more of his story, and the mother in her wanted to get Spencer his dog. "Okay," she finally agreed. "Just dinner and conversation, and I'll bring my checkbook for the dog."

"But what if it isn't my dog?" His voice had a teasing tone to it.

"Does he go by Bart?"

Gavin nodded.

"Then he's probably your dog. Where do you want to meet for dinner?"

"Meet?"

She nodded firmly. "Look, Mr. Barnes, I'm a city girl. I would *never* go out with a guy I'd just met without driving separate cars. Take it or leave it."

He grinned. "Okay, I'll take it. Since there's no good place to eat in Pine Mountain, I'd suggest Jasper's in Byron. Do you know the place?"

"I've seen it. What time?"

"Seven?"

"Fine. I'll see you at Jasper's at seven."

Gavin climbed into his Suburban. "Pleasure to meet you, Maggie. See you later."

She watched as the cloud of dust enveloped the back of his rig. What had she gotten herself into?

"Everything okay?" asked Spencer, opening the door.

"The coast is clear, Spence."

Bart pushed his way out the door with Spencer behind him. "I was trying to listen through the door, Mom, and I couldn't hear everything. But it sounded like you agreed to have dinner with the creep."

She shook her head. "I think it was temporary insanity, Spencer. He said he would consider my offer to buy Bart if I had dinner with him. And he's not really a creep."

"Man, what a hard-up way to get a date!"

She chuckled. "Or we could say, what a hard-up way to get a dog!"

"Well, you're not going, Mom!"

She blinked in surprise. "But what about Bart?"

Spencer rubbed his hand down Bart's back. "As much as I like Bart, I'm not willing to trade him for my mom."

She laughed. "Well, that's a relief, but I don't think Gavin was thinking of a trade. And actually, honey, I'd like to hear what he has to say. I've heard so many things, and I want to hear his side too. I'd like to see if I can figure this thing out between him and Clyde."

"But what if he's some sort of crazed, lunatic, mass murderer or something?" Spencer's words were light, but his eyes were serious.

"Oh, Spence. I think he's just made some bad choices in regard to his uncle. There are folks in town who think Gavin is just fine."

"Yeah, like the crazy postmaster. And you know how scary those postal workers can get."

She laughed again. "That's not fair. Even Jed said that Greg was okay."

"Yeah, but Jed's a pastor. He *has* to say good things about people."

She considered that, remembering Jed's reaction to her coming out of the Eagle. "I don't necessarily think so. I think Jed feels pretty free to speak his mind."

Spencer glanced at his watch. "Well, he's coming over here at three to help me work on the porch. I'll ask him what he thinks about this Gavin person myself."

"Do that if it makes you feel better. Now, if you're okay about being here alone, I think I'll head back to the paper. I've got a big project I'm working on."

"I'm fine, Mom. He just kinda took me by surprise. And I didn't want him taking Bart."

"I know." She reached out and patted his shoulder. "I'll do what I can to see that we keep Bart all fair and square."

As she drove back to the office, she wondered about the agreement to have dinner with Gavin. Was she a complete fool? She wanted to discuss it with someone, but didn't dare share the news with Abigail, knowing how the older woman despised and probably distrusted Gavin. And she certainly didn't want to tell Clyde. What in the world would he think of this unusual development? And where was he anyway? She'd halfway expected him to hop in his old truck and zip over to meet her at the house. When she reached the office, she saw his truck pull up behind her. He climbed out and greeted her as if he had no idea of what had just happened. With relief, she thought that might be for the best for the time being. What Clyde didn't know wouldn't hurt him.

Fifteen

Maggie stopped by the deli for an afternoon latte. Since the place was nearly empty, she hoped to use this opportunity to tell Rosa about her strange encounter with Gavin earlier. Perhaps Rosa might be able to shed some much-needed wisdom on the whole thing. For Clyde's sake, Maggie had managed to hush Abigail about the incident, brushing over everything by saying that Spencer had simply overreacted to a strange vehicle that had parked in their driveway. Abigail had still looked suspicious, but fortunately didn't question Maggie further. Perhaps after her meeting with Gavin tonight, Maggie could explain it all to Abigail on Monday.

Rosa had brought them both coffee and was now eyeing Maggie with concern after hearing the whole story. "I don't know about this," she said carefully. "Sam has known Gavin for years, and I know that he doesn't completely trust the guy."

"Don't get me wrong, Rosa. I don't trust him either. In fact, we're driving in separate cars. I told him it's only dinner and then dog negotiations."

Rosa smiled, then shook her head. "But you have to realize that Gavin may have other ideas—he's quite the lady's man. And you're an attractive woman. He's probably hoping he can sweep you off your feet with his wit and charm."

Maggie waved her hand to dismiss such nonsense. "It's nothing more than a business dinner. And I'm also hoping I can make some sense of whatever has happened between him and Clyde. It's so sad when things come between family members like this. And I feel that Clyde still cares about Gavin."

Rosa sighed deeply. "I probably shouldn't say this. And I wouldn't even mention it if you weren't considering going out with him, but Sam thinks Gavin might be into something...something somewhat disreputable."

"What do you mean?"

"Oh, it's pure speculation on Sam's part. And I hate getting gossip started. So just keep this completely between you and me, okay?"

Maggie nodded, then sipped her latte.

"Sam thinks that Gavin might have been involved in some sort of organized crime or something like that."

Maggie sat down her cup and stared at Rosa in disbelief. "You've got to be kidding."

"I know it sounds pretty silly. Especially here in the bustling metropolis of Pine Mountain. But for some reason Sam suspects *something*. He hasn't given me any details. The only reason I'm telling you is so that you will be careful."

Maggie tried not to laugh at the absurdity of Rosa's implication. "Okay, I'll keep my guard up. If I see any mafia men hanging around, I'll get out of there in a hurry."

Rosa laughed. "Now, I feel really silly for telling you this."

Maggie reached over and patted her hand. "Don't worry, Rosa. I know you're just looking out for me. I appreciate it."

"What's Spencer doing tonight?" asked Rosa suddenly. "You don't want to leave him home alone..."

"Why? Do you think some mafia men might come and kidnap him? Hold him for ransom until we turn over the dog?"

"All right," Rosa grimaced. "I know I asked for this. But, actually, I was thinking that Spencer might like to come over tonight. Scott invited Chloe for dinner and Sierra rented some new video they all want to watch. Spencer would probably like it too."

Maggie considered this. She really didn't like the idea of leaving him all alone. Especially after the strange visit from Gavin. What if he was involved in something? "That sounds like fun, and I'm sure Spencer would love to come over. Can I drop him by around six-thirty?"

"Perfect."

⟋

As Maggie drove to the Galloways' that evening, she received a lecture from her son. It was hard not to laugh at his parent-like concern, but he was perfectly serious.

"Now, whatever you do, Mom, don't get in his car with him. And when you get there, park close to the restaurant, where it's well lit…"

"Good grief, Spencer. The man's not a serial killer."

"You don't know that for sure, Mom."

She suppressed a smile as she pulled into the Galloways' driveway. "Well, don't worry, Spence, I'll be careful. And remember, I'm doing this for Bart."

He frowned. "You don't have to, Mom."

"I know. I'm also doing it for Clyde. You know how I'd like to see him patch it up with his nephew. He really doesn't have any other family to speak of."

He opened the car door. "Okay. But watch your step."

She nodded briskly, as if taking orders from her superior. "Have fun. I should be back around nine or so." She watched her son walk up to the house, wishing she were joining them tonight. It looked so cozy and sweet inside as Rosa opened the door and waved from the porch.

On the way to Byron, Maggie noticed that her palms were growing moist. Nerves. She often felt this way right before a difficult interview. Maybe that's the way she should look at this evening—like an interview. But the truth was, it did feel like a date. And she hadn't been on a date for ages, not since before she and Phil were married.

"This is *not* a date," she said out loud. "If I wanted to date, hopefully I could do better than Gavin Barnes!" But then she glanced down at her black silk pantsuit. If it wasn't a date, why was she so dressed up? "Because Jasper's looks like a very nice restaurant," she told herself, then clicked on the radio to drown out her apprehension.

Just as Spencer had suggested, she found a parking place close to the door, climbed out, and securely locked the car. She glanced over her shoulder and suddenly felt as if she were playing some spy role in a clandestine mystery movie. She took a deep breath and then walked into the restaurant. The lobby was softly lit, its wood-paneled walls glowing in the warmth of flickering candlelight. Fine art was displayed here and there, not in excess, but just enough to encourage interest. An antique Oriental rug covered most of the lobby's hardwood floor, giving the feel of old world opulence, something she had missed in Pine Mountain. Several well-dressed couples waited ahead of her. She glanced around but didn't see Gavin anywhere in sight. Suddenly, she wondered if she had been stood up. To her surprise, she hoped not—it had been awhile since she'd enjoyed a fine dinner in a good restaurant.

"Do you have a reservation?" asked the smooth-faced, expressionless woman behind the carved wooden counter.

"I'm not sure." Maggie glanced into the restaurant area. "I'm meeting someone."

"Name?"

"His name is Barnes."

The woman checked her list, then said, "Right this way." She lead Maggie through the main dining room, then off to a smaller one. There, seated at a corner table, was Gavin. He rose and politely greeted her.

"You came," he exclaimed as they both sat down. "I was worried that you might have changed your mind."

"I try to be a woman of my word," she said as she picked up the menu. "This looks like a lovely restaurant, Gavin."

"Wine?" He held up an already opened bottle of Merlot. "Excuse me for starting without you, but I got here early and was making myself at home."

"No, thank you. Water is fine." She wanted to make it perfectly clear that this was not a social occasion.

He frowned slightly, then set the bottle down. "So, what do you think of Pine Mountain? Quite a change from where you're from?"

"Yes, but I really love it. It's so fresh and clean—so beautiful."

He laughed and took a sip of wine. "Still in the honeymoon phase."

"Perhaps." She laid down her menu. "Or perhaps it's just the beginning of a wonderful marriage."

"I can see why my uncle lured you up here." A sardonic smile played across his mouth. "You sound like a perennial optimist, just like him."

"And what's wrong with that?"

"Nothing for those of you who refuse to take off your rose-colored glasses. It's the rest of us poor souls who have to suffer."

"Why not just get yourself a pair of rose-colored glasses?" she teased.

He laughed. "Oh, if only I could..."

"What are you doing now, Gavin?"

"This and that. Not really much of anything to speak of..."

"Do you ever consider returning to Pine Mountain?"

"For what?" He poured himself another glass of wine.

At that moment the waiter came and recited all the specials, then took their orders. By the time he had disappeared Maggie couldn't recall where the conversation had been interrupted, but she knew where she wanted it to go.

"Clyde says that you two never speak anymore. Is there any hope of mending your fences with him?"

Gavin shook his head and rolled his eyes. "Obviously my uncle hasn't told you much."

"He's been quite tightlipped about the whole thing, I think out of respect for you. Do you want to tell me about it?"

"Not really, Maggie. It's not a pretty story. I made some stupid mistakes, and I don't really blame Uncle Clyde for throwing me out. I deserved it."

"He threw you out?"

"Well, sort of..." Gavin swirled the dark, red liquid around in his glass, studying it in the flickering candlelight. "Sure you don't want some wine?"

She shook her head. "I certainly don't understand what went on between you two, Gavin, but I do sense that Clyde cares about you."

He set down his glass and looked intently into her eyes. For the first time she studied their color. It seemed to be a mix of browns and gold—a warm combination with his tanned skin and sandy hair. "Maggie, if I could do anything to undo the past, believe me I would. But I just don't see how. I don't think my uncle will ever give me the time of day again."

"Clyde seems like an understanding guy. Maybe you just need to give it time."

"Time..." He leaned back into the booth and sighed in resignation. "How much time do you think the old guy has got? He's already pushing ninety now. I just don't know what I'd do if he passed away before I had a chance to make things right with him."

She leaned forward, her expressive face reflecting her concern. "I see what you mean, Gavin. Maybe there's some way I can help... perhaps I could encourage him to reconcile with you..."

"Would you, Maggie?" His eyes lit up like a little boy who'd just been promised a pony. "You know, he might listen to you. I know he won't listen to me. But if you could bring him around...I'd be so grateful."

She was smiling now, happy to be involved in the restoration of this relationship. "I'd love to try. Perhaps it would help if you filled me in a little more on your history and things—you know, give me a better perspective of your relationship with Clyde."

"I knew you were special, Maggie. The moment I saw you back at the homestead, I knew you had a heart."

She blushed, then suddenly remembered the dog. Perhaps this was as good a time as any to broach the subject. "Before I forget, Gavin, I want to know if you're willing to sell Bart. I'll understand if you're not—he's such a sweet dog and all. But I can promise you we will give him a very good home."

Gavin smiled. "I know you will, Maggie. The truth is, I'm living in a condo right now where I'm not even supposed to have pets. You go ahead and keep Bart. Consider him a 'thank you' for your help with my uncle."

"But I'd like to pay..."

Gavin waved his hand. "No. He's yours. My gift to you."

She didn't know what to say. This man didn't seem anything like what she'd expected. "Well, thank you very much, Gavin. My son will be so happy."

Throughout their meal, Gavin talked almost nonstop, first about his childhood, which was similar to the version Sam had already told her, except that Gavin's was much more colorful, and perhaps slightly overblown. It seemed as if he grew up believing he was the fair-haired prince of Pine Mountain—the richest boy in town, the best athlete, all the local girls were in love with him and grew heartbroken when he and his mother moved away during his last year in high school year. Maggie couldn't help but smile as he told his story. But she grew worried as he emptied the last of the Merlot into his glass and took a swig.

"Are you driving tonight, Gavin?" she asked with concern.

He chuckled. "Sure, but don't worry about me. This stuff is like soda pop."

Maggie wasn't convinced, but held her tongue, relieved that he wasn't driving *her* anywhere. Still, she wondered how she might encourage him to take a taxi.

By the time dessert came, Gavin's life story had moved on to some of his disappointments, like never finishing college, some unhappy romances, and a string of disappointing jobs, finally ending with the newspaper. It seemed the wine had loosened his tongue considerably, and before long a sharp edge of bitterness began to permeate his words.

"It's just not fair," he said in an overly loud voice. "My dad gets killed over in Korea—just so he can live up to his hero brother—and what do Mom and me get for it? Diddly-squat! Uncle Clyde inherited every single penny!"

"I understood that Clyde was quite generous with you and your mom..."

"Oh sure, he sold off a scrap of land and gave my mom enough money to get out of town. Big whopping deal! She ran out of money before I'd even finished college."

"Really? I thought Clyde had given her a considerable sum..."

"Who you been talking to, Maggie?" His face was flushed from the alcohol now, and a mean look crept into his eyes. Suddenly she grew fearful. What had she gotten herself into? What if he got out of control?

"Would you like some coffee, Gavin?" she asked, trying to change the subject.

"No, thank you, I would not!" He thumped his fist on the table. "You know what I think, Maggie Carpenter?"

She shook her head, then glanced nervously around, certain that everyone in the restaurant would soon hear what Gavin Barnes was thinking.

"I think you and my uncle are plotting against me. I think you moved up here and took my job and my house, and now you think you're gonna get your grubby little hands on my uncle's money…"

She stood quickly. She'd had enough. "I think you're drunk, Gavin. And I am leaving right now. I'll ask someone to call a taxi for you." She waved to the waiter who nervously stood off to the side, as if afraid to approach their table.

The waiter met her as she crossed the dining room. She felt her cheeks blazing in humiliation as she fumbled in her purse for her credit card and handed it to him. "I'll pay the bill," she whispered. "Can you get someone to call a taxi for him?" She glanced over her shoulder and realized that Gavin too had risen from the table and was unsteadily weaving her way, bumping into tables as he went. She hurried to the front of the restaurant. "I'll be in the ladies' room," she whispered to the waiter, who was now explaining the problem to the smooth-faced hostess in the lobby.

She ducked into the bathroom, wondering if she'd ever be able to show her face at the elegant Jasper's again. She ran water in the sink, washing her hands as she stared at her shocked reflection. Her complexion was paler than usual except for two bright red spots across both cheeks, as if someone had slapped her. Her blue-gray eyes looked darker than usual and overly bright—probably from fear. She took a deep breath, willing herself to calm down. But her hands were still shaking as she finally dried them on a towel. Several minutes had passed. Would Gavin still be out there? Was he making a horrible scene? Was it her responsibility to see that he got home safely? Oh, why had she allowed herself to get into this mess? All for a silly old dog?

She peeked out the door, and the lobby seemed surprisingly quiet. She stepped outside and all appeared normal. She went up to where the smooth-faced woman still remained expressionless, as cool as the marble countertop resting beneath her folded hands.

"Did the waiter leave my receipt with you?" asked Maggie quietly.

Without speaking, the woman handed her the small leather portfolio that contained the receipt and her credit card. Maggie quickly added on a generous tip and signed the bill, then retrieved her card and apologized for any inconvenience. She sighed in relief and slipped out the door. It was dark outside and the cool air felt good on her face. But as she approached her car, she saw by the glow of the streetlight that someone was leaning against the passenger side of the Volvo. And she knew it was Gavin.

Her heart hammered as she walked slowly toward him. *Just walk past him and get in the car*, she told herself. She slipped her hand into her purse for her keys, ready to sprint past him to the driver's side if necessary.

"Hey, Maggie," he called in a slightly slurred voice. "How about giving your old buddy a ride?"

She stopped in front of the car, keeping a safe distance between them as she forced a smile to her lips. "I'm sorry, Gavin, but I need to go pick up my son right now. Do you want me to call you a taxi?"

His face crumbled like a disappointed child, and she felt an unexpected wave of sympathy wash over her. "You mean you can't even help out your old buddy Gavin?" he asked pitifully. "I know I wasn't very nice in there, Maggie. I'm really, really sorry. Will you forgive me, Maggie?"

She swallowed. "Of course, I'll forgive you, Gavin. But I need to go now. Do you want me to call a taxi for you? I have a phone in my car."

Suddenly he leaped forward and grabbed her arm. "I don't want a taxi!" he growled and his grip tightened as he gave her a sharp shake. "I want *you* to give me a ride! This whole mess is all your fault. That guy in there took away my car keys, and now you better..."

Just then someone slipped up from behind the car. And before she could see his face, the man had grabbed Gavin's free arm and given it a hard twist. In a flash, she remembered Rosa's warning about criminal connections. How had she gotten herself involved in all this? But in the same moment,

Gavin released her arm, and she leaped back. Cringing in horror to think there might be a gun involved, she ducked behind the other side of the car for safety. As she fumbled with her keys, she peered over the car to see that the man holding Gavin was none other than Jed Whitewater!

"Jed!" she exclaimed in shocked relief. "Thank God it's you!"

"Listen, Gavin." Jed spoke in a firm, authoritative voice. "You need to make a choice right now. Do you want us to call a cab or the police; or would you rather just take a hike?"

Gavin jerked his head around to see Jed's face. "Le'go of me, you stinkin' red-skin!" he yelled. "Lemme go right now, you dirty good-for-nuthin' injun!"

A small crowd of spectators had gathered, but Jed remained calm and in control. "I said you have a decision to make Gavin. If you can't choose, I'll choose for you—and right now I'm leaning toward the police." He glanced at the onlookers. "Anyone have a phone handy? I don't think the police will take kindly to drunken disorderliness, not to mention assaulting a lady like that. Now, what'll it be, Gavin?"

"I'll walk!" sputtered Gavin.

"You sure?" Jed still didn't release him.

"Yeah!" growled Gavin. "Now, lemme go!"

Jed let him go with a slight shove, then braced himself as if still expecting a fight. But Gavin just turned and staggered away. The crowd cheered.

Maggie was shaking so hard that her car keys jingled in her hand. "Thanks, Jed," she muttered as she leaned against the car.

"Are you okay?" He placed a hand on her shoulder.

"Just shaken," she said. "This is all so unreal. I can't believe it." Then she turned and looked at him curiously. "What in the world are you doing here anyway?"

"Just happened to be in the neighborhood." He gently removed her keys from her hand and unlocked and opened the door. "Why don't you sit down."

She slumped into the driver's seat and leaned her head against the steering wheel. She heard him open the door on the other side, slide in, and then lock the doors. "You seem really shaken. Maybe I should drive you home."

She shook her head. "No, that's okay. I'll be fine. Just need to get my bearings." She turned to look at him. His face, barely illuminated by the shadowy streetlight, reflected real concern.

"Have you been drinking, Maggie?" he asked softly.

She looked at him straight in the eye and sighed. "No, I haven't been drinking."

"Well then, do you mind telling me what's going on here?"

She thought for a moment. It was all so humiliating, and even more so since he had rescued her. She really appreciated his help, but it would have been so much easier to have gotten away without seeing anyone she knew. How could she possibly explain this whole thing to him? And why should she? Just because he'd rescued her didn't give him the right to nose into her personal life. And what was he doing here anyway?

As if reading her mind, he answered. "Spencer mentioned your little date with Gavin..."

"It was *not* a date!" she sputtered.

"Well, whatever it was, your son was concerned. And as it turns out, justifiably so. Why in the world would you agree to go out with someone like Gavin Barnes, Maggie?"

"We did *not* go out!"

"Well, you made an arrangement to meet him. You had dinner with him, he got drunk. And not surprisingly, he got out of hand. What do you call that, Maggie?"

"A disaster!"

He chuckled. "Yeah, I'd have to agree with you there. But *why* did you come?"

She shook her head. "I don't know. It was incredibly stupid, okay. But I wish you wouldn't lecture me about it. I made a dumb mistake. I appreciate your help very much, Jed, but it's really nothing for you to worry about."

He sighed. "Okay, Maggie. Whatever you say..." He reached over and opened the passenger door and climbed out. "You sure you can make it home okay?"

"I'm positive." The words came out shakier than she'd intended, but it was all she could do to hold back the tears. She felt discouraged and humiliated and she just wanted to be alone.

For a long moment, Jed stood there in silence with the door open. She couldn't bring herself to look up at him. Finally he spoke. "Sorry to have intruded. I was just trying to help."

Unable to speak over the lump in her throat, she just nodded mutely. He finally closed the door and she started the engine. As she drove away, her eyes filled with tears. She didn't even know exactly why she was crying. The whole night seemed so crazy and foolish. Nothing made sense. She told herself that by tomorrow she would be laughing with Rosa over the whole stupid incident. But tonight it all seemed very sad and tragic. And she wished that none of it had ever happened. Funny that she had left the Los Angeles area to get away from the frightening dangers of criminal elements, and here she winds up in a situation that could have been...she didn't want to think about what could have been. The whole thing simply made her sick.

After awhile, her tears dried. The calm of the beautiful night began to steal into her soul. She looked at the brightly shining stars overhead, and suddenly was aware that she had not bothered to ask for God's help or counsel in any of this little fiasco. Like a fool, she had eagerly leaped into a situation that was way over her head. And look where it had gotten her. What if something had seriously gone wrong? She was all Spencer had.

"Please, God, I need your direction. Show me the way *you* want me to go," she prayed out loud as she drove through the night. "I'm sorry I didn't ask before. I think I've learned a good lesson. Please, forgive me, and perhaps you can still bring some good out of the craziness of this evening." She sighed deeply, then added. "And thanks for sending help when I needed it."

Sixteen

aggie didn't mention the incident with Gavin when she stopped at the Galloways' for Spencer. They were just finishing their movie, so she slipped into an overstuffed chair and leaned back to relax. When the movie ended she noticed the curiosity in Rosa's eyes, but she deliberately steered the conversation away from her evening, instead checking on last minute details for tomorrow night's meeting.

"Did I tell you that the woman from Seattle, Elizabeth Rodgers, stopped by the deli yesterday?" said Rosa just as Maggie stood to leave. "She said she appreciated your invitation and that she's planning to come to our meeting."

"That's terrific." Maggie brightened. "I wasn't too sure she was interested when I spoke to her on the phone. I tried to be encouraging, but I had to be honest about the challenges in a place like Pine Mountain."

"Is that the lady who might open a coffee house?" asked Sierra hopefully.

"Not just a coffee house, Sierra," said Rosa. "It's a bookstore too."

"That would be so cool. I hope she decides to do it. Maybe I could get a job there..."

"Sierra," warned Rosa good-naturedly. "You already have a job!"

"Well, maybe *I* could get a job," said Spencer.

Maggie smiled. "What a couple of motivated kids we have."

"A paycheck seems to do that," added Sam dryly.

Good-byes were said and Maggie and Spencer drove home quietly in the car. She hoped that he wouldn't ask about her evening. She didn't want to lie to him. Just as she pulled into the driveway he spoke.

"Oh, yeah, Mom—how did it go tonight?"

She turned off the car and searched her mind for an easy answer. "Oh, I don't know... It was sort of different."

"Did you like him?"

She grimaced "Not really. I think he's a very troubled man."

Spencer nodded gravely. "Well, did he let you buy Bart from him?"

"Actually, he said we could have him for free." She sighed. She hoped Gavin wouldn't go back on his word now.

"That's great! I'd say that's mission accomplished! Thanks, Mom." He jumped out of the car, then added. "And since you don't like him, you won't ever have to go out with him again."

Maggie forced a laugh. "I think you can count on that, Spencer."

~

Maggie decided to devote her Saturday to creating a proposal that would hopefully procure some urban renewal funds for Pine Mountain. Spencer, involved in some big repair project at the house, came and went without disturbing her. From an early age, he had learned to recognize and eventually respect her need to concentrate if she were in the thick of some writing project. Phil used to say that even if the house came tumbling down around her ears, she wouldn't look up until she had finished that last sentence. But she had learned early that focus was a prerequisite for being a good reporter. Working in a staff room could be noisy and chaotic, and she had trained herself to tune everything out but her mind, her notes, and her computer screen.

She had taken a grant writing class in college, but until now had never put the training to use—had never wanted to. Now she just hoped she could remember the basics. She wasn't completely sure what the committee would be looking for, but hoped her approach was persuasive. She wanted to paint a positive picture of the town, but at the same time realized the importance of showing the dire need for some outside funding. And she had to do all this without making the town seem pitiful. It was a challenge, to say the least. But she was glad to have something this demanding to distract her from thinking about last night. The whole evening now seemed like a distasteful dream.

By mid-afternoon, as she proofed what she hoped would be her final draft, the phone rang. Still scanning the words on the computer printout, she picked it up and absently said hello.

"Hello, Maggie?"

She dropped her proposal and the pages scattered at her feet. "Gavin?"

"Yes. I'm sorry to bother you like this..." He paused.

She waited, almost afraid to breathe. Just the sound of his voice filled her with a tight apprehensive fear. After last night, she'd felt certain she'd never hear from him again.

"Maggie," he began again. "I just wanted to apologize for the rude things I said last night. I'm very, very sorry. I know I was a complete jerk."

She pressed her lips together. She wanted to agree with him about the "complete jerk" part, but knew that was unkind. "You were drunk, Gavin. When people get drunk they say and do some incredibly stupid things."

"I know."

She took a breath. As much as she disliked this man, she did feel sorry for him, and he was Clyde's nephew. "Gavin, I sense that you have some serious problems in your life. I don't know what they are, or how they all got started. But it seems quite possible that alcohol might be a part of them. Have you ever considered getting help?"

He made a moaning sound. "Oh, now you're sounding like my uncle…"

"Clyde cares about you, Gavin. If he's concerned, it's only because he loves you."

"I know. I know… It's just that he doesn't cut a man much slack. If he'd only given me another chance, I think I could've straightened out…"

She didn't know what to say. She didn't know enough about Gavin to know whether that was true or not. And the fact is, she didn't want to know. He scared her, and even though she felt sorry for him, she didn't want any part of his messed up life. "Gavin," she began slowly. "I'm probably not the best one for you to talk to about these things—you know, since I work for Clyde—but I do recommend that you get help. There are organizations, rehab centers…"

"Yeah, yeah. I know about that stuff. I just wanted to apologize to…"

"Apology accepted."

"Another thing…would you mind not sharing my little mess-up with Uncle Clyde?"

"I don't know why he'd need to hear about it, Gavin."

"Thanks, Maggie." He cleared his throat. "And just for the record, you're all right."

"Thanks." She smiled and shook her head. "But do look for help, okay?"

"I'll think about it."

"That's better than nothing."

Gavin remained silent on the other end, and she searched for a way to end this awkward conversation, then finally said, "Well, I better go. I've got to get some things ready for a meeting tonight."

"What meeting?"

"Oh, we're trying to get a business group together to see if we can revive this town a little. We're meeting at the grade school tonight to hear everyone's ideas and whatnot. And I need to get some things done before then. So..."

"So, you need to go." His voice sounded flat.

She felt bad. He probably needed someone to talk to. But she wanted him to find someone besides her. "Sorry." She thought for a moment, was there anything she could do for him? "Gavin, if you don't mind, I'm going to be praying for you."

"Now, that's a good one!" He laughed cynically. "Well, you go ahead and pray for me, Maggie Carpenter. Maybe we'll find out if the old man upstairs really gives a flying fig about the likes of someone like me."

Maggie sadly shook her head as she hung up. He might be messed up, but at least he wasn't in complete denial. She had no sooner hung up when the phone rang once more. Thinking it was Gavin again, she picked up the receiver and flatly said, "Hello."

"Is this Maggie Carpenter?" asked a woman's voice.

"Yes, it is."

"Oh, I'm so glad I reached you. My name is Susan McKay, and I'm the editor of *Western Life* magazine. Have you heard of us?"

"Of course," said Maggie. "I'm a subscriber, and I love your magazine."

"But you've never freelanced for us?"

"Actually, I sent you a submission about ten years ago. But I haven't sent anything since then. Why?"

"Well, an associate of yours who used to work at the *Times* recommended you for an assignment, and I'm just hoping that you're available because I need it on short notice."

"What did you have in mind?"

"We would like to run a piece about a small town in Oregon in our August issue. You know the section called 'Off the Beaten Path'?"

She laughed. "That pretty much describes Pine Mountain."

"And since you're living there now, I thought maybe you'd like to give it a try. I need about 1000 words."

Maggie tried to control her enthusiasm. Of course, she wanted to do this! "How soon will you need this piece?"

"That's the problem. We needed it last week."

"I see." She looked over at her stack of notes for the grant proposal. "Well, you're in luck, Susan. I've just been working on something that I might be able to adapt into a feature like that."

"*Really?* Oh, Maggie, you are a lifesaver. How soon can you get it to us?"

She scratched her head. "Well, lucky for you I'm a reporter—we're used to working fast. I think I can have it done by Tuesday or Wednesday."

"Great! Can you send it online?"

"No problem."

"You're an absolute godsend, Maggie."

As she hung up, she realized she'd forgotten to inquire about payment. Not that she cared. She'd have probably paid Susan just to get a byline in *Western Life*! She quickly jotted down some thoughts for the article, then forced herself to turn off her computer. If she got going on that there was no telling when she'd return to earth. And right now, she needed to get started on an early dinner before the big meeting tonight.

Spencer had unearthed their old barbecue from the things stored in the barn, and Maggie set it up next to the small front porch, along with a couple of patio chairs and a small table. Compared to their well-designed cedar deck back in California, this rinky-dink set-up reminded her of how the hillbillies might live, but the view was spectacular and the evening air fresh. As she grilled the chicken, she imagined adding a large deck or patio outside the dining room of the big house—maybe she'd get enough money from the article to tackle it. She didn't want to compromise the historical integrity of the old homestead, but at the same time it seemed a shame to waste the beautiful mountain views and cool summer evenings. Perhaps Jed would have some good design ideas for making the two worlds meet gracefully.

"Are you coming to the meeting tonight, Spence?" she asked as they sat down to eat.

"I guess so. Sierra's going to be there. And it might be kind of interesting. I heard a couple guys at the hardware store making fun of your flyer. You know you might get some opposition there tonight, Mom."

She smiled. "I'd be surprised if we didn't. But I think most of the business people are in favor of this organization."

As they ate, she told Spencer about the article for *Western Life*.

"Does that mean you'll be famous?"

She grinned then took a bite of salad. "Not hardly. But it's a great opportunity for me. I've been wanting to branch out with my writing. I just hadn't expected anything so soon." Then she explained about how working on the grant proposal would help her with the article too.

"So, these people with this grant stuff—do they just give you the money?" he asked.

She laughed. "Well, it's not quite as simple as that. But, yes, they do give some towns money—that is, if they feel it's a good cause and will be used well."

"Wow, that's cool, Mom. Everyone in Pine Mountain should be real happy."

"We haven't got it yet, Spence. And for now, let's just keep quiet about the whole thing. The submission deadline is next week so hopefully I should hear back from them in a couple of weeks."

Spencer cleaned up the dinner dishes while Maggie dressed for the meeting. Once again, she grew perplexed as she looked at her closet. She didn't want to overdress and look intimidating, and yet she didn't want to appear too unprofessional. Finally, she decided on khaki pants and an off-white sweater set with just a touch of silver jewelry. She pulled her dark hair back into a clip and said a silent prayer. Then she and Spencer headed into town.

Chloe had already placed a very visible sign, complete with balloons, at the entrance of the grade school, directing business people to the school library where the meeting would be held. Although there was still nearly an hour before the meeting, the Galloways were there setting up chairs. Maggie and Spencer placed a large wipe-off board in front of the room. She planned to use it to list concerns and goals during their meeting, and Rosa would take notes from the front row.

"Hi there," called Rosa from the back of the room where she and Chloe were arranging refreshments on a table covered with a colorful plaid tablecloth. "We wanted to make sure everything was all ready before anyone gets here."

"That table looks great," said Maggie.

"Hello there," called a female voice. Maggie looked up to see Kate and Jed walk in. Kate was carrying a huge basket of beautiful flowers. "Delivery for a Ms. Maggie Carpenter," sang out Kate as she presented the bouquet to her.

"They're gorgeous," said Maggie, looking up at Kate and Jed curiously. "Did you guys…"

"They're not from us," interrupted Kate. "The delivery guy just handed them to us…he came all the way from Byron. Open the card and see who it's from."

"Maybe Clyde?" said Maggie as she set down the basket and opened the little white envelope. Chloe and Rosa came up to admire the lovely arrangement as she removed the card, but as she read it, her cheeks reddened with embarrassment.

"Who's Gavin?" asked Chloe, reading the card over Maggie's shoulder.

"Gavin sent those?" said Rosa in surprise.

"Gavin Barnes?" echoed Kate. "You've got to be kidding!"

She quickly tucked the card back into the envelope. "That was nice of him. I had mentioned this meeting to him, and he probably wanted to do something nice for the whole town."

"Well, that would be a first," said Jed wryly.

She tossed a warning look his way, then turned her attention back to the flowers. "These are so pretty, why don't we put them on the table with the refreshments."

"Good idea," said Rosa as she picked up the bouquet. "That was very thoughtful of him."

Maggie slipped out of the library and down the hallway until she found the girls' restroom. Inside the safe confines of the pink-tiled room she took several deep breaths to calm herself. It was so childish to be embarrassed by a mere token of friendship. But somehow having Jed there watching and knowing how Gavin had behaved the night before just brought it all back with agonizing freshness. And even though it was silly, it was still painfully humiliating. And for this to happen tonight, just when she needed to be collected and in control. Now here she stood in the girls' restroom like an oversensitive schoolgirl!

She stooped over and peered into the murky mirror. "Grow up, Margaret LeAnn," she scolded. Then she glanced around the restroom and suddenly, despite herself, began to smile. The low sink, the painted plywood stalls, even the small bubble-glass window all reminded her of the time she was in fifth grade and Ronnie Williams had passed a neatly folded note with her name on the front, right in the middle of math class. But the note had been intercepted by old Mr. Sheldon. And she still remembered the shrinking feeling as those words expressing Ronnie's true love were read aloud for the whole world to hear. She had wanted to die right then and there! Later she'd sought refuge in the bathroom, certain that she would never show her face in public again. If only the note had been written by Paul Johnson, it would have been much more endurable. But Ronnie Williams was the class nerd!

Now she was giggling. She had survived Ronnie Williams and she would certainly survive Gavin Barnes. She glanced at her watch. There was still time to help with any last minute details before people would arrive for the meeting.

Seventeen

*E*verything in the library seemed to be in perfect order, and the folding metal chairs were slowly filling with various business people. Clara Henderson, immaculately dressed in a peach crepe pantsuit and matching shoes, sat with her husband, Lou, right in the center of the front row. And next to them sat the Mitchells from the Gas-n-Go. Maggie spotted Dolly and her husband making their way to the back row. It was the first time Maggie had seen Jinx and she was surprised to see that he was a thick, dark, stocky man, several inches shorter than Dolly. He had on cuffed jeans and a white T-shirt, reminiscent of the fifties, and looked a little like a portly James Dean. She also recognized Rich Stuart, from the Eagle Tavern, sipping a cup of coffee and chatting congenially with Sam in back. Shortly before seven, she noticed an unfamiliar woman enter the room.

"That's Elizabeth Rodgers," Sierra whispered to Maggie. "You know, the bookstore tycoon." Rosa had already made her way across the room to greet the woman. Elizabeth, looking elegantly out of place in a silk caftan with an Aztec-looking design, smiled confidently as she shook hands with Rosa, then found a seat off to the side. About that time, the room grew expectantly quiet as if everyone was ready to begin. Maggie had asked Clyde to open the meeting and then introduce her; and to her surprise he'd donned a clean white shirt, complete with a bolo-string tie, for the occasion.

He stepped to the front, loudly cleared his throat, then heartily welcomed everyone. He briefly recapped the town's history, not failing to mention the Oregon Trail and his parents' pioneer roots as well as the early sheep-herding industry. Then he covered the timber boom era that followed the war, and the time of growth and affluence during the tourism days of the next couple decades, and finally came to the bypassing of the highway and subsequent demise of the small town. "We've had us quite a time here in Pine Mountain. And as you all know, ever since Hugh Benson gave up his boot shop and moved over to Harrison, we've been minus one mayor." Clyde grinned mischievously. "Do I see any volunteers out there for a mayoral candidate?" A few self-conscious chuckles, but no hands went up. "Didn't think so," he quipped. "And for the record, I'm not volunteering either. But just the same, I do care about the future of our town, and I'm willing to roll up my sleeves and do whatever it takes to get us back on our feet. But to accomplish that, we're all going to have to get together and do us some planning and organizing. And that's why I want to introduce you all to our chairperson for tonight's meeting. I know most of you've already met her, but you may not know that she's also an award-winning writer." He glanced at Maggie as her brows lifted in surprise. She didn't realize that Clyde knew about her awards. He nodded smugly and continued. "That's right. While working for the *Los Angeles Times*, Maggie Carpenter received, not *one* mind you, but *two* Peter Hillman Awards—and for those of you who aren't aware, that's a mighty prestigious national newspaper award." He winked at her, then said. "And so I give you: Maggie Carpenter."

She stepped up amidst a politely enthusiastic applause. "Thanks, Clyde," she said. "If I'd known you knew about those awards, I might've asked for a bigger salary." The crowd chuckled at this, and then she grew more serious. She started out by praising the town in general; spotlighting its natural scenic beauty; acknowledging the hardworking, persevering citizens; and finally highlighting Pine Mountain's unrealized potential lying dormant like a hidden treasure. Then she invited the audience to begin sharing their concerns for the town while she listed them on the board. Mostly they worried that their own or other vital businesses might go under; that morale in the town had ebbed to an all-time low; that the meager population continued to dwindle; and that public services had diminished due to their shrinking tax-base and failing economy.

Suddenly Greg Snider stood up. Maggie noticed Cherise visibly shrink into her chair, almost as if preparing for an explosion. "Well, I have a concern too," he began in an overly loud voice. "And I know some of you don't want to hear it, but I'm going to speak up anyway. I'm worried about the effects of *over*-development. I don't want to see the mess we had back in the seventies and eighties happen all over again. Have you folks forgotten how overrun our town was with all those tourists and cars running through..."

"I'd take the prosperity of *those* years over *this* fiasco any day," growled Cal, the owner of the secondhand store.

"Let's not interrupt each other," injected Jed from the sidelines. "Go on, Greg."

Greg looked at Jed skeptically and then continued to speak quickly, as if he had rehearsed each sentence and wasn't about to let anyone get in a word edgewise. "Well, I know a lot of you are going to get swept away by this smooth-talking newspaper lady from Los Angeles. But, I ask you—when was the last time any of you saw what's going on down in California? Do we want Pine Mountain to become like *that*? Do you want to see strip malls on Main Street? Do you want to see the natural beauty of our wilderness spoiled by a bunch of outsiders coming up here from California and taking over..."

"Aw, put a sock in it, Greg!" snapped Cal. "I don't know why you even get to open up your trap in here—you don't even *own* a business."

"Well, Maggie Carpenter doesn't own a business, and it sure hasn't stopped her from vocalizing her pro-development opinions..."

Lou Henderson stood up. "Maggie's just trying to help the business people," he said. It was the first time she had ever heard Clara's husband speak.

"Well, there's a lot more people in this town besides just the business owners!" declared Greg.

"This town wouldn't be nothing *without* businesses!" growled Cal.

"Well, we sure wouldn't miss the likes of your place, Cal," sniped Greg. "It's nothing more than a dump site anyway."

Cal stood up with fists clenched, glaring across the room at Greg. Jed moved quickly to his side, and everyone began to murmur and talk at once, some voices rising louder than others. Maggie felt the tempers flaring, including her own. She glanced apologetically at the newcomer, Elizabeth Rodgers, who was looking on with what seemed almost an amused interest. She knew if they were to accomplish anything tonight she would have to calm this crowd down.

"Listen, everyone!" she yelled loudly over the din, and to her surprise they quieted. "Greg has made some valid points. And he has every right to make them. After all, his wife *is* a business owner, and his position as postmaster makes his opinion unique." She looked Greg squarely in the eye. "But his is only one opinion. We've heard his opposition to development. Now let's hear what some others think."

Greg glared at her then sank back down, folding his arms across his chest. Cherise glanced at her husband, then back at Maggie with a look of astonishment. It was probably not every day that someone shut down Greg Snider like that. Maggie studied his proud countenance briefly, wondering if another eruption was forthcoming. She was beginning to suspect that Greg took his responsibility as postmaster a little too seriously, almost as if he thought he should run the whole town. Slowly, more people began to open up and share their concerns again. And as a sense of hopeful optimism returned, Maggie gently directed the group toward the discussion of ways they might solve the town's problems, and then on toward actual goals they could set as a group. About this time, Greg noisily scooted back his chair and walked out, towing a reluctant Cherise along with him.

"I think it's time for a break and some refreshments," said Maggie as she laid down the felt pen she'd been using to jot down their suggestions. "And when we come back I think we should select our best ideas and make a plan to begin implementing them."

During the break, people continued to chatter with enthusiasm. A few naysayers still expressed concern and doubt, but it seemed that most had their hopes rekindled and were open to the idea of investing their own time and energy towards changing things in Pine Mountain. When the group reconvened, Maggie walked them through the entire list and they all voted to select their top priorities. First of all, it was nearly unanimous that the Pine Mountain Business Association be formed, and the only requirement for membership would be to own a business within the city limits. Next, a steering committee was nominated and voted upon to put together a plan for prioritizing and implementing the ideas brought forward tonight. To Maggie's delight, they chose Rosa Galloway to head this committee. Then they agreed to establish a Pine Mountain Days celebration to be held sometime in late July. And finally, after much discussion, they decided on a town-wide theme that they would try to build Pine Mountain's new image upon. Maggie had originally introduced this concept, thinking it was something they could determine over a period of time, but their enthusiasm was so great that no one would leave the meeting until it was all settled. After much discussion, the group voted that Pine Mountain's image would be similar to that of a Swiss village in the Alps. In the same way that the original Pine Mountain Hotel had been designed to resemble an Alpine ski lodge, the other business would likewise try to emulate the quaint style so common in European Alpine villages. They discussed using flower boxes, old-fashioned street lamps, and chalet styles of window trim. Clara even recommended a friend of hers to do some tole painting. Rosa and her committee would begin to compile a list of ways that businesses could utilize these ideas.

To Maggie's surprise, Elizabeth Rodgers spoke up. "I could have my bookstore in Seattle send Rosa some books on Alpine villages and Swiss chalets, and whatever else might be helpful."

"Thank you, Elizabeth. That's very generous," said Rosa.

"I don't want to sound like a wet blanket," began Al Mitchell from the Gas-nGo, "but how're we going to finance all these grandiose ideas? Some folks in town are barely hanging on by a thread as it is."

Maggie nodded. "I understand, Al. And I've been working on some financial possibilities. I hate to say too much about it right now, but there are some urban renewal grants available to rural towns like Pine Mountain. I'm applying for some and…"

"Is that a loan?" asked Al cautiously.

"No, it's more like a gift," said Maggie. "Some grants do require matching funds, but we'll cross that bridge when we get there."

"Don't you worry," said Clyde. "If we need matching funds, we'll find them."

As the meeting drew to a close, Maggie asked for volunteers or nominations for a member of the business community to chair the next meeting. But no one offered.

"You're doing such a good job, honey," said Clara. "Don't you want to continue?"

Maggie looked over the room of faces, searching for a likely leader. She paused on Jed, but the expression in his eyes told her he wasn't interested. Finally she held up her hands in submission. "Of course, I'm willing to continue, but I'm concerned that we need a business person to moderate this group."

"Well, isn't the newspaper a business?" chirped Clara hopefully.

"You bet it is," said Clyde. "And since I'm the owner, I don't know any reason why Maggie can't represent me in this whole thing."

"Maybe we should take a vote," said Maggie with uncertainty. "I don't want this to cause any problems down the line."

They voted and other than a couple of abstainers, it was nearly unanimous. Maggie thanked them all and promised to do her best to lead the group until they elected another chairperson. They agreed to meet again in one week. In the next few days, Rosa was to gather the steering committee to go over the notes from the first meeting, and hopefully refine everything into a workable plan. In the meantime, everyone would begin to spruce up their businesses, keeping the town theme in mind. The owner of the hardware store even offered to donate paint for those who couldn't afford it. And several volunteers, including Spencer and Sierra, offered to help on a painting committee.

"It looks like we've all got our work cut out for us," said Maggie in closing. "But if everyone does their part, I believe that Pine Mountain can make a fabulous comeback!"

People continued to visit after the meeting, still bubbling away on good ideas for fixing up the town, gathering outside resources, and thinking up creative ways to garner publicity. Clyde approached Maggie with a big grin. "Good job."

"Thanks. It feels like we're off to a good start."

"I just knew you could make a difference."

She smiled, looking around the room. "It takes everyone, Clyde."

"I know, Maggie. But they just needed a leader to get them going in the right direction."

She glanced at the basket of flowers and thought sadly about Gavin. Had Clyde, at one time, hoped that his nephew might be this leader? She thought about what Gavin had said about wanting to make things right with his uncle, and wondered how to broach the subject. "Say, Clyde, I ran into Gavin yesterday."

Clyde's brow creased. "What do you mean?"

"He stopped by for the dog..."

"Did he take it away?"

"No, we worked out a deal. Spencer gets to keep the dog."

"Did you tell Gavin I wanted to see him?"

"Yes. But I think he's concerned..."

"He ought to be concerned. We've got some unsettled matters to attend to."

She nodded. "It's none of my business. And I know Gavin has some problems, but he seems like a nice guy underneath it all."

Clyde scowled, then shook his head. "Don't let him fool you, Maggie."

She blinked in surprise. "What do you mean?"

"Believe you me, I know how Gavin can act real smooth and talk as slick as you please. But talk is cheap, young lady. And a tiger can't change his stripes."

"But he's your nephew, Clyde. Don't you care about him?"

"Caring and trusting are two different things. Just heed my warning, and stay away from him."

"You don't need to worry Clyde. We had a one-time encounter—one that I don't intend to repeat."

His brows raised with curiosity, but to her relief he made no inquiry, and instead changed the subject. "So, is Pine Mountain turning out to be all that you had hoped for?"

"It's certainly an adventure."

"Are you sorry you came?"

She shook her head. "Not at all. It's hard to explain, but Pine Mountain already feels like home to me."

He beamed. "I thought it would, Maggie."

That evening before starting to work on her magazine article, she decided to check her email. She was pleased to see that Rebecca had written again.

> MC
>
> Sounds like that postmaster is jealous of you. Maybe he is one of those guys who wants to be in control of everything. Or like you said, he may just want to prevent any kind of development. He's probably afraid it will increase his work load—too many letters to deliver. Ha! Well, hang in there, girl.
>
> RB

ᕤ

In the following week, Maggie saw actual progress, not only in town, but also at home. Jed and Spencer had finished repairing the front porch, and were now tackling some larger projects inside the house. Jed explained that his furniture shop was over-stocked with merchandise right now and until some customers came his way to reduce his inventory he might as well take on a paying job. Maggie was more than glad to have his expertise, and Spencer seemed to enjoy working with him. Yet as much as she appreciated his help, she tried to avoid him when possible. Ever since the incident with Gavin, she had steered clear of any in-depth conversations with him. She respected him, but somehow his quietness and penetrating gaze made her extremely uncomfortable. Sometimes it almost seemed as if he was trying to read her innermost thoughts, and she didn't like it. She believed that his interest in her was purely neighborly and perhaps even pastoral, but for some reason it always felt like more than that. And that made her uneasy. It was just simpler to avoid him.

Sam had been out to examine the plumbing and, to Maggie's relief, it wasn't as bad as she had feared. Sam worked up a reasonable estimate for some repairs, mostly to the downstairs bath, and she told him to begin whenever he had time. As much as she liked the little carriage house, she was already starting to resent its confining spaces. The only place she could be alone was in her bedroom, which was overly crowded with her large bedroom furnishings. And poor Spencer didn't have any privacy to speak of. His loft bedroom was open to the downstairs, and if she was working on the computer he usually tried to keep his music or video games turned down, but sometimes he forgot. Yes, it would be good to have a little more space.

She'd finished her article for *Western Life* on Monday night, immediately sending it online as promised. She hoped they'd be pleasantly surprised by her prompt response—it had cost her two very late nights. But she thought it was well worth it. Hopefully they would too. Fortunately, she didn't have the luxury of spare time to fret over when or how Susan would respond to her efforts. Instead Maggie focused all her attention on supervising every last detail for her first edition of the *Pine Cone*.

The paper came out as planned on Wednesday. And on Thursday afternoon she threw her staff a little party to celebrate.

"Great job, everyone," she said as she toasted a cup of sparkling cider to the small crew. "Congratulations for getting out our first edition as a brand new team."

"Congratulations to you, Maggie," said Clyde. "The paper was terrific. Several people have already commented favorably on it."

"Well, I hate to rain on our parade, but we did have one unhappy response," said Abigail as she held up a letter. "But when you consider the source, it's not surprising."

"Let me guess," said Maggie. "Does he work for the postal service?"

Scott laughed. "You know, we should probably watch out for that guy. You know what they say about postal workers…"

"That's not fair," chided Maggie. "Just think of the hundreds of thousands of postal workers who faithfully do their jobs day after day without a single problem." She turned to Abigail. "Okay, what did our sweet postmaster have to say?"

Abigail grinned slyly. "Do you really want me to read it?"

"Why not," said Clyde. "Then we can all have a good laugh."

"All right. Here goes." Abigail cleared her throat. "'Dear Editor, it appears our town is being taken over by aliens. At least one foreigner has invaded our fair city and is now forcing her pro-development ideals down our uninformed country bumpkin throats. Unfortunately, most Pine Mountain citizens are unaware of her hidden agenda. Like stupid sheep they blithely follow her down her lily-lined path. But when they wake up, they'll be sorry. When they see our lakes and mountains spoiled and polluted by tourist abuse, when our normally quiet streets are choked with traffic, exhaust, and tourists—mark my word, citizens of Pine Mountain, you'll be singing a different song then! I just hope you wake up before it's too late!'"

"Whew," said Scott. "I think that guy's just a few cards shy of a full deck."

"What do you think, Maggie?" asked Clyde, his wrinkled brow creased with what almost seemed a fatherly concern.

She smiled reassuringly. "Well, I don't think much of his writing ability—he certainly likes to mix his metaphors. But as for the general content, he's entitled to his opinion. And we all know that Greg Snider definitely has his opinion."

Clyde nodded grimly. "And I know that you're aware that being editor means taking flack from people like Greg."

"Don't worry, Clyde," she said. "I can take it."

Abigail patted her on the back. "I thought you could, dear. I just figured it would be easier to take it with your friends gathered around you. We're used to Greg and his kind. There are always a few crazies in a small town like this. It just takes a little controversy to stir them up out of the woodwork."

"You mean like creating the business association?" asked Maggie as she reached for a chocolate chip cookie.

"That'd do it," said Clyde.

"Well, let 'em send in their big guns," said Maggie. "I'm ready for them."

Just then the phone rang and Abigail reached behind her to pick it up. "Yes," she said. "Ms. Carpenter is right here." She pushed the mute button then turned to Maggie. "It's a Susan McKay from *Western Life*. Do you want to take it in your office?"

"No, I can take it here," she said, reaching for the phone. But as she took the receiver it occurred to her that Susan could have bad news. She might even hate Maggie's article... "Hello, Susan. This is Maggie."

"Hey, Maggie. Great story! Thanks for getting right on it. With a few little tweaks it'll be perfect. I want to send a photographer out the weekend after next. Is that okay? Can you sort of show him around? His name's Buckie Porterfield."

Maggie was almost too stunned to answer. Susan liked her article! "Yes, yes, yes, to all your questions," she answered. "When will he arrive?"

"Next Saturday around eleven, I think. You're sure it's no problem?"

"Not at all." She hung up and turned a beaming smile to her crew. "Good news! I just sold an article to *Western Life*."

"You mean that nice, glossy magazine about the West Coast?" said Abigail.

"That's the one. And guess what the article is about?" She waited, but no one ventured a guess. "It's about Pine

Mountain! And a photographer is coming next Saturday to take photos."

"Oh, my," said Abigail. "It's too bad we don't have more time to really spruce the place up."

Maggie nodded. "I know. But I think we should be happy to get whatever exposure we can. This will be some major coverage for us."

"How about if we have an emergency meeting of the Pine Mountain Business Association?" suggested Scott. "If we let people know there's a photographer coming, maybe everyone will try a little harder to get things ready."

"Good idea, Scott." Maggie turned to Clyde. "Can we use a little bit of newspaper time to let people know?"

"You're the chief," he said. "It's your call."

She thought for a moment. "I don't want to do anything to jeopardize the paper, but next week's edition is shaping up pretty well. I think we could afford to give the town some time next week to help out."

Clyde grinned. "I think that sounds real smart."

Within minutes, Abigail had notified Rosa and the entire steering committee. By the end of the day, Rosa had put together a complete and detailed plan for a work party to begin a massive overhaul on Pine Mountain during the upcoming weekend.

"It sounds like a brilliant plan, Rosa," said Maggie on the phone.

"Thanks," said Rosa. "I'm having a lot of fun with this. And I have to admit it's nice to finally be taken seriously by this town."

"Well, you've certainly paid your dues. It seems to me that you're well respected around here."

"Or maybe I'm just a sucker for work." Rosa laughed. "But it's worth the effort to see this town get a second chance."

"Spencer and I will devote most of our weekend helping on your cleanup committee. And I wanted to let you know that we've decided to donate some staff-time next week too."

"Oh, that's so great. We can use every possible hand right now."

"We'll be there first thing on Saturday morning."

"Great. And don't worry about food," said Rosa. "We've got that covered."

"I figured you did. But I hope you're letting everyone chip in for expenses," said Maggie with concern.

"So far, I'm just chalking it all up to business expense. It's an investment in our future. If we can't stir up some serious business this summer, it may be time to move on..."

She swallowed. "Are you serious, Rosa?"

"I didn't wanted to mention it to you—what with you just getting here and all—but last winter, Sam and I decided if things didn't change by the end of this summer we'd have to sell."

"Oh." Maggie didn't know what to say. She couldn't imagine Pine Mountain without the Galloways. And what would Spencer do without Sierra around to brighten his world?

"But don't worry," said Rosa cheerfully. "I haven't had this much hope for this town since before they moved the highway."

Eighteen

*C*an you believe what we've accomplished in just over a week's time?" said Sam as the Pine Mountain cleanup crew headed toward the deli for a celebration dinner. It was Friday evening, the night before the magazine photographer would arrive to take photos of the town.

"Rosa should be crowned the Cleanup Queen of Pine Mountain," said Chloe as she adjusted a loose strap on her paint-splattered overalls. "The way she organized everyone and everything was amazing!"

"And the town looks absolutely incredible," said Maggie as she gazed down the transformed streets in wonder. "I'm so glad I took those *before* photos. The grant committee might not have believed me otherwise."

"And it's so great we're a finalist for that grant money," said Scott.

Maggie nodded. "I think it worked in our favor to be one of the last submissions. I only hope it comes through. Clyde's been extremely generous to back us financially during this first stage of renovation, but I'd really like to see him paid back in full."

Sam waved his hand in dismissal. "Oh, don't worry about old Clyde. He can afford to be generous."

"It's not just that," she said as they stopped in front of the deli. "I think the whole town needs to feel like they've invested in Pine Mountain."

"Don't worry, Mom," said Spencer. He had a streak of dark green paint across his nose that matched the color of the benches. "I think they do. Just look around."

They paused in the late afternoon light to enjoy their handiwork. Shops with clean windows and freshly painted trim now boasted neat flower boxes that had just been filled with colorful blooms donated from several local gardeners, including Abigail and Clara. Thanks to Jed and Lou, touches of Alpine-inspired architectural trim had been added to gables, windows, and doorways. Clara's artist friend had donated various accents of tole painting on doors and shutters. Shop signs had been repainted in old-fashioned lettering; wooden garbage receptacles were repaired and repainted; and old oak barrels, donated by Cal from the secondhand store, had been planted with flowers and shrubs and set upon street corners in the spots where they eventually hoped to see old-fashioned street lamps placed. Even the face of the old Pine Mountain Hotel had been painted and tidied so that the casual observer might not know it was currently uninhabited. And despite the fact that nearly half the businesses were vacated, the town seemed to sparkle with energy, hope, and promise. A facade perhaps—or hopefully it was a sign of what was to come.

"There's Jed and Kate," said Chloe as she waved at the two across the street. "Can you believe how many flower boxes Kate managed to throw together this week? That woman's amazing!"

"Not to mention the benches that Jed built," said Maggie.

"Hey," called Rosa from inside the deli. "What are you all gawking at out there?"

"Our beautiful little town," said Maggie. "Come join us and bask in our praises. Chloe thinks we should crown you the Cleanup Queen."

Rosa just laughed as she joined them, and together they all stood and reminisced about the events of the busy week. They laughed about how Cal had tried to talk them into utilizing his worthless fifty-five gallon drums for planters, but then Sam had spotted those dandy oak barrels instead and had somehow persuaded Cal to donate them to the cause. Or the time Clyde sat on Jed's freshly painted bench, then walked around for several hours with dark green stripes across his backside. Or even how surprised everyone was when Rich from the Eagle Tavern pitched in by helping to paint new signs. No one had realized before what a talented sign-painter he was.

"This is all fine and good," Rosa finally said. "But I've got a huge spaghetti dinner in there just waiting to feed all you hard workers."

They laughed and joked as they heaped their plates with spaghetti and then filled the tables of Rosa's little restaurant. Maggie sat down with Chloe and Scott, and then Elizabeth Rodgers joined them. To everyone's pleased surprise, Elizabeth had decided to open her bookstore in Pine Mountain after all, and had given up her vacation to spend the entire week helping on their work crew. Only yesterday, her full-price offer on the old drugstore building had been accepted, and she planned to begin interior renovations as soon as she found a good contractor.

"I'm glad I waited until tomorrow to have my grand opening," said Chloe as she took a bite of garlic bread. "Maybe that photographer will manage to get a shot of it—good publicity, you know."

"Maybe I should have Rich whip me up a sign for my new bookstore," said Elizabeth. "After all, no one would guess that building is actually vacant."

Maggie smiled at the older woman. "It's so great to have you here with us. You've been a real morale booster this past week."

"Yes," chimed in Chloe. "And I can't believe how helpful you were with all this cleanup. It couldn't have been much of a vacation for you, though."

Elizabeth chuckled. "Well, they say the best vacations are those that provide a drastic change of pace. And that pretty much describes my week!"

"Sounds like good tourist enticement," joked Scott. "Come to Pine Mountain for a *drastic* change of pace."

Everyone laughed. Then Clyde held up his glass and spoke loudly so as to be heard over the noise. "I'd like to make a toast: To our two ladies of the hour, Maggie and Rosa." He glanced at the two women. "Here's to all the work you two have put into this town the past couple weeks."

"And here's to a great beginning," added Maggie as she raised her glass. "May it get better and better."

Everyone helped clear the tables after dinner. And to Maggie's surprise, Jed was back in the kitchen with an apron tied around his waist as he vigorously scrubbed pots and pans. The scene, so unexpected, brought a smile to her lips. She glanced around to see if Kate was around to lend a hand but didn't see her anywhere.

"Need any help?" she offered, almost hoping he'd decline.

"Sure." He gestured to a pile at his elbow. "Those are ready to be loaded in the dishwasher."

She began to load the pots, carefully fitting in as many as possible while searching for something trivial to say. "Well, tomorrow's the big day—Pine Mountain meets the world."

He nodded somewhat soberly. "I hope that it's a good thing."

"Meaning you're not convinced?" She stopped loading the pans and stared at him curiously. "Don't tell me you're thinking of joining forces with Greg Snider?"

"The truth is, I don't want to see this place overdeveloped either, Maggie. Sure, I would like more traffic in Pine Mountain so I can sell furniture and all, but I can understand some of what Greg is saying. I don't want this place to grow too big or too fast."

"Then I suppose you liked his letter to the editor this week." Her voice went flat.

The corners of Jed's mouth turned up slightly. "I have to admit it was slightly amusing, but a little mean-spirited, if you ask me." He looked intently at her. "I do appreciate that you printed it, Maggie. That took guts."

"He has a right to his opinion."

"Are you aware of the main reason he's so put out with you?"

"Because I'm from California, I suppose." She slid the loaded rack into the dishwasher and leaned back against the counter. She pushed a stray strand of hair out of her eyes and suddenly realized that she was exhausted. It had been a very long week.

"Being from out of state doesn't help," continued Jed. "But besides the development issues, Gavin and Greg were best friends for years. I'm sure he resents you for having what he still thinks of as Gavin's job."

"I know they were friends. But Greg needs to realize that Gavin messed up his own life long before I ever got here."

"Have you seen Gavin since..."

"No." She felt too tired to have this conversation. She glanced around the kitchen. "Looks like that's the last of the pans. I should probably get going. I have a big day tomorrow."

"Do you know where you're going to take your photographer?"

She shrugged. "I just thought I'd show him around town, then maybe out to the lake and up to the ski area."

"You might want to take him on a hiking trail," suggested Jed. Just then Kate came in.

"What're you two up to?" she asked with wide blue eyes.

"Just finishing up in here," said Jed. "And I was telling Maggie she might want to take that photographer on a hike."

"That's a good idea," agreed Kate.

"I don't know any hiking trails." Maggie was getting exasperated now. She didn't want to take anyone on a hike. She just wanted to go home.

"Maybe I could help out," offered Jed. "I could take you guys up Silver Creek Trail. It's only about two and half miles, and the view from the top is spectacular. A real photo opportunity."

"Well, I could suggest that to him as sort of a back-up plan or something."

"I'll be free after two," said Jed. "Just stop by the shop." He glanced at Kate. "You're working tomorrow afternoon, aren't you, Kate?"

"I guess so." Kate pouted prettily, reminding Maggie of a disappointed child.

"Thanks for the offer, Jed," said Maggie. "I'll let you know if he's interested."

"What have you done in here?" asked Rosa as she stepped into her nearly clean kitchen. "I thought I'd be here until midnight."

"It was Jed, mostly," said Maggie. "And now I'm going to say goodnight."

When she got home, her answering machine was blinking. She rewound it and listened to the message. It was from her mother.

"Hi, my sweeties. How's everything in beautiful Pine Mountain? I've been thinking I'd like to take you up on your offer to come for a visit. How does mid-July sound? Let me know if you have room for me. I know you're working on that big old house. Is it done yet? Maybe I can help out. I used to be fairly handy with those kinds of things."

"Is Grandma coming?" asked Spencer eagerly as Maggie shut off the machine.

"Sounds like it." She glanced around the crowded carriage house. "But I don't know where we'll put her. How soon do you think it'll be until we can start using the big house?"

"You could start using some of the rooms right now," said Spencer as he opened a can of food for Bart. "There's several bedrooms that are just fine. That is, unless you want to do anything else to them like paint or wallpaper or anything like that."

She thought about that for a moment. "You know your grandma loves doing those kinds of things..."

"Maybe you should invite her to come help out."

"Like that kind of vacation that Elizabeth was describing?"

Spencer laughed. "Yeah—a *drastic* change of pace."

She considered this. Her mother had seemed a little blue the last few times they had spoken. "You know, Spence, that might be just the ticket."

He smiled. "It'd be nice to have her come visit."

She decided to call her mother before she went to bed. They talked at length about all the things that Audrey could help with. They agreed that mid-July was perfect, that would give Audrey plenty of time to take care of some things and hopefully Maggie would have moved, at least partially, into the big house by then. It seemed a good plan.

The next day, she got up early to inspect the condition of the big house. She wanted to determine how realistic it was for them to move in. She took a notepad to list all the things that needed to be finished, as well as to make a list of things she should purchase for the various rooms, things like window coverings and towel bars. It was the first time she'd allowed herself to feel very involved with the house. She wasn't sure if her neglect was a result of being so busy or due to her first sad introduction to the place. But today, as she walked through the rooms, she felt surprisingly hopeful. With all the dreary drapes removed and the many repairs finished or in progress, the house seemed, for the first time, to have great potential. In fact, she felt excited about the prospect of bringing the old place back to life.

"So, what do you think, Mom?" asked Spencer from behind.

She turned in surprise. "You're up awfully early—for you that is."

He rolled his eyes as he took a bite of an apple. "I heard you sneak out and I wondered what was up."

She smiled. "It was nice of you to check up on your old mom."

"So," he said again, "what do you think?"

She grinned. "I think it's absolutely wonderful. I'm so pleased! I hadn't really taken time to check out what was going on in here, and now I'm just so happy with it."

He nodded. "Yep, she's coming right along. Jed is really good at this kind of stuff. You should see where he made this piece of molding to perfectly match the old one—you can't even tell where the two meet. He could do this remodeling stuff for a living."

"He seems to enjoy working with wood." She glanced at her watch. "I didn't realize I'd been in here for so long. I guess I better go make us some breakfast before the photographer arrives."

"What's his name again?"

"Buckie Porterfield. And he's supposed to stop by our house first thing. Then I'll take him into town. Do you want to come with us? I'll probably take him to the lake and the ski area—and maybe even a hike."

"Maybe. Sounds kinda interesting."

"I just hope he likes everything," she said nervously. "I want to put our best foot forward so he doesn't think that Pine Mountain is a waste of his time."

"Well, Mom," said Spencer in a philosophical tone. "I think you and everyone else have done just about everything possible. And I remember how Dad used to say something like 'do your best and let God do the rest.'"

She blinked in surprise, then poked him playfully in the arm. "You're just too amazing, Spencer Clay Carpenter. When did you get so wise?"

Spencer grinned. "Sierra says it's okay to let people know if you've got something upstairs as long as you don't get a big head about it."

"That Sierra's a smart little gal."

Nineteen

This is quite a place you have here," said Buckie Porterfield as Maggie showed him around her property. "Is this homestead listed on the historical registry?"

"Not yet, but I've thought about inquiring into it."

"Hmm." He squinted up at the house as if framing it through the lens of a camera. "You might want to investigate it first. I have an aunt in Vermont who listed her house and has been sorry ever since. She says she can't even prune her shrubbery without getting someone's approval first."

"That's something to consider." She led him up the porch steps, grateful that the repairs to the porch were now complete. "I suppose it could get even more complicated if I ever decided to use this place as a bed and breakfast."

Buckie looked surprised. "You'd want to run a B & B?"

"Maybe someday..." She turned to admire the view from where they stood. Pastoral and green, with mountains rising off to the right. She could imagine a nice porch swing up here, and maybe some comfortable wicker chairs and a rocker or two. "It sounds sort of interesting," she continued absently, "you know, running a cozy bed and breakfast while you leisurely write the great American novel..."

"You want to write the great American novel?"

She felt her cheeks grow warm as she realized she'd never actually admitted this secret desire to anyone. Not even to Phil, although he had suggested it a time or two. "Oh, I don't know..." She laughed nervously. "Maybe the novel thing just seems to go with the bed and breakfast. Besides, isn't that every writer's dream?"

Buckie smiled. "And some photographers'."

She looked at him skeptically. "You mean you want to write the great American novel too?"

He laughed hard over this. "No. I meant the part about running a bed and breakfast."

"Really? But wouldn't a bed and breakfast tie you down? And I thought you photographers had to be on the go all the time."

"Well, I think the idea of owning a B & B appeals to me because I've always enjoyed staying at them while I'm on the road. They're so much homier and more personal than hotels. Maybe I'm just looking for a place to come home to."

She laughed. "I think I know just what you mean."

"Say, would you mind if I took a few shots of your place?" He began to slide his camera bag off his shoulder. "Not for the magazine article—at least I don't think so—but just for the fun of it."

"Shoot away. And if you get any good ones, maybe I could buy some copies—you know, to use for advertising in case I ever get my bed and breakfast off the ground. But you won't want to take any interior shots of the house. It's sort of a work-in-progress right now. We're still repairing a lot of things inside. Want to see?"

"You bet!"

Maggie showed him her house, and he, too, could see the potential beneath years of neglect and the current stages of renovation. He even shared some ideas he'd picked up from various bed and breakfasts over the years. She studied him as he carefully examined the hand-carved mantle on the front parlor fireplace. At first she'd been slightly put off by what she'd perceived as an overly assertive busybody. With his short-cropped reddish hair, ruddy complexion, and bright blue eyes, he had reminded her of an obnoxious uncle on her father's side who was always poking his nose in where it didn't belong. She had observed Buckie from a safe distance as he parked his dark green Explorer right in front of the barn, then hopped out and immediately began to stroll around investigating the exterior of the old building, almost as if he owned the place. After she'd gone out to introduce herself, she stiffly asked if he wanted a tour, as if to hint that he was being somewhat intrusive. But he eagerly accepted, and as they walked around the outbuildings he had asked a lot of good questions about the history and ages of each one. She decided right then to ask Clyde to write it all up for her. She knew he wouldn't be around forever, and she doubted that Gavin would be much help in this area. And now she realized her first impression of Buckie had been all wrong. He actually seemed to be a fairly likable guy, open and easy to talk with, plus he had a good sense of humor. And he was interested in the things that interested her. Suddenly, she found herself looking forward to spending the day with him.

She left him on his own to shoot his photos while she returned to the carriage house to finish cleaning up the breakfast dishes. Then she decided to spend a few extra minutes on her own appearance, even taking time to change into a fresh shirt and a new pair of khaki walking shorts. Buckie had arrived earlier than expected, and although she hadn't cared much at the time, now she wanted to look good. When she went back out to find him, he was taking photos of Spencer and Bart posed out in front of the barn.

"Are you about ready to head into town?" she called out.

He looked up. "Sure, just let me get a couple more shots here."

She smiled at the picturesque scene before her. Spencer had on the same paint-splotched overalls he'd worn for the work party all week. He was bent over with one foot on a split log bench that looked almost as old as the barn. Bart sat next to him, head held high as if posing for the photo. Behind the two loomed the old barn, its red paint faded into an interesting patina.

"That looks like a great picture," said Maggie. "I hope I can get a copy."

He snapped the lens cover back on his camera and turned. "No problem." He glanced at his watch. "Guess we better go see this town of yours. Since I came straight to your place I haven't seen it yet."

"What did you think of the road from the highway?" she asked cautiously.

He laughed. "You call *that* a road? I thought I was four-wheeling."

"We're hoping to get some funding to fix it."

Maggie and Spencer rode with Buckie. She tried to briefly explain the history of the town, including it's more recent hard times, and why it was so important that they get some positive exposure in *Western Life*.

"We're going to have Pine Mountain Days in late July," she said as they approached town. "I just hope this issue will be out before then so we can draw some more traffic this way."

"It might be on the rack by then," said Buckie. "I know the magazine has to be laid out before the fourth because I have a killer deadline on these photos. And it usually comes out the end of the month to beat the issue date. You could get lucky."

"Do you do a lot of work for *Western Life*?" she asked.

"I try to—they're great folks to work for. But I freelance for a lot of others too. And I've been trying to build up my own photo collection. Hey, is this it?"

"Don't blink," warned Spencer, "you might miss it."

Maggie tossed a warning glance her son's way as she quickly said, "Pine Mountain is definitely small, but that's part of its charm. Why don't you park by the newspaper office, Buckie, and we'll start there."

"Hey, this is an attractive little town," he said as he glanced at the newly painted shop fronts. "It looks like they keep things fixed up pretty nice around here. Some small towns can be real eyesores."

Maggie didn't mention their very recent, mad-rush efforts to prepare for this photo session. "Yes, we want people to know that Pine Mountain is a great place to visit while they're on their way to the mountains or the lakes or whatever."

Spencer left them at the newspaper office and went to find Sierra. Then Maggie began to show Buckie around the town, introducing him to various business people and waiting patiently as he shot rolls and rolls of film. He appreciated everything from their flower boxes to the Alpine theme.

"It looks like there's some vacant businesses," he noted as he arranged his tripod to take some shots of the Pine Mountain Hotel.

She cleared her throat. "Well, yes. As I mentioned earlier, the town was hit with some hard times when the highway was relocated. And it's still recovering. But with the new business association that I told you about, I think things are on the upswing now."

"But maybe the real estate prices are still on the downswing?"

"Well, perhaps," she said somewhat defensively. "But I think that will all change as soon as people begin to realize what a great place this is." Just then, she noticed Greg Snider walking down the street toward them. She locked eyes with him for a moment, bracing herself for a scene, but hoping desperately that he would pass by quietly.

"What's going on here?" asked Greg as if someone had just appointed him the official street patrol.

"Hi, Greg." Maggie forced a smile and formally introduced the two men, hoping for the best. "Buckie's taking some photographs for *Western Life*. Have you ever heard of that magazine?"

Greg rolled his eyes. "I don't live under a stone, Ms. Carpenter."

She blinked and took an involuntary half-step back.

"Why does *Western Life* want pictures of Pine Mountain?" demanded Greg.

"Maggie wrote a great little article about your town," began Buckie as he polished his camera lens with a piece of soft flannel. "And I'm taking the photos to accompany her story. This ought to be a real nice boost for tourism here."

"Just what we need!" snorted Greg as he walked off.

Buckie looked at her with raised brows. "Is that the official Pine Mountain welcoming committee?"

She frowned. "Unfortunately, he's the postmaster."

"Who put the burr under his saddle?" asked Buckie as he bent over to refocus his camera lens.

She shook her head. "I don't know. I think he's just a perennial sourpuss."

"Maybe he's worried that Pine Mountain's population is going to grow so much that his work load will increase at the post office."

She laughed. "You're not the first person to suggest that."

He snapped a few more shots of the hotel. "Well, I think I've got enough of the town now. You mentioned a ski area and lake?"

"That's right. Let's stop by the deli first. The owner, Rosa Galloway, has put together a lunch that we can take on the road."

"Great," said Buckie. "Maybe I should get a couple of interior shots of the deli while we're there. I've only gotten interiors of the antique shop and Chloe's new clothing shop so far."

Maggie chatted with Rosa in the kitchen while Buckie snapped some photos inside the deli. "It seems to be going well," said Maggie quietly. "I think he likes Pine Mountain."

"Good." Rosa put their lunches into a small cooler and handed it to Maggie. "Spencer said to tell you that he and

Sierra want to help Chloe with her grand opening today. They thought if they hung around and looked like customers it might seem as if she was busier than usual."

Maggie laughed. "I saw those two in there when Buckie was photographing her place. Spencer was trying on goofy hats."

"Do you mind going all by yourself with him?" asked Rosa with sweet concern.

Maggie glanced at Buckie who by now had moved outside to shoot the seating area by Rosa's pretty herb garden. "Not at all. He's really a nice guy. Hey, it looks like he's giving your deli some good coverage too. Just think, you might be in *Western Life* magazine!"

Rosa beamed. "Now, wouldn't that be something!" She peeked out the side window. "Say, Maggie, he's kind of cute. Is he married?"

Maggie playfully poked Rosa in the arm. "You should be ashamed Rosa Galloway—and you a happily married woman."

"Oh, I wasn't thinking of me..." said Rosa, her dark eyes sparkling.

⌒

Buckie seemed suitably impressed by Silver Lake. "I'd like to see if I could reserve one of those cabins for later this summer," he said as he packed his camera away after his final shot. "This place is unbelievably beautiful. You know, there are some gorgeous lakes up in Washington, but it seems like it's always raining there, even in the summertime. Is this day a fluke, or is it really true that you get a lot of sunshine here?"

"Actually, we just ordered this sunny day especially for you," she teased as she unpacked their picnic lunch. "We have a direct line to the weather man upstairs."

"Well, I appreciate the trouble you went to. Good weather always makes my job a lot easier."

"Some folks boast that this area gets 300 days of sunshine a year, but I haven't been here long enough to verify that yet. They say it's due to the mountain range. A lot of rain gets dumped on the west-side of the Cascades, and then more right on top of the mountains, and a smaller amount falls on this side—just enough to keep the forest green and healthy."

They ate at a lakeside table, and Buckie told her about his work in Seattle. "I do a lot of corporate work, advertising and the like. Not my favorite, but it pays the bills. And of course I get some interesting assignments that take me off to other countries. I just got back from a photo shoot in northern China."

"You mentioned 'your own collection.' Do you show your photos anywhere?"

"There's a gallery on the waterfront that exhibits my photos once in awhile. But the competition in Seattle is something fierce. I've been thinking of opening up a small gallery of my own somewhere, someday...it's one of those photographer dreams, kind of like the bed and breakfast idea."

They finished lunch and headed on up the highway to the ski resort. The mountain looked slightly bleak with the snow-pack melting to expose bare, rocky slopes, but the manager assured them that it would be hopping up here by Thanksgiving if not sooner.

"We're not the biggest ski resort around, but we're steadily growing. We're putting up two more chair-lifts this summer," he explained, pointing to the construction crew halfway up the mountain. "One lift will go all the way to the top. It'll be an advanced run for more experienced skiers and riders."

"Riders?" asked Maggie.

"You know, snowboarders," said Buckie informatively, and the manager nodded in agreement.

She tossed Buckie a sideways glance. "And how'd you know that?"

He grinned. "I happen to be a rider myself."

She laughed. "Somehow that doesn't surprise me, Mr. Porterfield."

As they drove back to town, she told him about the possibility of an afternoon hike to another scenic area, that is if he was interested, and she almost hoped now that he wasn't.

"Sounds terrific," he said. "Although I haven't made any reservations for spending the night yet. Do you think that the hotel has any rooms available?"

She grimaced. Rosa had secured permission from the hotel owners to remove the boards from the windows and hang curtains to make it look more habitable. But Maggie hadn't realized that Buckie didn't know that it was really vacant. "Well, actually, the hotel isn't open for business right now." She thought for a moment. "But I do have an idea that you might like. I'll check on it while we're in town."

She left Buckie to visit with the ever-congenial Kate up front while she slipped into the back-room of Jed's shop to quickly call Clyde at home. Fortunately, he had just stepped in from fishing and everything was quickly settled.

She went to the front of the shop to find Buckie. "Say, you mentioned you'd like to stay at a cabin on the lake," she said. "It's not exactly the Ritz, but Clyde Barnes, the owner of the *Pine Cone*, has invited you to be his house-guest tonight—if that sounds okay to you."

"Sounds great. Sure it's no problem?"

"Not at all. Clyde said he just caught a mess of trout, and he wants us both to come for dinner." She turned to Kate. "Isn't Jed here yet?"

Kate frowned. "He said he'd be here by two, and it's a quarter past..."

"Hey, there," called Jed from the back. "Sorry I'm late. Everybody ready for a hike?"

"You bet," said Buckie, extending his hand for introductions.

Jed looked at Kate, then frowned at his watch. "I suppose you'd like to join us, Kate."

She smiled beguilingly. "It's been a good morning, Jed, but it's really slowed down this afternoon."

He thought for a moment. "I suppose it won't hurt to close early today." He glanced at Buckie. "That's one of the perks of running your own shop in a little town like this. You can keep your own hours and usually no one complains."

"This small town life is sounding more and more appealing all the time," remarked Buckie as the four of them headed out the door.

Maggie couldn't recall a better hike. The steadily rising trail was immaculately maintained, and pristine ferns and wildflowers lined it all along the way. The weather was perfect, warm in the sun, refreshingly cool in the shade. And the scenery was amazing. They stopped at various waterfalls and panoramic viewpoints along the way, giving Buckie ample opportunity to take some gorgeous shots as well as providing much-needed breaks for Maggie. It seemed to her that everyone else was in good shape. She had to push herself to keep up, but she tried not to let it show, and she didn't want to slow them down. She also tried not to compare herself to Kate, who easily led the way with her long legs moving like steel pistons steadily up the trail. Maggie knew that Kate was still in her twenties and a regular sportswoman, but just the same (and she knew it was silly) she didn't want to be shown up by this young woman. By the time they finally stopped, Maggie's legs felt like overcooked spaghetti and she wasn't even sure she could make it back down in one piece. Nonetheless, she was extremely glad she'd made it all the way to the top.

"Isn't this view spectacular," she said breathlessly as she studied the snowcapped mountains before them. "The peaks seem so close."

Buckie had already pulled a portable tripod out of his pack and was quickly setting it up. "They're fantastic," he commented without pausing. "I've got to get them with the sun at this angle."

Kate watched intently as Buckie arranged his camera on the tripod and tested several different lenses. "That must be a fun way to make a living," she said with admiration. "I took a photography class once, but I wasn't any good at it."

Jed removed his backpack and set four bottles of water, power bars, and several packs of jerky on a large stone. "I've got some refreshments if anyone is interested," he called.

"Why, Jed, you're a regular boy scout," teased Maggie, instantly regretting her words as she remembered her knack at offending him. But to her relief he only smiled.

"It's surprising how a short hike like this can really take it out of you," he said as he handed her a cool bottle of water.

"Thanks." She took a swig, then said quietly, "I'm glad you thought to bring this. I probably need it more than the rest of you. I can see now that I'm really not in very good shape."

"You did just fine on the trail, Maggie. You seem like a natural hiker."

"Honestly?" She looked at him skeptically, but he seemed perfectly serious as he nodded. "Well, I really enjoyed the hike. I'd like to get Spencer up here."

"There's a lot of good trails around. I'd be happy to show you and Spencer some other ones too."

Kate walked over and took a bottle of water, wiping it across her forehead. "Hey, we should take Maggie and Spencer up Mount Jackson this summer."

Maggie looked at the mountains. "Which one is that?"

Jed stood beside her and pointed out the peak just right of the middle. "It's a relatively easy climb. You don't need ropes or anything, but you and Spencer would need to work up to it. Maybe by August we could plan a trip."

"That'd be great," she said. "I've never climbed a mountain before."

"Hey," said Buckie, walking over to join them. "That sounds like fun. Can I come too?" He casually threw an arm around Maggie's shoulder as if he'd known her all his life. Maggie laughed. Buckie reminded her of a little boy who didn't want to be left out of the fun.

"I don't know why not," she said, glancing at Jed for approval.

"The more the merrier," he said, but his voice sounded flat to Maggie's ears and she wondered why. Didn't he like Buckie?

"Why don't we invite Scott and Chloe along too?" suggested Kate. "And maybe Sierra would like to come to keep Spencer company." Kate was counting people on her fingers. "That makes four couples. A perfect climbing party."

Maggie suddenly flinched at the word "couples," but wasn't even sure why it bothered her so much. Turning her back to the group, she pretended to study the remarkable view once more. But her mind was not on the mountains. As much as she liked Buckie, she didn't want to be paired off with him, or anyone else for that matter! She just wasn't ready for that yet. A lump grew in her throat as she thought about Phil. He seemed so far, far away. But, oh, wouldn't he have loved it up here!

Twenty

That night Buckie and Maggie enjoyed a delicious pan-fried trout dinner at Clyde's little cabin next to the lake. Clyde proved to be an excellent cook and not a bad housekeeper, either. His hand-hewn log cabin was charming with its humble log walls and golden wood floors worn smooth with time and use. On a sturdy maple kitchen table sat a small canning jar filled with wild forget-me-nots and purple asters, a thoughtful gesture that made Maggie smile, but she was careful not to draw undo attention to it. An old leather couch and a bearskin rug were comfortably arranged before a big river-rock fireplace, and a large oak rocker sat off to the side. Several other attractive antique pieces nestled against the pine log walls, probably family heirlooms that had once inhabited what was now Maggie's house.

All through dinner, Buckie and Clyde happily swapped hunting, fishing, and traveling stories, and although Maggie enjoyed listening, she felt her presence wouldn't be greatly missed. So after lending a hand cleaning up Clyde's rustic kitchen, she decided to excuse herself early, saying she wanted to get on her way before dark. She thanked Clyde for the excellent meal and then Buckie walked her out to her car.

"Maggie, I want to thank you for a truly great day," he said as he opened her car door for her. "I really like your town."

She chuckled. "It's not exactly *my* town. In fact, I'm one of the newest newcomers in Pine Mountain right now."

"Well, you've sure settled in nicely for a newcomer." His face beamed happily in the blue, dusky light. "The amazing thing is…" He paused as if weighing his words. "I really feel at home here."

She smiled knowingly. "I know what you mean. That's exactly how I felt when I came to Pine Mountain."

"And I've been doing some serious thinking…" He leaned his head back and sighed deeply. "I know it's real sudden and all. But I think I want to look into buying some real estate here—one of those vacant business properties. I think I'd like to put a gallery in it."

"Oh, what a good idea! And would you show your photos there?"

He nodded enthusiastically. "I can just imagine it, Maggie, and I think I know exactly which building I want. And believe it or not, I've already got a name for the gallery—it just hit me as we were hiking today. I'll call it *The Blue Moose*. You see, I have this photo I took up in Alaska—one of my best wildlife shots ever—it's a moose in the early dawn, all misty and blue, and I call it the Blue Moose."

"That's a terrific name, Buckie."

"And if things pick up in this town like everybody's hoping, this whole thing could prove a very sound investment for me."

She grew thoughtful. She had no desire to lure *anyone* into Pine Mountain under false pretenses. "Buckie," she began slowly, "you need to be fully aware that Pine Mountain has gone through some very serious financial struggles in the last few years. And as hard as we're all trying, we are not out of the woods yet."

"I know that, I'm not blind. And I realize it's a risk. But I have a good feeling..." he pointed to his chest, "in here. I think I want to throw my lot into this town and work together with the rest of you to help bring it to life."

"That would be so great. You'd be such a good addition to this town—and to think—a gallery!"

"Another thing, Maggie," his voice grew more serious now, "I'd really like to get better acquainted with you too. Do you think that's even a possibility?"

She sighed deeply. "Of course...it's a possibility... But you should know that even though my husband's been gone for two years, I still struggle with the whole thing sometimes. Just today I found myself missing him... And anyway, I haven't had a serious relationship with a guy since his death."

Buckie smiled. "It's okay. I know it's not the same thing, but I went through a grueling divorce a few years back and I've been kind of gun shy ever since. And I know I can come across as a pushy sort of guy, but I wouldn't push you, Maggie. I just wanted to make sure that there wasn't someone else in the picture." He looked down at his feet. "I couldn't help but notice how Jed seemed pretty friendly with you today..."

"Jed?" Maggie laughed lightly. "Oh no, you don't need to worry about Jed. I'm pretty sure that he and Kate are an item."

"Really? Kate and Jed?" Buckie looked curiously into her face. "I guess I didn't get that impression at all."

Maggie shrugged then glanced at the quickly darkening sky. "I think I better get going, Buckie. I'm really not very familiar with the roads out here at night."

"Well, thanks for everything, Maggie. I'll be seeing you."

She climbed into her car then added, "Hey, if you tell Clyde about your interest in a gallery, he'll give you the low-down on the available real estate and recommend a good realtor."

"Thanks."

She pulled out of the driveway and onto the gravel road. For some reason it seemed as if her pulse was racing as she drove through the shadowy pines. What in the world was wrong with her? Of course she was thrilled that Buckie might open a gallery in Pine Mountain. What a boon that would be to the community right now! And she was pleased and flattered that he wanted to get to know her better. He seemed like a fun and interesting guy. But what moved her the most was that he had assumed that Jed was interested in her! Whatever would make him think something like that? And as much as she found herself wishing it might be true, she felt just as certain that Buckie had simply imagined the whole thing.

ᴄ⁓

Maggie and Spencer joined the Galloways as they celebrated the Fourth of July at Silver Lake. The lake was more crowded than usual, resulting in more than a few disgruntled fishermen as the wakes rocked their little boats each time the motorboats and jet-skis whizzed by. Maggie felt sorry for them, and hoped things would quiet back down after the holiday. It would be hard to see a way of life deteriorate. Even Clyde, with his pro-development rhetoric, was known to lament the cost of growth from time to time. But he was also quick to point out that there were still plenty of quiet fishing lakes to be found within a ten-mile radius. Of course, Clyde also knew enough to keep tight-lipped about his favorite spots. He was probably spending his holiday at one of them right now.

As the sun began to set, the boats slowed their speed and turned on their running lights, motoring to various niches along the shore where they would wait for the fireworks show to begin. All across the still lake could be heard the sounds of "ooh" and "ahh" as the spectators enjoyed the spectacular bursts of color and light, this sound quickly followed by loud booms that echoed and reverberated off the water. But best of all, as the brilliant display flashed in the sky it was simultaneously reflected upon the obsidian-like water. It was like seeing two fireworks shows at once!

"That was the best fireworks I've ever seen," exclaimed Maggie as they climbed from the boat to the dock. "It may not have been the longest or most expensive, but it was by far the best!"

"Wasn't it great!" said Rosa. "Too bad we couldn't have a photo of *that* for the *Western Life* article."

"I don't think a photo could begin to capture the magic of what we witnessed tonight," said Maggie as they walked toward the graveled parking area.

"Speaking of photos," said Rosa, "I heard that Buckie Porterfield bought the old McFadden building for his gallery."

"Word sure travels fast," said Maggie. "Actually, he called and told me that he'd made an offer, but I hadn't heard that it was accepted. And he asked me to keep it under my hat. I think he was worried someone might make a better offer and steal it out from under him."

Rosa laughed. "I can see that Buckie still doesn't quite realize how easy it is to acquire real estate here."

"Oh, it won't always be like that. The day will come when people will be fighting to buy property in this town." Then Maggie lowered her voice. "Now, Rosa, if you can really keep *this* a secret, I'll tell you something else. Buckie thinks he might have a potential buyer for the Pine Mountain Hotel."

"You're kidding! Oh, that's such good news!"

"But please don't tell anyone. He said that a very wealthy friend in Seattle, a guy who used to be with that mega software company, wants to retire and buy and run a hotel in a small tourist town."

"Now wouldn't that be something." Rosa patted Maggie on the back. "Ever since you came, it seems things have just gotten better and better."

"Well, like Jed said in church this week, let's just remember to give God the credit and that'll take the pressure off us." Maggie opened her car door. "Thanks for letting us join you tonight."

Before going to bed, Maggie emailed a quick note to Rebecca.

RB

Happy 4th! I'm really too tired to write much, but wanted to catch you up on the latest. My mother will be here in about ten days! Am I crazy? Sometimes we get along so well, and others... Oh well, I'll hope for the best! Just now I feel so overwhelmed with all that's going on in my life. And I wonder, what have I gotten myself into? Like even tonight, my friend Rosa acts like everything that's changing here in town is a result of me. It makes me feel awkward, and more than that it makes me nervous—as if everyone's fate is riding on my shoulders. What if it all falls apart? Will it be my fault? I even had a dream the other night that the townspeople decided to stone me because I'd done something wrong, and the postmaster was leading them. I know it's silly, but I do feel some pressure. Fortunately, I had the sense to refuse to head the planning committee for our upcoming event, Pine Mountain Days. Poor Elizabeth, the bookstore lady from Seattle, has taken that on. But of course I'm on her committee, and doing all I can to help out. I may need some lessons on how to say no. But right now I just feel so responsible. And tired. I'm going to bed now.

mc

The next day, Maggie was surprised to see an email from Rebecca just as she was getting ready to go home from work. She decided to take a few extra moments to read it, and had to laugh at her friend's response to last night's cry for help.

MC

Stop whatever you're doing right now and listen to me! You've got to slow down, Maggie! It sounds as if you're trying to kill yourself! Working your head off for a silly little paper with a circulation of 500, trying to remodel an old dinosaur house, and on top of all that saving the town, raising a teenager, and having your mother come visit. You are nuts, my friend! And you DO need to learn to say the word "no." Right now practice it with me— NO, no, NO, no! Very good. Now I want you to go upstairs and draw yourself a nice bubble bath in that claw-foot tub you told me about. Light some candles and play some relaxing music. Now, get into the tub and don't get out for at least an hour (adding hot water as needed). An hour! I mean it, Maggie. And while you're in there, you are to think of nothing. NOTHING! You understand? Not your job. Not your house. Not the town. Not your mother. Not even your son. Just breathe deeply and relax. Do you understand???? I will be checking on you. And if you don't follow my orders, I may have to come out there and pay you a very embarrassing visit. And you know I can do it. Don't you? Okay, that's all I have to say about that.

RB!

Maggie followed Rebecca's orders. At first it was very difficult not to think about anything, but after ten minutes she fell into the pattern of breathing deeply and listening to the music. And finally she actually managed to relax. That night she went to bed calmly refreshed. And the next morning she emailed a sincere thank-you to Rebecca.

RB

Perhaps you should give up your law practice and take up medicine. I tried your prescribed remedy and it worked wonders. I'm ashamed to think that I was in such pitiful need of help. But your advice was well timed. I do need to slow down and stop thinking that I'm carrying the whole world on my shoulders. I've promised myself to take time to enjoy the beautiful place I live in more, and not to fall back into the old workaholic ways that I was hoping to escape. And, I'll be taking more therapeutic baths. It's funny, I always think of you as working too hard. But then you always seem to remember to take better care of yourself than I do. I used to think it was because you weren't so busy taking care of a husband and children. Now, I just think it's because you're smarter! Thanks again.

mc

~

The next week and a half seemed to be busier than ever, but Maggie tried to remember Rebecca's advice to pace herself. Somehow everything fell into place getting her house ready, and she and Spencer managed to move in with the help of a moving party organized by Rosa. And even though there was still a lot left to be done in her house, Maggie knew her mother would probably enjoy pitching in to help. Finally the day came for her mother's arrival and Maggie was glad to see her car pull into the driveway.

"That was some road into town," said Audrey as she climbed stiffly from her low-to-the-ground Honda.

"Oh, I'm sorry about that, Mom." Maggie hugged her mother. "I forgot to warn you about the road conditions here. Even in the summer we should have travel advisories for *that* particular road. But we're working on some public funds to get it fixed, hopefully before winter sets in."

Audrey looked around expectantly. "Where's my grandson? Do you keep him tied up in the barn or something?"

Maggie laughed. "No, Mom. I quit tying him up a few weeks ago. Like I said, he's made a miraculous adjustment to Pine Mountain."

"I think that had more to do with that girl than any miracle."

"I think it's a combination of both." Maggie pointed to the Ponderosa Pine woods on the north side of her property. "Spencer just took Bart for a walk in the woods. That's all National Forest over there and it has lots of great trails. Bart just loves to romp and if he doesn't get his daily workout, we all pay for it."

"Well, Maggie," Audrey looked at the house approvingly, "this is quite nice. After all you said, I was expecting to see a real wreck."

"I probably made it sound much worse than it was to start out with, but I was so shocked at the time. And don't get me wrong, it has required a fair amount of work. Spencer and Jed have done a lot of repairs."

"Who's Jed?"

"You'll meet him soon enough. He's been helping Spencer fix things. He's an excellent woodworker and furniture maker. Plus he knows a lot about renovating old houses. He's a handy guy to have around."

"You know, your brother would love this place, Maggie. He's just nuts about old houses."

"I told Barry he's welcome anytime, and not to forget to bring a hammer."

Then she led her mother through the inside of the big house, proudly showing the changes and repairs and explaining how things used to be and what still needed doing.

"The kitchen still needs the most work. But at least it's usable now."

"It's certainly big for an old home. Often the kitchens were cramped because they were only used by cooks and servants."

"I know. Clyde told me that his mother had the kitchen made to her specifications. Apparently, she liked to cook. And although she only had the two boys, and they were born a ways apart, she always longed to have a big family."

"When was the house built?"

"Around 1910 or 11."

"So, how old is this Clyde fellow anyway?"

"He's actually in his eighties, but he seems a lot younger when you get to know him. He's sharp as a tack and leads a very active life." She showed her mother the freshly painted dining room. "I wasn't sure about this color at first—butter yellow—but now I'm finding I absolutely love it. It's so warm and inviting, and I like how it sets off the dark mahogany wood." She opened the glass doors to reveal a framing project still in progress. "Jed and Spence are building a deck out here. Cedar. It should be finished in the next week or two." She smiled proudly. "It was financed by the payment for my article to *Western Life*."

"That's wonderful." Audrey drew a deep breath. "The view of the mountains is gorgeous from here. You know, I've only been here a few minutes, and I have to admit, I'm already falling in love with the place."

Maggie beamed as she showed her mother the rest of her house, finally stopping in the guest room that she had just finished fixing up for her. She'd even splurged on a hand-made quilt to cover the bed. After that, they toured the out-buildings, finally stopping at the carriage house. "This is where Spence and I stayed at first," she said as she opened the door. "It was a real life saver."

"This is adorable! What will you do with it now?"

"I don't know yet." Maggie glanced around the small spaces and remembered how thankful she'd been when they'd first arrived, but how after a few weeks she'd been ready for more room. "I actually thought about fixing it up for you to stay in, but then I thought you might prefer to be with us in the big house..."

"Oh, I'd absolutely love it out here!" Audrey ran her hand along the granite countertop and smiled. "But then again, it might not be such a good idea. Once I got settled in you might not be able to pry me out of here."

Maggie laughed. "That would be just fine with me, Mom. You're welcome to stay as long as you like."

"Hey, there," called Spencer from outside. He and Bart burst into the carriage house and more greetings and hugs were exchanged.

"Like my new digs, Spence?" asked Audrey.

"You're going to stay in here?"

"Not really, but I was just telling your mother how much I like this little house. But you wouldn't want me to get too settled. I might not ever go back home again."

Spencer grinned. "Okay by me, Grandma. I already think you should move up here permanently anyway."

Maggie glanced at her watch. "Well, if you're thinking of becoming a permanent resident you might want to come with us to the Pine Mountain Days meeting. It's our last one before the big event. That is, unless you're tired and need some rest."

"There's plenty of time to rest later. I'd like to come and see what you've got going. Maybe I can help out with something."

"You can count on that, Grandma," said Spencer.

As they drove into town, he spoke up. "Hey, Mom, I just remembered that I was going to tell you something, but I forgot all about it when I saw Grandma here."

"What's that, Spence?"

"Well, it's probably nothing, but it seemed kind of strange. When I was walking Bart in the woods we came across this guy, and Bart started barking."

"What's so strange about that?" asked Audrey.

"Well, the guy looked like he was scared or something and then he took off running. Bart started to chase him, but I called him back to me."

"It might just be a homeless person," suggested Maggie.

"Or a criminal hiding out," said Audrey suspiciously.

"You read too many mysteries, Mom," teased Maggie. "Besides this is not L.A., or even San Jose, for that matter. Just the same, Spence, maybe you shouldn't go into the woods until we figure out who it was."

"Oh, he's probably harmless, Mom," said Spencer, backtracking. "I'm sure it's perfectly safe out there. Besides, nobody would mess with me when I've got Bart the bodyguard by my side."

"I suppose," said Maggie as she parked in the school parking lot. "After all, this is Pine Mountain."

Audrey laughed. "Yes, I doubt too many serious criminals would be attracted to a sweet little place like this." She looked around as they got out of the car. "And this is a very charming town. I like it already!"

To everyone's pleased surprise, Elizabeth Rodgers was proving highly capable and adept at leading the Pine Mountain Days committee. Since she'd already rented a small house in town and was quickly setting up her book and coffee shop, she explained that she had something of a selfish interest in helping to ensure that this celebration went off without a hitch. And although she occasionally came across as slightly bossy and domineering, most folks understood that she meant well and only wanted to see the celebration succeed. It became obvious that she'd had previous experience with such committees as she had already managed to organize a group of Northwest crafters and antique dealers to hold a country fair in the tiny city park. She'd also invited a folk band from Byron to come and play music during the day for a very minimal fee, with the understanding that they would sell lots of tapes and CDs and then perform for a dance on Saturday evening. Her plans also included colorful banners to hang along Main Street, various food vendors, and even some carnival games for kids.

Just as the meeting was winding down, Maggie spotted Buckie Porterfield and two people unknown to her slip into the back of the school library. Just as Elizabeth finished her last bit of business, signing up some additional help for setting up the food booths, Buckie spoke up.

"Sorry to interrupt your meeting, Elizabeth," he said. "But we just got into town and before everyone leaves, I have some special friends I want to introduce." He asked the couple to stand. "This is Brian and Cindy Jordan. And you'll be pleased to hear that they've come to sign the closing papers for the purchase of the Pine Mountain Hotel!"

Everyone burst into loud cheers and hearty applause. Buckie then turned to Brian. "Anything you'd like to add?"

Brian smiled and straightened his well-cut sports coat. "Only that I'm very happy to be a part of all this, and it looks as if Pine Mountain has some really great potential. I hope to reopen the hotel sometime in August if all goes well. And we may even try to get the restaurant opened before that." This was followed by more applause, then Buckie waved his hands and said he had another announcement.

"It's not 100 percent for sure yet," he began, "but I told a TV news buddy of mine about what's going on down here in Pine Mountain, and he thought it would make a good feature story. He's the roving reporter for the biggest station in Portland, and if his manager approves, he wants to bring his entire TV crew down here for Pine Mountain Days!"

Again the enthusiastic crowd burst into fresh applause, even louder this time. Elizabeth quieted them and finally spoke. "Well, isn't this simply providential? It almost seems as if someone is watching out for us here in Pine Mountain. I want to thank you all for coming tonight. And thank you again, Mr. Porterfield, for sharing this tremendous news."

After the meeting, Buckie found Maggie and introduced her to the new owners of the Pine Mountain Hotel, and then Maggie introduced the three of them to her mother.

"And I have even more good news," said Buckie quietly. "But I didn't want to steal the whole show from Elizabeth."

"What is it?" asked Maggie.

"I've got everything squared away for the Blue Moose and it looks like I'll be able to open in time for Pine Mountain Days."

"That's great," said Maggie. "You missed it, but Elizabeth announced that she plans to be open too. This town is growing by leaps and bounds."

"Maybe I should get into the action," said Audrey. "I wonder what kind of business I'd like to run?"

Maggie laughed. "Maybe you should just take up counseling again. I'm sure there's some folks around here who could use it."

Cindy Jordan perked up. "Are you a counselor too? I'm feeling a little sad about leaving my family practice in Seattle, but it's become such a rat race up there. We're ready for a quieter, simpler life."

Maggie chatted with Brian and Buckie about the future of Pine Mountain, while her mother talked counseling with Cindy. Then suddenly, she noticed Cherise Snider standing by herself at the refreshment table. Dressed, as usual, in bright-colored lycra and spandex, she was hard to miss. It appeared that she'd come alone tonight. Poor Cherise. She seemed genuinely enthusiastic about all the plans, but people kept her at a distance. Maggie suspected it was because of Greg. Some even claimed that Cherise was a spy at these meetings, and it was rumored that Greg might be seeking some political clout to slow down some of the progress and development direction that Pine Mountain was quickly taking.

"Excuse me," said Maggie as she left the two men and began to make her way over to Cherise.

"Hi, Maggie," said Cherise, smiling brightly—almost too brightly.

"How's it going, Cherise?"

"Okay, I guess. Looks like this Pine Mountain Days deal is going to be fun."

"Are you going to help out?"

Cherise frowned momentarily. "Greg doesn't want me to get involved. He doesn't even know I'm here tonight."

"I see." Maggie felt sorry for her, and she searched for something reassuring to say. "How's your business doing these days?"

"Not so good. I think Greg may have scared off some of my regular customers with all his anti-development talk. He can get a little carried away sometimes."

Maggie thought for a moment. "You know, Cherise, I've been wanting to get into shape for some hiking this summer and then skiing in the winter. Do you have anything to recommend?"

"Sure!" Cherise brightened. "Come on in and I'll put you on a program."

"Is it all right to come during my lunch hour?"

"You bet. I used to have several people who came during their lunch hours." Cherise's face grew cloudy again.

"You think this thing with Greg is really the problem?"

Cherise nodded. "I don't know what else it could be. I have the best equipment, and even though some people think I'm just an air-head, I really was trained in this. I suppose it seems silly to someone smart like you, but it's what I love to do."

Maggie smiled. "It doesn't seem silly at all. And I'm looking forward to coming in. Not only that, but I'll tell you what. If I enjoy your facility and the workout, you can count on me to spread the word around."

"Really?" Cherise's heavily mascaraed eyes opened wide.

"You bet."

Cherise glanced around as if to see if anyone was listening, then she whispered. "I don't know why Greg thinks you're such a terrible person, Maggie. I guess it's because of what happened with Gavin, plus all this development stuff. But I keep telling him he's all wrong about you." Then she reached over and squeezed Maggie's arm.

"See you on Monday, then," said Maggie.

Cherise pointed her finger and winked. "See ya!"

Twenty-One

Maggie dedicated two full pages of the *Pine Cone* to the coverage of the upcoming Pine Mountain Days, featuring several local businesses plus a small slice of Pine Mountain history. And Scott sold twice as much advertising space as usual. The paper would be a little fatter this week, and for the first time ever, thanks to Scott's computer savvy, it would also appear on the Internet.

"Oh dear!" said Abigail as she lowered her rhinestone-rimmed reading glasses and waved a letter in the air.

Maggie looked up from her final proof of an article about antique preservation contributed by Clara Henderson. "Let me guess," she said, recognizing the familiar border of Greg Snider's favorite printer paper. "A letter from our biggest fan. What does the postmaster have to say this time?"

"I can barely stand to read it, Maggie. It's so nasty and negative."

Scott poked his head out of his office. "Go ahead, Abigail. We need some entertainment." Maggie nodded to Abigail to read.

"Okay." Abigail drew in a deep breath. "'Dear Editor, who would have thought that in less than two months you could have turned our quiet community into a gaudy circus town? Everywhere I look I see ugly banners hanging over my town's streets. And if that's not enough I now hear that some cheesy Portland TV channel is coming here to film the whole stupid spectacle. When will the madness end? All of you Pollyanna do-gooders need to know that not everyone in Pine Mountain backs your childish circus plans. Some of us don't care to see our town turned into a statewide laughingstock. And some of us are ready to fight back in order to preserve our quiet way of life here. This is not California, Maggie Carpenter! And it never will be. Mark my word, Ms. Editor, we will be heard!'" Abigail shook her head sadly as she folded the letter. "I just don't know what gets into that man."

"He likes attention," said Scott simply. "My dad says he's always been like that."

"I think he just enjoys stirring up his tempest in a teapot," said Abigail, shaking her head. "But unfortunately, he's got a few cohorts following his lead. I heard Bill Tanner talking at the grocery store. He was acting like they have some big plan that'll put a stop to everything we're trying to accomplish. Bill actually had the nerve to blame our business association for the poor fishing season this year."

Scott laughed. "Now, that's a good one. Why don't we put that in the paper? 'Pine Mountain Business Association Ruins This Year's Fishing Season.'"

"Greg would like that." Abigail dangled the offensive letter over the waste basket. "Want me to just toss this into my *oops I can't find it* file?"

Maggie frowned. "I sure don't like running it in this week's edition. It's so contrary to everything we want to establish. But as bitter as he is, Greg has the right to be heard."

"No, Maggie!" groaned Scott. "Don't put it in. Or at least sit on it until next week. He's had a letter in every edition so far. Why don't we give this town a break from Greg

Snider? Or else maybe we should just give him his own opinion column. How about *Snider's Snipes.*"

Maggie smiled. "But...maybe this town needs to hear from the likes of Greg. I mean, just think how many others have written positive and supportive letters in reaction to Greg's little gems. My old editor at the *Times* always said to get both sides, especially if it stirs people up. That's what a good paper is supposed to do, Scott."

"I suppose you're right."

"Of course she's right," said Clyde, stepping into view. "That's why I hired the woman. She's a smart cookie."

"I just wish I could delete his nasty comments about the banners," said Maggie with a sigh. "My mother's on the banner committee now and she's worked so hard sewing those things. You should see the carriage house. It looks like a kite factory."

"Those banners are absolutely gorgeous," declared Abigail. "The ladies did a fine job on them. Who gives a hill of beans over what Greg thinks? He isn't exactly the epitome of good taste, you know. Goodness, have you ever seen his house?"

Scott chuckled. "Or his wife?"

"Okay," said Maggie in a mockingly stern voice. "*That's* enough."

"Oh, that's right," teased Scott. "I forgot that you and Cherise have become all buddy-buddy ever since you started working out at her little fitness club."

Maggie made a face at him. "For your information, Cherise is a very sweet person. And her club is quite well run." She poked him in the midsection, which was as flat as a breadboard. "Who knows, someday you may need to get into shape too, Scotty boy."

He grinned. "I'll keep that in mind."

Maggie glanced at her watch. "Okay, enough fun and games. We better get to work if we're going to get this paper out by Wednesday. Did those photos of the folk band come in yet, Abigail?"

Just then the phone rang and Abigail politely answered. After a brief moment she hung up and growled. "*Another hang-up call!* I must get at least two or three of those each day." She peered up at Maggie with concern. "Do you suppose it could be Greg and his boys just trying to aggravate us?"

Maggie shrugged. "That seems pretty childish, if you ask me."

Scott chuckled as he returned to his office. "Just consider the source, Maggie."

⌒

The paper came out on Wednesday with Greg's hostile letter intact, but Maggie no longer concerned herself with what the townsfolk might think, because it was plain to see everyone was too distracted with preparations for the weekend festivities to even notice. On Thursday afternoon, Maggie stopped by the Blue Moose where Buckie was frantically trying to set up his gallery. Spencer, after helping both Chloe with her clothing store and then Elizabeth Rodgers with her bookstore, was now assisting Buckie.

"Need a hand in here?" asked Maggie as a little brass bell tinkled on the glass door.

"You bet," said Buckie. "And I hope you're not just teasing." He nodded toward the back of the store. "Your son has been a lifesaver. He's out there stacking the packing crates right now."

"Actually, we're all taking the afternoon off at the paper so we can help out for Pine Mountain Days. Abigail's helping Clara and Lou with the antique and craft show. Scott's over at Chloe's setting up a hot dog stand. And Elizabeth has placed Clyde in charge of the cotton candy booth."

"Clyde and cotton candy...sounds like a Kodak moment to me." Buckie laughed. "Well, Maggie, if you're serious about lending a hand, feel free to grab that broom and I'll put you in charge of floors."

"How very glamorous." But she went right to work sweeping up a neat pile of debris and packing materials that had collected on the wood floor during the unloading of all the photos. "Buckie, it looks really nice in here," commented Maggie as she swept her last pile. She'd heard that he'd hired a paint crew to paint the old ceiling black and the walls white, and had wondered what the finished product would look like, but with numerous spotlights carefully positioned on the darkened ceiling it seemed the perfect way to show off his large collection of photos. The wood-plank floors added a golden warmth to the room. The overall effect was surprisingly refined and uptown.

"Well, hopefully I can take more time to polish the gallery later." Buckie looked around the room with satisfaction. "But for now it's just fine. Actually, better than I'd even hoped."

"These photos are really good," she commented as she paused by a black and white shot of a cityscape. Then she noticed an attractively framed color photo of a covered bridge set against a stand of fall foliage. "This is gorgeous, Buckie. I might be interested in purchasing this one, myself. Do you take checks?"

"Hey, that reminds me, did you get your copy of *Western Life* yet?"

"You're kidding!" exclaimed Maggie. "Is it out now?"

"Yes. I got mine last weekend in Seattle. I think I brought it with me. I'll dig it out and show you. I'm surprised you didn't get your complimentary copy yet."

Maggie thought about Greg at the post office. Surely he wouldn't dare to tamper with her mail. But then again, would he be tempted to sneak a peek at the magazine featuring Pine Mountain? Maggie shook her head as if to erase her suspicious thoughts. "I'd love to see your copy, Buckie. I'm just so glad that it came out before the celebration. Who knows, it might even pull in a little extra traffic. I heard the weather in the valley is extremely hot and humid right now. Those folks might enjoy coming up to the mountains for a little relief."

The bell tinkled on the door again and Maggie looked up to see Jed walk in. "Are you open for business yet?" he asked as Buckie greeted him.

"Come on in and have a look around," said Buckie.

"But watch out," called Maggie from the back where she was still sweeping. "Or Buckie might put you to work."

"Oh, hello, Maggie," said Jed. "I didn't realize you were here." He peered at her curiously, then turned his attention back to the display racks of photography. "These are excellent, Buckie. You're a very talented guy. I wouldn't mind hanging this one in my house."

Maggie glanced over to see which one Jed was admiring. "Hey, you might have to take bids on that one, Buckie," she teased.

He laughed. "Yeah, that's the photo that Maggie wants. I can easily make a duplicate so you can both have one."

Jed moved to another section. "Well, you've got a lot of good ones to choose from. But I'm supposed to help Kate rearrange some things in my shop this afternoon. She has some new idea for decorating that she wants to finish up tonight. Maybe I'll stop by during the weekend though. Hopefully your stuff won't all be picked over by then."

"You do that, Jed. I'll make you a good deal."

For an afternoon break, Maggie stopped by Elizabeth's new shop to pick up coffee. To her surprise, Sierra was behind the counter. "Hey, why aren't you at the deli helping your mom?" asked Maggie.

Sierra grinned. "My dad's helping her this afternoon. And since Elizabeth is so swamped with Pine Mountain Days, I offered to pitch in over here." Sierra glanced around to see if anyone was in earshot. "Don't tell Mom, but I wish I could work here instead of the deli. My friend Cara is applying for a job here, but I'd switch places with her in a minute. Don't you just love the smell of books and coffee mixed together?"

Maggie laughed. "It *is* pleasant in here. And that music is delightful. Say, does Elizabeth sell any good CDs?"

Sierra pointed to a small display by the cash register. "Want coffee? Our specialty for Pine Mountain Days is the Hazelnut Vanilla Latte."

"Sounds good. Give me three specials to go—I don't dare return without bringing them a treat. And I'll take this CD too."

Maggie returned to the Blue Moose with coffees for Buckie and Spencer. "And here's a shop-warming gift," she said as she handed Buckie the new CD.

"Brilliant idea, Maggie. I brought my CD player, but forgot to bring any CDs with me. I'll use this tomorrow when I officially open. Thanks so much." He smiled warmly at her. "You are a truly amazing woman, Maggie Carpenter—a real visionary."

"Wow, all this praise just for getting coffee and a CD."

"No, I don't mean that. I mean everything you've done for this town. Others have been talking too. Right now, I'd say you're first in line for the Pine Mountain Woman of the Year Award…"

Her laughter cut him off. "As if they even have one! And just for the record, some of my motives are not very noble. When I came here originally it was to escape the rat race of L.A., but when I found this place floundering on the edge of extinction I decided to give it all I had to save it—just so I could stay here. Pretty selfish, huh?"

Buckie shrugged. "I don't know. When your motives manage to rescue a whole community, I can hardly classify them as selfish."

"Well, it took almost everyone to rescue this town. And besides, there are some that wouldn't agree with you that it's such a good thing."

He nodded. "Yes, I've heard some whimpering from the dissenters. But you'll find that anywhere. There are always those who will fight against any kind of change. That's life."

"I suppose. But to be honest, it bothers me to know that my efforts have made some people pretty angry, even if it's only a small handful."

He grinned at her. "I'll bet you're one of those people who wants everyone to like them all the time."

She bristled. "No, actually I'm not. You couldn't be in my line of work if you were. I don't mind controversy over some things. It just makes me uncomfortable to think I might be spoiling what Greg Snider thinks is a just fine status quo. I mean, I do understand what it's like in California. I've seen the changes over the last three decades. Development can be devastating..."

"*Poor* development can be devastating, Maggie. Face it, this town would develop one way or another no matter what you did or didn't do. But you're helping it to develop in a positive way. You've managed to get the local folks involved and they are very thankful for all you've done."

"Well, as my mom would say, the proof is in the pudding. We'll see how it all comes together in the next few weeks, starting tomorrow. For everyone's sake I hope you're right, Buckie. I have to admit, worrying about all the things that could still go wrong has kept me awake a few nights. But that's when I pray about it."

"You pray about it?"

She nodded. "Yes, one thing I didn't mention about this whole venture is that from the very start I felt that God had led me here. And when you think about it, so many impossible things have happened, it's really nothing short of miraculous."

Buckie scratched his head. "Interesting... I've never actually imagined God getting involved with our daily lives like that."

"Maybe that's because we usually forget to ask him."

He nodded thoughtfully. "Maybe so..."

Twenty-Two

*T*he phone rang sharply and Maggie, still half-asleep, fumbled for the receiver and muttered a groggy hello.

"Maggie!" Rosa's voice sounded urgent. "Are you awake?"

"Just barely. What's wrong, Rosa?"

"Everything! Oh, absolutely everything. It's just horrible, Maggie, unbelievable! You've got to get to town immediately!"

She leaped out of bed, heart pounding. "What is it, Rosa?" she cried. "Is someone hurt? Please tell me what's going on."

"No one is hurt." Rosa's voice calmed, but only slightly. "Not physically anyway. But a lot of people are about to be severely hurt..."

"Rosa, please! Tell me what's wrong!"

"The town!" Rosa's voice choked and Maggie could tell she was crying now. "I came in early to finish up my baking and...and the entire town has been completely vandalized! It looks like everyone's been hit. The deli is a mess! Broken windows! Glass everywhere! Flower boxes overturned.

238 ⌒ Melody Carlson

Spray paint all over and trash strewn about...you name it, they did it!"

She sank back onto her bed speechless, attempting to process all she'd just heard as she imagined the pretty little town in ruins. Who in the world would have done such a thing? Then, like an electric jolt, she remembered the TV crew that was scheduled to arrive around nine to film Pine Mountain Days. She looked at her bedside clock. Not yet six, but still not enough time to repair the kind of damage Rosa had just described. "What about the TV crew?" she asked weakly.

"Oh, no!" cried Rosa. "I completely forgot about them...I was only thinking of the business owners and the Pine Mountain Days festivities. Oh, Maggie, can you call the TV crew and beg them not to come?"

"I can try. But they may be on the road by now." She took a deep breath and closed her eyes, hoping this was all a bad dream, but when she opened them she was still awake, her heart was still pounding, and she could still hear Rosa's quiet sobs on the other end of the phone line. "I'll call the station," she said quietly. "And then I'll be right there. Maybe we can salvage this...somehow."

After unsuccessfully trying to reach the TV crew, she left a short message with a receptionist who sounded as if she was filing her nails and then raced to town. She didn't wake her mother or Spencer. She wanted to see the damage for herself first and then try to determine their best course of action. As she drove she wondered who could have done this and why. Surely Greg and his boys wouldn't resort to anything this low and actually criminal. Or would they? What if they'd been out drinking and things had gotten out of hand? Cherise had mentioned to her how Greg liked to drink with his friends, and often became a different person while under the influence. She certainly remembered how hideous Gavin had become that night she'd had dinner with him. And then she wondered, where had the sheriff been last night while all this was taking place? Wouldn't the sound of breaking glass have alerted him of a problem? She knew Sheriff Warner was good friends with Greg, but surely that wouldn't cause him to turn a blind eye to something as horrible as this. Still, things like this sometimes happened in small towns. She muttered a quick prayer as she turned her car down Main Street. And then she gasped.

The devastation was obvious at first glance. Torn banners hung limply, some on the ground and some even burnt. Garbage cans were tipped over, flower boxes spilt, and ugly streaks of bright paint were everywhere. It looked even worse than Rosa had described. As Maggie parked in front of the deli, careful to avoid shards of broken glass, her eyes filled with tears and the ugly scene blurred before her. Was this her fault? A result of trying to change things? Even the old "status quo" would be preferable to *this*. With heart pounding, she forced herself out of the car and stood on the street looking first one way, then the other.

Several discouraged business owners were already walking about, gaping at the vandalism with a mixture of shocked and angry faces. Maggie spotted Rosa and went immediately to her. "This is so appalling, Rosa! I don't even know what to say. I couldn't reach the TV crew, but I left a message."

Cal, from the secondhand store, walked up to Maggie. "My place is a wreck!" he complained. "Every durned window's busted! I wish we'd never started this whole doggone business of fixing up the town—just look where it's gotten us! I can't afford to replace those plate glass windows—I don't even got insurance on the place. I'm finished for sure now."

"I'm so sorry, Cal..." She turned back to Rosa, tears welling in her eyes again. "This is all my fault..."

"No!" Rosa interrupted her. "This is *not* your fault, Maggie Carpenter, anymore than it is my fault or Cal's. The only ones to blame are the ones who did this!"

Maggie looked down the street toward the Blue Moose and Elizabeth's Window Seat, their two latest business additions. "Shall we see how the others fared?"

The two women walked down the street in aggrieved silence, as if participating in a funeral procession. Behind them, Cal continued to bemoan his loss along with several other business owners. "I was better off before we ever started that business association," Cal said bitterly and loud enough to reach Maggie's ears. "Things might've been slow, but at least I had windows!"

"I wonder if Elizabeth has heard the news yet," said Rosa, as if to block out Cal's harsh criticism. "I'm fortunate to have my whole family to help clean things up at the deli, but Elizabeth doesn't have anyone."

"Has someone notified all the business owners?" asked Maggie, her voice flat.

"Sheriff Warner has called some. I think he's pretty busy just writing up reports, and he gave me a form to fill in. Scott's already snooping around town, taking photos and trying to play investigative reporter."

"Good. I was just thinking we need to cover this in the paper. Obviously, it's a big story. But what I'm most concerned about is whether we can somehow pull this place together before the film crew arrives..."

"Oh, dear!" cried Elizabeth Rodgers as she burst out of the Window Seat wearing a purple chenille bathrobe. "Can you believe this? I came straight over. It's so utterly ghastly! I didn't think things like this happened in little towns. I'm just so upset, I don't even know what to do first! There's the festival, and the TV people, and my shop!" Suddenly Elizabeth, usually so dignified and in control, burst into loud sobs.

Rosa put her arms around the older woman. "It's going to be okay, Elizabeth. At least no one was hurt. And I think it may look worse than it really is."

"We need to pull ourselves together and make a plan," said Maggie with fresh urgency. "Maybe we can still beat this." Then and there, the three woman began to confer right on the street. Maggie pulled her ever-present note pad from her purse and began to jot down all their ideas and prioritize the steps needed to bring order back to their town. Soon, they were joined by Chloe and several others, and it was quickly decided that for starters everyone should work fast to do whatever possible to inventory the damage, and then clean up their own businesses. Sam was already checking on new windows for the deli, and Rosa would put him to work on everyone else's too—maybe they could get a group rate. After two hours of cleanup they'd all regroup and focus their energy on the celebration and any damage that needed to be addressed. A list of potential helpers who were not business owners was quickly made, and Maggie offered to make phone calls to them and any other business owners who hadn't yet heard the news. While everyone dispersed to their own tasks, Maggie took a moment to glance into Buckie's gallery and survey the damage. One of his display stands had fallen, knocked down by the large stone that had shattered his front window, and a number of framed photos were in various pieces on the floor. She quickly turned away and hurried over to the newspaper office where she would use the phone, and then begin her own clean up efforts as Rosa had already warned her that the newspaper had been hit as well.

When she reached the porch Abigail was already there, dressed in yellow and blue sweats and sweeping broken glass shards into a large dustpan. "No time to waste," said Abigail as she stood to her full height. "Clara called me a few minutes ago. Oh my, was she ever upset. So, I thought I better hop on over and see what could be done, and when I finish up here I'm going over to help Clara. And I thought maybe I could take charge of repotting all the planters around town."

"Bless you, Abigail," said Maggie as she looked forlornly at the graffiti sprawls splattered across the natural wood siding of the building. "I wonder how we'll ever get *that* off?"

"Maybe we should just cover it up for today, dear."

"Good thinking," said Maggie. "I've got to make some phone calls, then I'll be back to help you with this."

After waking up several sleepy business owners who were unaware of the catastrophe in town, she reached Buckie and quickly broke the unfortunate news.

"You're not serious, Maggie!" he said in a sleepy yet skeptical voice.

"Buckie, I'm dead serious. The whole town has been horribly vandalized. As far as I know, no one was missed. Your shop mostly suffered broken windows and one of your display stands is down."

He moaned. "All of my savings are in that little gallery, Maggie. It took every penny just to cash it out, I don't even know if my insurance is good yet."

"I'm sorry, Buckie. I hope none of your photos are irreparably damaged. Don't you keep the negatives anyway?"

"That's not it. It's just that I thought coming to a small town like Pine Mountain was a guarantee that something like this would never happen."

"I guess there are no guarantees. The fact is everyone is hurting right now. And on top of the vandalism, we still have the TV crew and the Pine Mountain Days festival to contend with."

"I know. I know." He sighed deeply. "What a stupid, senseless mess!"

After hanging up, she called home. Then, leaning back in her chair, she suddenly longed to be home. Not here in Pine Mountain, where everything was suddenly going all wrong, but somewhere safe and secure, protected and sheltered from all of this. Maybe there was no such place on earth, maybe it only existed in heaven...

"I wondered where you'd gone off to in such a hurry," said her mother pleasantly. "What's up, honey?"

She groaned. "Oh, it's so horrible, Mom." Then she poured out the whole awful story.

"Even the banners?" exclaimed her mother. "They destroyed my banners?"

"Mostly. And the TV crew will be here in a couple of hours."

"A couple hours?" Suddenly Audrey's voice grew hopeful. "Well, I still have lots of materials, and even a couple of partially sewn banners that Elizabeth thought were unnecessary. Maybe I could get Spence to do some cutting while I try to throw some together and then we'll pop into town and put them up, and after that we can help out with some of the cleanup too."

"That would be so wonderful, Mom. Do you really think you can do the banners that quickly?"

"You know I'm a fast seamstress. And we'll do our best. It would probably be encouraging for everyone to have the banners back up." Her mother cupped her hand over the phone as she yelled. "Hey, Spence-buddy, time to get up and do your part to save Pine Mountain!"

In spite of everything, she smiled. "Thanks, Mom. You're a real trooper." She hung up the phone and looked up to see Clyde standing in her doorway, a dark shadow of concern across his face.

He shook his head. "This is unbelievable, Maggie. All my years in Pine Mountain, and I've never, ever seen anything like this. Never."

She nodded glumly. "I know. And the truth is, I feel sort of responsible, Clyde. Like, if I hadn't started this whole business association thing, maybe everything would be just fine right now. Normal. Status quo."

"Now, don't you go blaming yourself, young lady. Everything was going great guns until this happened. And there's no use crying over spilt milk right now. The thing is we've got our work cut out for us today, and I suggest we get right to it, and let the chips fall where they may."

She had never known anyone to utilize as many adages as Clyde Barnes, and on a normal day it might even be laughable.

"Thanks for the pep talk, Clyde. And I suppose it doesn't do any good for me to sit around here feeling guilty."

"That's the spirit. We can't let this get us down."

"But you know what's bugging me most?" She suddenly slammed her fist down on her desk. "Just who the devil do you think pulled this little stunt anyway?"

His brow furrowed as he hooked his thumbs into his suspenders and blew out a long puff of air. "Don't s'pose you noticed that Cherise's little exercise place wasn't even hit?"

Her eyes opened wide. "You don't really think...?"

He shrugged. "I don't know. But if you ask me, it's fishy. Mighty fishy."

"But Cherise's place isn't on Main Street. Perhaps the vandals only went after the Main Street businesses. Did you notice if any other businesses off Main Street got hit?"

"We sure did," he said wryly.

"I know, but we're pretty close to Main." She frowned. "Do you think the post office got hit? It's not on Main."

His brows lifted. "Now that might be worth checking into."

"I have to admit that Greg was the first person I thought of too," she confessed. "But it seems so crazy. He's supposed to be a responsible person...he's the postmaster!"

"What about those poison-pen letters, Maggie? Remember, you even printed one this week."

She took a deep breath. "Let's be careful before we start throwing around accusations."

"I reckon you're right. And right now we just need to pull ourselves up by our bootstraps and put this town back together...if we can."

After working with Clyde and Abigail to clean up the newspaper office, Maggie went over to see how Elizabeth was faring. To her relief, Sierra had already come by to lend a hand and Sam was there measuring her windows while talking on his cell phone to a friend in Byron who owned a window and glass company. Elizabeth was out on the sidewalk painstakingly salvaging her pansy plants, then carefully tucking them back into the flower box beside her door.

"My mother's sewing up some new banners," said Maggie as she picked up a broken pansy bloom from the sidewalk.

Elizabeth looked up with a faint flicker of hope in her eyes. "That's good of her." Then she slowly stood and brushed the potting soil from her hands onto her purple bathrobe. "I suppose I should run home and get dressed." She smiled ever so slightly. "Back in Seattle I would never have gone out in public like this."

Maggie reached over and squeezed Elizabeth's hand. "Well, you're with family here." Then she glanced at the broken window. "Albeit a slightly dysfunctional family."

Elizabeth sighed. "Aren't they all? Somehow, we'll pull this off, Maggie. I guess my shop is under control now. Sierra has offered to help out this morning." She glanced at her watch. "I'll go get dressed, and then let's all meet at the deli in twenty minutes to see what needs to be done for the festival. Hopefully the TV crew won't be here by then."

Maggie went back outside and glanced over to Jed's shop. Kate had on heavy leather gloves and was carefully removing the remaining glass shards from the broken window frame and placing them in a trash bin. Maggie called out to her, and Kate turned with a frown.

"Sorry to bother you, Kate," she called from across the street. "But we're all going to meet at the deli in about twenty minutes—that is, if you and Jed want to join us."

Kate nodded mutely, then returned to her task. She and Kate had never been chummy, but this cool encounter filled her with a fresh load of guilt. Perhaps everyone secretly felt this was all her fault, that their town would still be intact if not for her interference and meddling. She decided to stop by the Blue Moose and inform Buckie of the meeting too. At least his sidewalk was swept clear of glass now. She poked her head in and spied Buckie in the back of the shop holding two pieces of a broken picture frame together as he gently tapped in a nail.

"Hey, Buckie," she called. "We're going to have a little meeting at the deli in about twenty minutes, if you'd like to come."

"Uh, yeah, sure," he said, without looking up.

She stepped back outside and tried not to look at the destruction all around her. Why had everything suddenly gone so wrong? It reminded her of the other times in her life when things had quickly spun out of control. One moment everything is fine, the next it is changed forever. Sure, no one was dead. That was something to be thankful for. But why did this have to happen at all? Why here? Why now? Maybe it was her. As ridiculous as it seemed she wondered if perhaps she was some sort of jinx.

"Oh, *there* she is," came a loud voice.

She looked up to see Greg Snider and Bill Tanner quickly approaching. They stopped in the middle of the sidewalk, as if to block her way.

"Well, here she is, the woman of the hour," said Greg. "So, are you pleased with the results of all your hard work, Ms. Carpenter? Ready for your TV cameras to start rolling now?"

She blinked at him, searching her tired mind for an answer, when something inside her just snapped. "I'll bet you're pleased...aren't you, Greg?" She stepped up and stared him right in the eye. "This was just what you'd hoped for, wasn't it? You should be real happy right now! One would almost wonder if you had something to do with it, Greg. Are you the mastermind behind this little piece of work? By the way, I heard Cherise's place wasn't even touched. Funny, isn't it?"

Greg leaned forward, eyes narrowed. "Are you accusing *me* of doing this?"

"I'm not accusing anyone, Greg. I'm just pointing out that this whole thing should make you very, very happy. It fulfills all your gloom and doom prophecy, doesn't it? Very convenient for you."

Greg's fists clenched. "I don't like want you're insinuating, Ms. Carpenter."

"Well, if the shoe fits, wear it!" she exclaimed as she tried to push past the two men. Suddenly, Greg grabbed her by the arm.

"Not so quick," he snarled. "I want you to see something."

"Let go of me!" she said firmly.

"Not until you see something first." Then he proceeded to forcibly walk her down the sidewalk and around the corner. Her heart beat furiously, and she even considered crying out for help, but it was broad daylight with people all around. What could he possibly do? He stopped right in front of the post office and released her arm, pointing to the broken windows. "There! If I was responsible for the vandalism, would the post office have been hit too?"

She was fuming now. He had no right to drag her over here against her will! And she could care less whether the post office was vandalized or not. She was fed up with this guy and his egotistic power games.

"I don't know, Greg!" she exploded. "I guess you *might* break your own windows in order to cover your trail. And besides, you don't even *own* the post office. Uncle Sam will pay to have all those windows replaced, not you!" She turned and glared at him. "This doesn't prove a single thing! And I would thank you, Mr. Snider, never to lay a finger on me again! Is that clear?" She turned in a fury and ran smack into Jed.

"Easy does it, Maggie," he said soothingly. Then he looked past her to where Greg was still standing. "I suggest you listen to her, Greg. I didn't see the whole thing, but I didn't like what I did see. Tempers are running hot and heavy around here today. I suggest you keep yours under control." Then Jed took Maggie gently by the arm and guided her down the street and away from the postmaster.

"You're shaking, Maggie," he said quietly.

Hot angry tears were now cascading down her cheeks. "I'm just...very, very upset."

"Come on, let's see if we can calm you down." He led her toward his shop and around to the back where he sat her down on a log bench in the cool shadows, then he sat beside her. "You want to talk about it?"

She took a deep breath. "Everything's just so upsetting right now, and then Greg Snider has to go off like that! It was just more than I could handle, and I guess I just lost it. I know I said some bad things, but I'm sure he asked for it."

Jed smiled. "I've no doubt that he did."

She peered up at Jed. "Do you think Greg is responsible for the vandalism?"

He paused for a moment, then answered slowly. "Just because he's the most likely suspect doesn't make me think he did it."

She nodded. "I know what you mean."

"Did you accuse him?"

"Not in so many words, but..."

"I see."

She sighed. "I'm sure I came across as *very* accusatory. And you know what's really weird now?" she looked at Jed, "I don't think he did it after all."

"Why?"

"I'm not sure. Something about the way he acted just now. Or maybe just a gut feeling. I do think he's a boorish and disagreeable lout, and a lot of other nasty things, but somehow I don't think he's really a criminal." She glanced at her watch. "I better get to the deli for the meeting."

"You sure you're okay, Maggie?" She'd never seen his dark eyes look so warm and compassionate.

"I'll be fine. Are you coming to the meeting?"

He nodded. "I'll be along in a few minutes."

"Jed," she smiled up at him. "Thanks."

"No problem."

She hurried over to the deli. The room was already crowded with business owners, with Elizabeth up in front, no longer in her bathrobe but now dressed in a sophisticated ethnic-print dress and expensive-looking stone jewelry. "Listen, people, we need to stay focused on our celebration," she said in a slightly strained voice. "We can't keep getting distracted by these useless accusations. It will get us nowhere..."

"But are we just going to sit on our hands and watch Greg Snider freely walk the streets after he's done this?" yelled Cal from the back. "Sheriff Warner's acting like he's gone all deaf and dumb about the whole thing! He won't even question Greg."

"Yeah," chimed in another. "I don't think Warner even bothered to read Greg's letter to the editor in yesterday's paper. Now *that* says it all."

"That's right," said the owner of the hardware store as he waved the newspaper. "Greg framed himself with his own words..."

"Order!" yelled Elizabeth as she banged a coffee mug on the counter. "We're just wasting our time arguing about Greg Snider. The important thing is to get back on track in time for the festival."

"*Why?*" yelled Cal. "Just so the likes of Greg and his boys can come in here and mess it all up again?" He stood up and shoved his old dusty felt hat onto his head. "I'm finished—through—I give up!"

"Wait a minute!" called Maggie. Everyone turned to see her, still standing by the front door where she'd come in. "As you know, Greg and I aren't exactly best buddies. In fact, we just had a little altercation over at the post office a few minutes ago and I would have liked to punch him. But just the same, I don't think Greg is the one behind this." She could tell she had the attention of some of them.

"But just look at the evidence," cried Cal. "His wife's place wasn't even hit!"

"And what about this letter in the paper?" asked Al. Several others chimed in.

Just then, Maggie noticed something from the corner of her eye. She turned just in time to see a large white van pulling slowly down Main Street. Painted boldly across its side were the call letters of the Portland news station.

"They're here!" she announced over the din of voices. "The TV news crew is here!" The deli grew unexpectedly quiet as everyone turned to look out the window.

Elizabeth stepped forward. "Maggie, would you like me to join you in greeting them? We have a lot of explaining to do." Maggie nodded and the two women stepped outside and waved to the van as it parked on the other side of the street. Several men climbed out looking around at the town in bewildered amazement.

"I'm Glen Robertson," said a familiar-looking dark-haired man in a chambray shirt and tie, "the roving reporter for Channel Four News. What happened here? It looks like a bomb went off."

Elizabeth quickly explained everything to Glen, finally pleading with him to turn the van around and come back on another day—any other day.

"I understand your concern, Ma'am," said Glen, eyeing the remaining shredded banners flapping limply overhead. "But you must admit this makes for a pretty interesting story." He glanced over to his camera and sound crew. "Okay, guys, let's get unloaded and get some footage of this vandalism."

Elizabeth groaned loudly as the crew began to arrange cameras and equipment on the sidewalk. Just as Maggie was about to make another plea, Rosa came running out of the deli with the cordless phone in her hand. "Maggie!" she exclaimed. "It's your mother. Something is wrong!"

Maggie grabbed the phone, wondering what more could possibly go wrong today, then listened as her mother quickly poured out a strange and frightening story. Maggie hung up. Forgetting all about the Portland reporter, she thrust the phone back to Rosa and exclaimed, "Call the sheriff right now, and then the state police! Send them to my house *immediately!*"

Rosa's dark eyes widened in fear. "What? What is it, Maggie? Is Spencer—"

"Spencer's fine. It seems he and Bart uncovered some big drug operation in the woods behind our property—even guns! I've got to get home right now!"

Maggie dashed for her car, but as she was pulling out she noticed that the TV crew was now rapidly reloading their cameras into the van. In the next instant, they managed a U-turn and began to tail her. Just what this town needed! Vandalism, drug operations, all about to appear on the six o'clock news across the state. All this in little Pine Mountain, Oregon! Why, she might as well be in L.A.!

She prayed silently as she drove. Prayed for the safety of her son and mother, the future of the town. And amazingly, she even prayed for Greg Snider!

She tore into the gravel driveway, leaving a trail of dust behind her, but not thick enough to obscure the white van that must've also exceeded the speed limit. She ran into the house, relieved to see Spencer, her mother, and even Bart all safe and sound in the front parlor. She closed the door behind her, locked it, then collapsed onto the couch.

"Are you okay, Mom?" asked Spencer with concern.

"Considering the past few hours, I guess I'll survive. Now, tell me Spencer, are you absolutely sure it's a drug operation? That can be very dangerous. Did you see anyone? Did anyone see you?"

Spencer waved his hands. "Too many questions, Mom."

"Okay. Let's do the most important one. Did anyone see you?"

He shook his head. "I don't think so. You see, I wanted to take Bart out for a quick run before Grandma and I went into town. And Bart took off into the woods like usual, but then he just took off a different way. It was weird, it's like he led me straight to them, almost as if he knew they were there.

And at first I thought it was just some campers, 'cause there were tents and cooking stuff. But then I saw all these big glass jars, you know, like in chemistry class, and then there was a whole bunch of camp stoves like the one Dad used to have. And then I saw the guns and stuff, and that's when I got a little scared. I think the guys must've been asleep in the tents. I'm telling you, I never ran so fast in my life." He reached over and patted Bart's head. "And you were real good, boy. He just ran with me—didn't bark or make any noise or anything."

Maggie sighed. "Thank goodness."

"I see flashing blue lights," said Audrey from her self-assigned post by the front window. "Hey, Maggie, did you know that the Portland news team is parked in your driveway?"

She groaned. "I know. What a great publicity story for the charming little town of Pine Mountain! Vandals, drugs, what next?"

"Here comes a state police car now," said Audrey. "They'll probably want to question you, Spencer."

Maggie looked her son in the eye. "Answer all their questions and give them good directions, but you are *not* to go back out there with them into the woods, do you understand?"

"Aw, Mom!"

"I mean it, Mister! They can take Bart if they want, but I refuse to let you go." She felt tears building in her eyes again. "I have already given up one man in the line of duty. I simply cannot afford another."

Spencer nodded. "Okay, Mom. I got ya."

Twenty-Three

*I*t's been an exciting day for this normally quiet little mountain resort town," said Glen Robertson from the screen of the big TV set up on the counter of the deli. "The people of Pine Mountain began their morning with the startling discovery of a vandalism rampage that nearly brought this tiny town to its knees, and this on the eve of their much-planned Pine Mountain Days celebration. And then, just as local citizens were recovering from that shock, a major drug operation was uncovered just outside of town." The camera shot changed from downtown Main Street to the drug manufacturing site in the woods so near Maggie's home as Glen continued. "Tucked away in the Ponderosa Pines of the beautiful National Forest was one of the biggest drug operations ever uncovered this side of the Cascades. Unknown quantities of crack-meth amphetamines were seized today, along with hundreds of live marijuana plants growing right in the woods. But probably of greatest interest to the citizens of Pine Mountain were the empty cans of spray paint that matched the graffiti found all over town this morning." Now the camera zoomed into a pile of spray cans lying next to a trash heap. "Apparently, the alleged drug man-ufacturers had been using the quiet town of Pine Mountain to traffic their drugs for several years now, and didn't want to see the isolated town grow or change in any way. Three arrests were made at the drug site, but state police are on the lookout for others believed to be involved." This was followed by a brief interview with Spencer, who explained how he and Bart happened to come across the drug site in the first place, then Glen paused as the town of Pine Mountain reappeared on the screen, looking slightly neater than in the first shot.

"It's actually been a rather amusing visit," he continued. "Our news team thought we were coming out here to cover a folksy little festival in a sleepy little town, but that just goes to show you how even small towns can have their problems. However, we did find some pleasant surprises along the way. We discovered a group of citizens who know how to hang in there together and weather the storm. And by the end of the day, they had nearly restored their little town to rights." Now the cameras began to flash candid shots of various people diligently working to repair the damage. Viewers in the deli shouted out names as they recognized familiar faces. There was Sierra painting out the graffiti on the exterior of Elizabeth's Window Seat; Abigail kneeling on a rubber knee pad as she repotted pink petunias in front of Clara Lou's antique shop; and even Spencer again, this time perched high on a ladder as he replaced one of the banners sewn by his grandmother. Now the camera tightened back in on Glen Robertson's face as he continued his live coverage from the streets of Pine Mountain. "And even as I speak, people are gathering tonight for potluck victory dinners at the various local businesses—probably even watching Channel Four News just like you. And the truth is, we've had such an interesting time here in Pine Mountain, that we plan to stay for the entire weekend. Watch us tomorrow at six as we cover the Pine Mountain Days Festival, and then tune in at eleven as we show you some footage from the Pine Mountain Moonlight Dance. And I promise you city dwellers, if you want to have a good time, come on over to Pine Mountain—

where the people are friendly and you never know what might happen next!"

The crowd laughed and cheered as the scene on Main Street faded on the screen and another reporter in the Portland station began to talk about a city official accused of sexual harassment. Sam stepped up and turned off the TV, then grinned. "Well, it looks like we finally made the big times!"

Maggie shook her head in wonder. "What a way to get there!"

"I wonder if *all* small towns have to work this hard just to get publicity," said Chloe.

As everyone continued to chatter and replay all the various events of the day, Maggie noticed Clyde sitting by himself in a corner of the room.

"What the matter, Clyde?" she asked as she pulled up a chair next to him. "You should be feeling pretty happy right now. After all, you're the one who wanted to put Pine Mountain on the map, and now we've certainly managed to do it."

He nodded absently. "That we have."

She frowned. "Well, what's wrong then?"

Clyde sighed sadly. "I feel bad."

"What about?" She leaned forward in concern. "Is it your health?"

"Oh, I'm healthy in body, Maggie. It's my spirit that's lagging." He looked around to see if anyone else was listening. "I'm afraid that Gavin may be involved in this drug business."

"Oh, dear." She didn't know quite what to say. She knew that Gavin had his problems, but she'd never suspected anything as serious as this.

"You see, that was the last straw when I made him leave. I found out that he'd been using the newspaper office to transport drugs. I honestly don't know if they were really his, or if he was just helping someone else. But I *had* to put a stop to it." He looked down at his hands folded on the table in front of him. "For years I've thought of Gavin almost like my own son. Oh sure, I've had to overlook a lot of things, and he's had a lot of trouble. But when *this* happened, I couldn't ignore it." He looked her straight in the eye. "Drugs are serious. They can really mess up kids." He glanced over to where the young people were sitting.

"I know, Clyde," her voice was quiet.

She glanced around the room, making certain that people were still involved in their own conversations, but still she whispered, "And so you really think that Gavin is involved somehow?"

"The fact that this drug operation was so near the old homestead makes me think he has something to do with it."

"Are you worried about him, Clyde?"

He sadly shook his head. "No. I guess I'm beyond that. Gavin's a grown man, he makes his own choices, good or bad. The thing that upsets me most is that I feel it's my fault that everything happened the way it did today...the vandalism, the drug operation... I feel lousy that everyone worked so hard and then, perhaps due to my nephew, the whole future of this town was foolishly put into jeopardy."

"But you don't know for sure that it's Gavin. And even if it is, that's not *your* fault, Clyde."

"But I'm the one who brought Gavin back here. I encouraged him to come."

"You were trying to help him. And besides, you said it yourself, Gavin's a grown man, he makes his own choices. Not you."

He nodded. "But to think, there I was blaming Greg Snider for all this. Sure Greg may have his personality problems, but now I seriously doubt he had anything to do with this. In fact, I remember a time when Greg raked Gavin over the coals about a situation something like this. And even though they were friends, I honestly don't think Greg was aware of Gavin's little problems when I made him leave."

"I heard the police have searched Greg's house without success."

Clyde sighed. "What a mess."

"Well, you don't know for sure that Gavin was involved. Only time will answer that question. And even if he *is* involved, maybe the best thing would be to get caught and come clean. And if he's not involved, who knows, maybe it'll give him a good scare."

Clyde perked up a little. "It just might."

She poked him gently in the arm. "Now, no more feeling guilty. Things are looking up for Pine Mountain. Don't be all gloomy. Haven't you ever heard that old saying, 'all's well that ends well'?"

He looked at her with his pale blue eyes and then smiled ever so slightly. "Maybe you're right, Maggie girl."

"Of course, I'm right," she teased. "Isn't that why you hired me in the first place?"

"I hired you because I wanted you to make a difference."

She grinned at him. "Well, what do you think now?"

"I'm not disappointed."

Later that night, as tired as she was, Maggie had to let her friend in L.A. know the latest news.

RB

You're not going to believe this but today, the day before our big celebration, we were first hit with a horrible case of vandalism that nearly destroyed our town, and then one of the biggest drug busts ever! I'll share the details later if you want, but the thing that's so weird is the irony of it—to think I left L.A. to get away from just that type of thing and here in beautiful Pine Mountain, Oregon—here it is again!!! I guess you just can't run away from anything. I think that instead of running away, we need to run TO God. Also, instead of putting all our hopes into an earthly home (even one as lovely as Pine Mountain) we need to put them in a heavenly one. And on that sweet, but tired, note I shall first take a therapeutic bath and then collapse into bed.

mc

ᦂ

The town was alive with people during the first official day of Pine Mountain Days. Apparently many visitors had been drawn there by curiosity after Glen Robertson's unusual report. But even as workmen replaced windows, shops managed to turn a good bit of business—far better than ever before. And the antique and craft show was a big hit. Even Clyde, wearing a sticky veneer of pink cotton candy, boasted that his booth had made more money than Scott's hot dog stand.

At the end of the day, Maggie, Audrey, and Spencer went home to eat a light dinner and rest briefly before the evening's festivities began.

"I'm exhausted," complained Maggie as she loaded a plate into the dishwasher. "I might just have to beg out of the dance tonight. Would you take Spencer with you, Mom?"

"You've *got* to go to the dance!" exclaimed Audrey. "It's going to be such fun, and you've been working so hard. You'll be sorry if you miss it, Maggie."

"I don't know why. I'll probably just end up being a wallflower anyway."

Her mother laughed. "I seriously doubt that, dear. Buckie Porterfield certainly wouldn't allow you to be a wall flower for long."

"I don't know. Buckie seems rather preoccupied with his gallery right now," she said, trying not to sound too concerned. "I think our little crime wave has really shaken him up."

"Well, you can always dance with your son, Maggie. Surely you wouldn't want to miss an opportunity like that." Her mother smiled enticingly.

"You're stooping pretty low when you drop a mother-guilt bomb just to get me to go to this silly dance."

"Whatever it takes, dear. You've invested so much into this town. It won't hurt you to have a little fun. Now," she gave her daughter a gentle shove, "I'll finish up in here while you to go put on a pretty dancing dress."

Maggie laughed as she went up the stairs. "I don't even *own* a dancing dress!"

But she managed to dig out a raisin-colored silk dress with a long full skirt that swooshed nicely when she turned. She took a few moments to apply a little make-up, and instead of tying her hair back as usual, brushed it out and let it fall softly over her shoulders. "That should make Mother happy," she said to herself as she turned from the mirror in satisfaction.

The dance floor was a large wooden platform situated in the center of the park. It was lit by tiny white lights strung around from post to post which added to the electric feeling of festivity already in the air. Maggie was glad she'd come as she listened to the folk band pleasantly play—they were really quite good. Everyone seemed happy and relaxed. Even Cherise Snider was there and actually dancing. Of course, Greg was nowhere in sight. Naturally, he'd think it an admission of defeat to openly enjoy the fruits of development. Oh well, at least his wife was having a good time. Maggie chuckled to herself as she remembered Greg's shocked expression when she'd introduced him to the film crew today. After several hours out at her place covering the drug story, the crew had finally been enticed back to town with the promise of a complete tour and free lunch at Rosa's deli. During the tour, they'd come upon Greg outside the post office cleaning up broken glass. At first he seemed, not surprisingly, irked, but as soon as Glen began to ask questions with cameras rolling, Greg warmed right up. He actually smiled and talked into the camera, confidently espousing his views about over-development and environmental concerns. Maybe Scott was right, maybe all Greg really needed was attention. As the camera crew moved on, Maggie quickly apologized to him about the earlier flare up. And while he didn't apologize for his behavior, he nodded brusquely to her, almost as if to acknowledge some sort of unspoken truce, or at least she hoped that's what it was. How long that would last, she didn't know and, for the moment, she didn't care.

She spotted Chloe and Scott, already on the dance floor too, and doing a pretty good looking two-step. Audrey, on her way to get some punch, had become happily ensnared in a conversation with the Jordans, who had recently purchased the Pine Mountain Hotel. Maggie smiled as she watched her mother fitting in so seamlessly into this funny little town. She wondered how long she would stay. Like radar, Spencer had already found Sierra and was hanging with her and several of her friends. It was nice to watch the kids taking turns dancing with each other, but so far Spencer had remained on the sidelines. Like mother like son. She actually toyed with the idea of inviting him to the dance floor herself, but would that embarrass him? Suddenly, Spencer stepped up to Sierra and mustered the nerve to ask her to dance. Maggie's eyes grew misty as she watched the two teens move awkwardly across the dance floor. Her little boy was growing up.

"Care to dance?"

She turned to see Jed facing her. In the shadowy light his eyes seemed darker and deeper than usual and his angular jaw-line firm against his white shirt.

"I'd love to dance," she said, wanting to ask, *but where is Kate and why aren't you dancing with her?* Instead she suppressed the urge and, as soon as they were dancing, forgot all about Kate. She breathed in the delicious smell of his clean shirt as it mingled with an indistinct woodsy fragrance, almost like cedar. It was somewhat intoxicating. Jed was a very good dancer, and they moved gracefully together. She liked the feeling of his strong hand supporting her back. But then the music stopped and the dance ended too quickly. Without hesitation, he asked her again, and they danced several more times together and were still on the floor when Buckie walked up with a bright smile.

"Mind if I cut in, Jed?" he asked boldly. "I just got here and it looks like you're having all the fun tonight."

Jed nodded politely, then thanked Maggie for the dances.

"Sorry I was so grouchy today," said Buckie as they danced to a peppy two-step number. "I guess I'm just a little worried about risking everything I have for this gallery."

"How did it go in your shop today?"

He smiled. "Great. I think everything's going to be just fine after all."

After several dances with Buckie, she took a break to dance with Clyde and then passed him off to her mother while she grabbed Scott Galloway.

"Did you get some good shots for the paper today, Scott?" she asked.

"You bet I did. I think I'll even send some online to the Associated Press."

She laughed. "Still thinking about the *L.A. Times*, Scotty boy?"

"Actually, I'm thinking I might like to spend a little more time around here."

"Really?"

"Yeah, I think there's still a lot for me to learn at the old *Pine Cone*. And I'd like to keep getting better acquainted with Chloe. It seems there's some friend-of-the-family *old* boyfriend who's planning to come out and visit her this fall. I might want to stick around and see how that goes."

Maggie looked at him with understanding as the dance ended. "Sounds like a wise plan. Now, if you hurry, you might be able to catch Chloe for the next dance."

Just as she considered taking a break, Rich, from the Eagle Tavern, shyly approached and politely invited her back out on the floor. She couldn't refuse.

"Remember when you told me that miracles can happen, Maggie?" he asked as they danced to a slow number.

She smiled. "Yes, I remember."

"Well, I'm starting to wonder…"

"About miracles?"

"I still have my doubts, mind you. But at least I'm considering the possibilities. I thought you'd like to know."

At last, she got to dance with her son, and she was certain it was the highlight of the evening for her. "So, are you having a good time tonight, Spence?"

"I guess so, Mom." His voice wasn't convincing.

"You guess so? What's wrong?"

"Well, I don't exactly like seeing Sierra dancing with that Kurt Gilbert so much."

She stifled a giggle, then said, "Well, maybe you should try dancing with someone besides Sierra for a change. How about Cara?"

"Really? You think so?"

"Try it and see what happens." She smiled at her son. So wise about some things, and yet still so naïve. Still a boy. Enjoy it, she reminded herself.

ᴑ

For the rest of the night, Maggie never missed a single dance. But she never got to dance with Jed again. In fact, although she saw Kate, she couldn't spot him anywhere.

After the dance, they drove slowly through the town on their way home and Maggie suddenly remembered how dreary and sad the town used to look when they'd first arrived here only a couple of months ago. But now sparkling strings of white lights, heartily recommended by the Pine Mountain Business Association and funded by an anonymous donor, glimmered cheerfully from trees and around roof-lines of the shops. So enchanting! And even with the windows in their various states of repair and some boarded up, the town looked brighter, more hopeful than ever before! And as Maggie silently thanked God for what she believed to be a real miracle, somehow she knew. She knew in her heart that this was only the beginning.

About the Author

Melody Carlson is an award-winning author of more than 30 books, from novels to children's stories, including *Homeward* and *Wise Man's House*. When not writing, she enjoys skiing, hiking, and boating. Melody and her husband live in Oregon and have two teenage sons.